Redeeming the Prodigal

Cross Family Saga, Volume 1

Jodi Basye

Published by Jodi Basye, 2021.

This is a work of fiction. Similarities to real people, places, or events are entirely coincidental.

REDEEMING THE PRODIGAL

First edition. September 1, 2021.

Written by Jodi Basye.

For Matt. My mountain man and my inspiration. If it wasn't for your love and support I never would have been able to bring this dream to life.

Chapter 1

Cripple Creek, Colorado 1897

Jo slipped a tot of brandy into the steaming cup of hot, Oolong tea she poured herself from the sideboard. It wasn't right. But what in her life was right anymore? She had sunk so low. What was a little brandy going to hurt?

She quickly slipped the small flask back inside a fold in her gown and stole a glance over her shoulder in Hazel's direction. The new madam of the well-known parlor house would turn a blind eye to a little discrete imbibing, but there would be no tolerance for a girl who drank openly or showed any sign of drunkenness.

Surveying the sitting room, Jo took a long sip of the tea, despondency wrapping itself around her like a cloak. The exotic carpets, electric chandeliers, and rich fabrics of the high-end brothel had once seemed so grand. Now she only saw faded oriental rugs, gloomy lighting, and heavy drapery. The weight of them pulled her deeper into the abasement that overwhelmed her more and more each night. The heavy aroma of perfume mingled with the opium smoke that hung thick in the room. She longed for the fresh scent of grass and the solid feel of a good horse under her. She longed for home.

The bawdy laughter from the courtesans and patrons was an abrasive contrast to the feigned tone of refinement set by the pianist playing Chopin in the corner. How much longer could she go on with this? There had to be another way. She lifted the cup to her lips. The warmth of the liquor burned in her chest, bolstering her nerve to get through another night.

When she had first arrived in Cripple Creek, she'd been destitute and afraid. She had spent the previous year living with the notorious Blake Gang, sleeping on the rough ground, eating nothing but poorly cooked beans and corn dodgers, and drinking gritty camp coffee. After escaping Kane Blake and that outlaw life, she'd been penniless and starving. That was when Pearl DeVere, the former madam of the parlor house, had discovered her and offered her work and a safe place to stay. Pearl had since passed, having taken too much laudanum one night after a Friday night soiree, never to wake again.

In light of such a dramatic transition, Jo's first year at the brothel had been spent in relative comfort, despite the part of her that ached to go back to the life she'd once known. However, as time had dragged on, the glamour of her elevated, though fallen position had faded rapidly, leaving her consumed by regret. There was no going back. All she would bring her family now was shame.

Jo sauntered across the sitting room to the green, velvet chaise lounge by the open fireplace. At least here, she wasn't required to deal in volume-trade like in the cribs, cottages, and low-end brothels. A parlor house specialized in fine wine, champagne, good food, and counterfeit romance.

She sat, careful to position herself attractively, putting herself on display like a china doll on a shelf. She arranged the red silk overskirt to drape across the cream skirt, highlighting the contrast of the lace-trimmed bodice intricately embroidered with flowers.

The tight bodice and hoop skirt of the princess gown made every movement stiff, increasing the sensation of being on display. This dress was her most recent purchase from a traveling salesman who had come from New York. It had pained her to pay the high price, a double-eagle gold piece, for the dress. She'd never had any real love for gowns, but if she ever wanted to make enough money to leave the brothel behind, she needed to keep her services in high demand. The dress was eye-catching, cut low in the front, and sported only a light rim of tassels at the shoulder, leaving her arms bare. It was quite the contrast to the leg-o-mutton, puffed sleeves that were the more typical fashion among the district's proper ladies but not as overtly distasteful as the chemise-clad girls in the cribs and cottage houses on the row.

The tinkling doorbell sent a shock of panic skittering over her. The guest list for the evening was full. Whoever was at the door was uninvited. Every muscle stiffened, and she held her breath as Bernard, who was pouring drinks, moved swiftly to the door.

A man walked in and removed his hat. Jo released the breath she held. He wasn't the man she'd feared.

The new guest was quite tall, with a dark, manicured mustache, bowler hat, and a gray suit. He looked straight past Bernard and flashed a charming smile at Hazel, who came to greet him. The puzzled look on Hazel's face confirmed Jo's suspicion that this gentleman hadn't made an appointment.

The brothel's steadfast rule that customers must have appointments in advance was well known. If the man were a stranger, a letter of reference would also be required. This standard provided the establishment with a level of safety for the boarders and madam that lower-end brothels could not.

To Jo's surprise, the stranger took Hazel by the hand, covertly slipping something into it, bent his head near her ear, and whispered. She hesitated for a moment but smiled and escorted him to the bar, instructing the bartender to pour him a glass of fine champagne.

A knot hardened in Jo's chest. Hazel's apparent disregard of the brothel's rules left her vulnerable and exposed. The only solace she had of living in this sordid place was the protection and anonymity it afforded her.

Jo continued to watch the man from her perch in the corner. Was this dandy in his fine clothes a fox in the henhouse? The Old Homestead Parlour House was the finest establishment of its kind in Cripple Creek. The high price for a night's entertainment ensured the average patronage was wealthy, prominent men—the older, pudgy sort. This man couldn't be more than thirty years old and was much more attractive than her usual clientele. Maybe she was overreacting.

Nothing about this profession held any enjoyment, but she knew the business well. She needed to play her part, one night, one trick at a time. She lifted the china cup to her lips and met his eye over the edge of the cup, cocking a feathery eyebrow and giving him a coy smile.

The stranger's eyes flashed. His upper lip curled in a predatory sneer like a cat who had found its mouse. A cold chill trickled over her as her stomach tied itself into a knot. She knew that seductive smile too well. She had experience with this type of man before. A man like this could turn from mild-mannered to monstrous in the blink of an eye.

Fool. Why had she been so bold? Displayed on the lounge, she was exposed, vulnerable now. Jo froze in place, dampening her usual beacon of flirtatious charm. Could she fade into the hand-painted, French wallpaper behind her?

No. Jo already had the man's attention. She had intentionally placed herself beneath the electric lights knowing her striking, strawberry blond waves would shine like a siren calling out across the sea of salacious women and drunken men.

She lowered her eyes and began studiously counting the number of brass rivets along the upholstery edge of the chaise lounge, bolstering her courage. One, two, three ... Each tick of the mantel clock above the fireplace sent a jolt of dread up her spine. Would this ever get any easier? She'd been here too long. The weight in her heart wasn't going to get any lighter as long as she was here. She had to find a way out.

A weight shifted on the plush, velvet seat beside her, and her fingertips shook over the brass rivets. She turned to find the dark-haired stranger seated beside her. He smiled charmingly, but there was something feral in his eyes that struck a chord of panic in her.

"W-Well, hello there." Jo mustered up a pleasant smile.

"Hello, yourself," he teased, his voice smooth and low. "I'm told you go by the name Copper Kate." He sat close enough that the sickly-sweet fragrance of his cologne was overpowering. The scent of it turned her stomach, and she closed her eyes, holding her breath for a moment. She took in a shallow breath, steadying herself, letting it out slowly. She opened her eyes again and smiled with a bland mask of calm.

"So I see an introduction of myself is no longer necessary, but what is your name?" She did her best to sound lighthearted, hoping that she was wrong about the type of man she feared he was.

"You don't need my name." The statement was abrupt, lacking any charm.

"Well, now, how can we go on about our evening if you don't have a name?" She brushed past the sudden change in his mood, remaining as cordial as she could. "Why don't you just give me something I can call you?"

"Carver. You can call me Mr. Carver." His smooth, warm tone was back, and he smiled as though finding something funny. Had she misjudged his character? A little more relaxed now, she motioned to the decanter on the side table.

"Mr. Carver, would you care for a drink?"

She guessed the transitory shift in his mood might have to do with nervousness. Maybe a nip of whiskey might calm him. He nodded, and she poured him a glass. After handing it to him, she reached out and placed a calming hand over his. A twitch of tension ran through him at her touch. He tossed back the glass of whiskey and jerked his head to one side. An audible crack released from the bones of his neck as they popped with the quick motion.

"It's time," he said in a low voice, standing up abruptly and pulling her toward the stairs. No, she hadn't misjudged him after all.

She frantically searched the room for Hap, the big man who guarded the girls. Where was he? Hap always sat at the end of the bar and monitored the comings and goings from the room. He wasn't there. She hesitated, hoping to find a way to stall their ascent of the stairway. Hap was a caring soul and all-fired protective of his girls. He never left them alone.

The bouncer's job was to move from his post at the bar only when one of the girls had a customer in her room. At that point, he would follow the pair and take up residence on the stool in the hall.

She breathed a quick sigh of relief. *The hall.* He must be at his post upstairs.

"I said it's time." The man clipped the words behind his gritted teeth and guided her by her elbow to the stairs.

Her legs shook as she climbed the stairs and walked down the hall to the door to her room. As she crossed the threshold, she glanced back to Hap's stool. It was empty.

The door slammed behind her, jarring her nerves. At a loss of what else to do, she moved forward with her usual routine. She crossed the room to gain some distance and her bearings.

"I assume you paid Ms. Hazel downstairs? Us girls can only accept tips, you know. She handles the transactions."

"Oh, I paid highly for your services tonight." He sat on the bed and leaned forward. "And I know it will be worth every copper."

"Well, then." She pulled the skirt of her dress above the knee and propped her foot up on an ottoman to unbutton her shoe. "What'll it be?"

"What'll it be?" He repeated her words over to himself as if weighing them on some unseen scale.

Jo finished the buttons on the first shoe and paused to look up at him. "What's your pleasure, mister?" She spoke bluntly, impatient with his repetition of her words. His eyes narrowed, and he stood up from the bed, cracking his neck as he had done earlier.

"You're no different than those whores down on crib row." His voice was low and had lost its former smoothness. The feral look she'd seen before snapped to life in his dark eyes. Her heart stopped beating for a moment, then started back with a thunderous pounding in her chest. Her stomach tied itself into a knot, and a bead of sweat trickled down her spine.

"I-I beg your pardon?"

"You're nothing but a filthy, lying harlot." He came closer, and she stood erect, standing at her full height. She refused to show the terror that caused her heart to beat against her chest like a battering ram. He towered over her. "You paint over your filthiness with powder and call yourself a lady, but you're just as ugly as all the rest."

He stood between her and the door, and she glanced over his shoulder, gauging the distance, weighing her chances of getting past him. She reached under the overskirt of her dress for the dirk she carried. She slipped it from its sheath and bolted for the door, hoping she wouldn't have to use it. He caught her by the hair. Twisting against his grip, she slashed the knife in his direction. The knobby metal handle was slick with sweat, allowing him to jerk it free from her hand. The blade sliced down her palm with shooting pain. She tried to scream, but he clamped a cold, clammy hand over her mouth so hard her top lip split against her teeth. Tasting metal from the blood, she struggled and fought with every ounce of strength in her. The man's arms were like iron bonds. She was helpless.

He ripped the voluminous lacy frill from the bodice of her gown and crammed it in her mouth, silencing her and almost choking her on it. She was jerked back, and the sound of tearing of fabric preceded her being slammed face down on the wooden plank floor. His boot heel dug into her back, and he pulled the strings of her corset with all his might. The air was forced from her lungs, and black-red pain engulfed her vision as a rib cracked under the force. He released the ties and jerked a fist-full of hair, lifting her head off the floor. The glint of shining metal flashed in the corner of her eye as he twisted a knife back and forth in his left hand.

"I'll show the world how ugly you really are." His voice dripped with disgust.

Her back arched as he yanked on her hair even harder and dragged the knife across her skin in an excruciating arc of hatred.

Chapter 2

The sound of a woman humming brought Jo to the murky surface of consciousness. She tried to open her eyes, and a stinging sensation like a line of fire shot down the left side of her face. She gasped and sat up.

Her cry of anguish was barely audible as a sharp, stabbing pain shot through her right side. She froze in place, careful not to move more than necessary. Drawing in slow, shallow breaths, she reached up to her face, only to realize her hand was wrapped in a bandage. More cloth bandages also covered the entire left side of her face.

She tried to speak, but her throat was dry and cracking, unable to form clear words. More cautiously this time, she opened only her right eye, and a blurry, bright space began to reveal itself around her. Across the room, a woman was arranging something in a cabinet. The humming once again registered as her senses began to clear.

"Wh-Where am I?" Her parched throat strained to utter the words at anything above a whisper. She cleared her throat and tried once again to get the woman's attention. "Ma'am," she said in a raspy tone but more clearly this time.

Still no response. Jo looked around the room again now that she seemed to have gained some clarity in one eye. On the right side of the narrow bed was a side table with a glass of water. Struggling to rise, she managed to pick up the glass and take a drink. At once, her throat was soothed, and she nearly shouted.

"Ma'am!"

The woman across the room jumped and turned to face her. The soft light streaming in from the window seemed to illuminate the weightless, butter-yellow curls escaping from a long braid giving her the appearance of a celestial vision. With a genuine smile, she quickly crossed the room and knelt beside Jo's bed.

"Oh, my sweet girl, you're awake. Hallelujah!"

Still quite confused at this strange place and the sharp pain in her side, Jo wrinkled her forehead, which again sent waves of stinging pain across her face.

"What? Where am I?" Jo was finally managing clear words but not yet clear thoughts.

"You are at Dr. Thornton's place." The woman paused, pursing her lips. "You had a run-in with a very bad man, my dear. You're lucky to be alive."

Jo settled back on the pillow once more and tried to gain some mental clarity.

"My name is Mrs. Thornton. You may call me Abigail. I'll go get John, that is, Dr. Thornton. He'll be so pleased to know you're awake."

She touched Jo's arm gently and whisked out of the room in a flutter of light cotton. Jo closed her unbandaged eye again and tried to make sense of all this. What had happened? Still images came to her one by one, but it was like a puzzle beyond her ability to put together. The sitting room of the parlor house, brass rivets set in green upholstery, an empty stool in the hall.

She opened her eye again, seeking to escape the confusion of choppy memories. A black and white photograph of Abigail posing formally next to a handsome man with neatly combed brown hair and wire-rimmed glasses sat on the table next to the water glass.

"Well, well, look who decided to join us today, Abigail." The man from the photograph entered the room, followed by his wife.

Again, these people spoke to her with such kindness, and it seemed as though they had been old friends, which was impossible. In exchange for a six-dollar monthly tax, Jo and the other girls were allowed to frequent the shops and businesses on Bennett Avenue. Still, they were only allowed to do so "after hours" so the civilized ladies of Cripple Creek wouldn't be subjected to their presence. As a result of the restriction, Jo knew few people from the town unless they visited the brothel.

She had seen a doctor before who would routinely come to check on the girls, but he had been an older, sweaty, fat man who smelled of pipe tobacco. This doctor must be new in town.

He pulled up a low, wooden stool beside the bed and listened to her breathing with a stethoscope. Apparently satisfied with his observations, he smiled again.

"How do you feel?" he asked, leaning back on his stool.

"I hurt," Jo answered bluntly, resisting the urge to raise a sarcastic eyebrow.

The doctor nodded. "Yes, that is to be expected for quite some time. You have a long road of healing ahead of you. But don't worry, we'll take good care of you."

"How did I get here?" Jo's voice shook with fatigue.

"A big gentleman, but a kind soul." He rubbed his chin. "Hap, I believe, brought you to us. He told us your name and what had happened to you. He was mighty worried about you."

At this, he allowed Abigail to sit down. She set a basin of water with a cloth in it on the side table.

"I need to change your dressings now, Miss Kate."

This woman was calling her Kate, not Jo. With Hap bringing her here, they must know what she was. Why were they treating her with such kindness?

"This might sting a bit, but I will be as gentle as I possibly can."

Abigail assisted her in sitting up by propping several pillows behind her neck and back before unwinding a long bandage from around Jo's head, then another that started at her neck and transitioned under her arms and around her chest. Whatever the large wound was, it stung like fire, and Jo bit her lip, trying to fight back the tears.

A wave of nausea overcame her when she looked down at the ugly red line across her chest covered in dozens of stitches like a railroad track. She retched into the basin on Abigail's lap. The heaving pressure made the pain in her side unbearable. She stifled the sickness as quickly as possible to avoid any more agony from what must be a broken rib.

The cut ran across her chest in a downward motion and stopped between her breasts. Abigail kept the sheet discretely pulled up to preserve what modesty she could, and Jo held back an urge to laugh. What modesty was there to protect?

"You were quite lucky." The doctor interrupted her moment of ironic mirth. "No," he corrected himself, "you are quite blessed. The good Lord protected you from what could've been so much worse. While your wounds will scar, miraculously, the cut was not deep enough to damage your eye or cut your throat. And there is also no real damage to your breasts. You will still be able to nurse a child."

She looked at him with incredulity. "A child?" she scoffed. "You do know what I am, don't you?"

He sighed deeply, offering a sad smile and a thoughtful expression. He placed a hand on his wife's shoulder. "Yes, I do, but that doesn't mean it is who you have to be." He turned and walked out of the room, leaving the two women alone.

Abigail began gently cleansing the freshly stitched wounds with cool water and replacing the bandages with clean cloth strips soaked in medicinal liquid. Jo blinked at the odd smell.

"Carbolic acid." Abigail nodded to a brown glass bottle on the table next to them. She applied bandages with gentle pressure, but the solution stung like fire. "I know it's not pleasant, but it will keep your cuts from becoming inflamed."

The increased burning sensation from the medicine brought back the full force of her attack. Her memory was no longer separate puzzle pieces but an ongoing flood of images like the moving pictures she had seen when a wealthy customer had brought in a new gadget to boast on.

What came back to her terrified her all over again. She remembered the dark-haired man pulling her head from the floor by her hair, so far backward her back had strained and arched in agony as he ran the knife from her chest up her neck and face, ending above her left eye. He had then begun tugging her hair, yanking her head to and fro in a jerky motion. Suddenly, without any further attack or molestation, the man had fled the room, and she'd been left wheezing for every stuttering, painful breath. She lay staring at a pile of red-gold hair in front of her until blood blurred her vision, and the room faded into a red fog.

When the moving pictures of memory subsided, Jo reached a hand up and felt the ragged, short crop of hair where her luxurious locks had once been. She closed her unbandaged eye and fought back the stinging tears that threatened to break over.

GIDEON LISTENED IN the silent stillness of pre-dawn light for the high-pitched scream and chuckle that was the quintessential call of a Rocky Mountain Elk. The sound would set a plan in motion for this morning's hunt. It was yet a few hours before full light, and the air held the cold crispness of Colorado autumn at high elevation.

This time of year was the peak time to be hunting elk. For a few weeks each fall, the bull elk would be in a mad frenzy to gather their herd and build their harem. They would be exceedingly vocal, screaming out a spine-tingling bugle to call wayward females.

There. The adrenaline rush brought on by the elk's bugle caused a lightness in Gideon's chest that left him breathless. The call came from a bench far above the game trail where he had stopped to listen.

Taking a steadying breath, he checked his Sharps carbine rifle to make sure all was in order and began the ambitious climb. While the morning was still early, there was no time to waste. The moon had been full the night before. The elk would have fed all night and would soon retreat to the shadows of the darker timber to bed down before the mid-morning sun had a chance to warm the sloping mountainside.

Cold breath prickled in his bellows as he scaled the near-vertical terrain. Damp leaves, crushed underfoot, gave off an invigorating aroma that kept him moving. After an hour of arduous climbing, he was finally close to the area the bull's raspy bugle had come from. The sun had just begun to crest the craggy clifftops on the east side of the canyon, creating a faint pink glow, brightening the snowy peaks in the distance. He marveled in the grandeur of the mountains. This solitary life in the Rockies was far removed from the Kansas prairie.

The hillside he traversed remained in cool shadow, but it would not be so for long. He quietly removed his rawhide pack to keep it from snagging on the low-hanging branches and pushed himself the remaining twenty feet up to the edge of the bench.

He reached the top with the triumphant, fulfilling fatigue of conquering his goal. As he cleared the last of the golden aspen trees on the ridge, a small herd of elk, grazing in a clearing on the bench, startled and bolted at his sudden appearance.

He dropped to his knees and bowed his head in defeat.

Greenhorn, fool. There goes dinner. It was a good thing Clay wasn't here to witness his blunder. After all the time he'd spent teaching Gideon the ways of the mountain, he'd never let Gideon hear the end of it. Gideon rocked back on his heels and rubbed a hand over his jaw, aching from the tension there. The soft fullness of his beard had grown long, measuring the time he had been living on this mountain.

His heart had nearly burst with the commotion but now hardened in his chest. He released a slow breath. *How about not tramping about the woods like a stampeding buffalo next time, eh?*

Regaining his composure, he looked back where he had left his pack and landmarked the location in his memory. He laid a hand on the bowie knife at his belt and rested his rifle over his shoulder. He shouldn't need anything else for the time being. Even if he were blessed enough to harvest an elk this morning, he wouldn't climb any higher today. The cliffs above were growing too steep to pack an elk safely down. He ought to stick to areas where his mule, Jack, could pack out for him. But this vertical climb wouldn't have been safe for horse or mule, and Gideon loved the sheer physical challenge of a hunt like this.

He followed the bench in the opposite direction the group of cow elk had gone. It wouldn't do to continue bumping them and alarming all the other wildlife in the area. He'd missed his chance with that bunch.

He continued hiking through the fragrant pines, and within a quarter-hour, Gideon heard a branch crack. He stopped dead in his tracks, his heart racing, and listened closely. The distinct, drum-like "glunking" noise and a sharp, sweet scent in the air told Gideon not only had he located the bull, but he was extraordinarily close.

He willed his nerves to calm and gathered his wits. He could make out the faint impression of an old game trail working its way in the direction of the bull, and he thanked the Lord for the soft moccasins that allowed him to creep to the edge of a nearby clearing.

He checked that his Sharps was loaded and ready to fire and let out the mewing sound of a cow elk, hoping the bull would come looking to round up a lost cow. The bull responded with a sharp bark, demanding the wayward cow to join the others. Gideon picked up a branch from the damp forest floor and raked it against the tree beside him.

The raking did the trick. The thump-thump of the bull's cloven hoofbeats reverberated through the soft layer of soil and plant decay and into the soles of Gideon's moccasins.

Heart pounding, he raised his rifle and braced it in the gap of spruce bows on the tree he stood beside. He waited.

The magnificent creature made his appearance, blinded by his ambition to fight off the threat of another bull in his territory. One step into the clearing, two, and as soon as the lighter color of the hair on its shoulder cleared the tree line, Gideon slowly squeezed the trigger.

Chapter 3

Jo followed Abigail into the spare room. She had been a resident or guest at John and Abigail's house for a week now, but he had insisted she stay longer to give her cracked ribs time to heal and allow him to watch her wounds for any further signs of infection. Abigail had said moving Jo to this room would free up the bed she'd been occupying in the patient room while allowing her additional time to heal.

Abigail opened the curtains, sunlight casting a golden ray of sunshine on the bed. "That's more like it."

The cheery yellow-and-blue-patterned quilt and the vase of wildflowers on the bedside table warmed Jo's spirits. It was like being home again. Though she couldn't pinpoint any definitive similarities in the house or the Thorntons' themselves, there was something familiar with her home and her parents back in Kansas.

Abigail surveyed the room with authoritative hands on her hips. "Now, what you need is a hot bath and a change of clothes." She must've been a school matron in a former life. All orderliness and propriety—not in a brisk or unkind way—but in a way that said she knew her purpose in life.

Jo stepped up to the window and peeked around the sheer, white fabric. Had Jo ever known her purpose in life?

Outside the window, the Thorntons' shaggy, white cart-pony reached his soft nose as far as he could under the bottom board of the fence to get the last few bunches of grass available.

Once, Jo had thought she would explore the wild Rocky Mountains and build a life with Gideon. Perhaps she would've even trained horses. She sighed and lifted her eyes past the rows of houses that stretched out to the edge of the foothills surrounding Cripple Creek.

Beyond, the mountains sprawled, growing larger as the landscape expanded. Each mountain grew in stature until, at last, the formidable Pikes Peak showed itself in the distance, jutting far above the rest with its snowy cap purple in the afternoon light.

Her heart yearned to escape to those mountains so seemingly clean and untouched.

It's no use. There's no way out now. She exhaled slowly, leaving a hollow void in her chest and fog on the glass window that faded as quickly as it had appeared. Her dream and any purpose she'd once had were gone now, having vanished like a mountain mist.

She took in one last moment of the magnificent view and turned back to face the cozy room.

"I'll just be a minute." Abigail flitted out of the room, leaving Jo to take in her new surroundings.

She sat on the edge of the bed and ran her fingers lightly across the quilt, tracing its double wedding band pattern. She appreciated the reprieve from life at the brothel, but she was an imposter here. She had to avoid getting too comfortable. While she wasn't ready to face the ugliness of the real world yet, the extra time here must be racking up quite the bill. A bill that she couldn't afford. She had to move on soon. But how?

Working at the parlor house meant she made quite a bit more money than the average prostitute, but she also was required to pay rent and purchase the dresses, perfumes, and cosmetics that she was expected to use. By the time it was all said and done, she only ever broke even. She never had a half-cent to spare at the end of the month.

She didn't have money to move on from this town. She would have to go back to the brothel. Wouldn't she? Her stomach roiled, and the room tilted. She steadied herself with one hand on the iron footboard beside her. The cool metal grounded her, and she drew in a steadying breath.

Life at the brothel had been a vile necessity, not something she'd ever aspired to do. Becoming Copper Kate at the brothel had provided protection and anonymity that kept her safe from being discovered by Kane. She had only meant it to be a temporary solution after she had escaped Kane and the Blake Gang and had been left with no other options to stave off starvation.

Jo had fantasized about finding a way out of this mess but had never been able to save enough money even to begin to come up with another plan. Her hiding place had transformed into a prison.

Growing restless, she stood again, careful not to jostle her sore ribs, and began pacing. What was she doing here? She'd never be a proper lady in a fine house or even a suitable wife for any man. A life like Abigail had was beyond her grasp now, but if she could save enough money to get to

Denver and find work somewhere as a seamstress or washerwoman, she just might be able to find contentment. She detested the idea of city life, but maybe the throngs of people could help her disappear where she wouldn't have to live in constant fear of being found.

Would that still be an option for her now? Given a larger city, could she pass as just another face in the crowd?

Jo didn't even know what she looked like now. Dr. Thornton had removed the stitches the day before, but she hadn't yet had the stomach to look at her reflection. The mirror above the bureau taunted her from the corner of the room. She pressed her lips together, wincing at the sting of broken skin against her teeth. She dreaded what she would find in her reflection almost as much as she had dreaded her first night at the parlor house. But there was no more stalling. She had to know what she would be facing.

She wavered slightly but gritted her teeth and lifted her chin. *Come on, Jo, we've gotten through harder things than facing a mirror.*

It took four shaky steps to cross the room and stand before the bureau. Jo kept her eyes trained on the floor, taking in every scuff mark and crack in the wood. Slowly, she drew in a deep breath and pulled her eyes up to her reflection.

She gasped and jerked at the distorted face in the mirror, and the quick motion sent a shot of pain through her side. John had said her ribs likely weren't broken, only cracked, but the sudden move was excruciating. Her head was light from the sharp intake of breath, and she braced her palms on the bureau to keep from falling.

Her gaze wandered restlessly over the reflection, unsure where to settle first. The ugly, dark red scabbing ran the length of her face and disappeared in the neckline of the dressing gown Abigail had given her. She closed her eyes, willing her stomach to keep its contents in place. Releasing a shaky breath, she forced herself to look again.

Her hair—oh, the wreckage. The long, thick waves were now choppy swirls that stood out this way and that. A mere inch long in one particularly unseemly patch on one side and maybe three inches in other places.

Ugly. It was the only word Jo could conjure. She'd never been vain, but the crushing blow of the reflection staring back at her reduced her to ashes. With her hair so short, she looked masculine. And that terrible scar would always ensure she'd be the center of gossip and speculation. It wouldn't take much for folks to reason out what she was. Only certain women were at risk of the type of ruin she now wore as a flaming red banner down her face.

Abigail backed through the bedroom door with a bundle in her arms. "I've gathered everything we need to get you all cleaned up and—" Her customarily cheerful countenance fell when Jo looked back at her through the mirror. "Oh, my dear." Abigail dropped the armload of clothes, hair combs, and soap onto the quilt and gathered Jo into her arms.

No words could convey Jo's grief. She sucked in a breath and held back her tears as Abigail spoke soothing words over her and patted her back. As lost as a distraught child, Jo buried her face into the puffed sleeve of Abigail's blouse and bit her lip to distract herself from the desire to cry.

"Your hair will grow back, and your scar will fade." Abigail gently took Jo's shoulders and set her straight again, tucking a wayward strand of Jo's hair behind her ear. "It will always be there, but the redness and swelling will go down, and you'll feel much more like yourself in no time."

Jo scoffed. She hadn't felt like herself since she'd run from home. This scar was only going to make things worse.

"Come now, let's get you washed up, and I'll see what I can do to tame that hair of yours." Abigail scooped up the bundle from the bed and motioned Jo to follow.

The bathroom was modest but comfortable, sporting a washstand and an enameled rolltop tub emitting a hazy vapor of steam. A screen stretched across the corner of the room for privacy. Jo was vaguely aware as Abigail busily fussed with the buttons of Jo's dress. Abigail finished undressing Jo while she stood in a daze. When Abigail stepped away to hang clean clothing on the screen, Jo let the borrowed dressing gown slide to the floor and dipped a toe into the hot water. She longed to slip beneath the surface and disappear from this world into another where the waves would carry away the weight of her mistakes, and she could remain peacefully adrift and alone.

Pain pricked her skin from the heat, bringing her back to reality. She welcomed the sensation. She longed for a cleansing she wasn't sure could be achieved even if the water had been boiling. In these past quiet days at the Thorntons', Jo had no distractions and ample time to think about her present situation. It was quite the contrast to the life she'd led since leaving Kansas. The sordid filth of her relationship with Kane Blake, her time as an outlaw, then serving herself on a platter in the brothel, it all clung to her. She scrubbed violently with the soap and pumice stone, leaving red streaks down her arms.

"Stop that!" Abigail snatched the pumice from Jo's hand.

"I can't—" Jo sobbed, the tears stinging the wound that scabbed across her eyelid. "I can't get clean." She forced herself to stop the tears. "It's not enough. I'll never be clean."

Abigail pulled up a stool behind Jo and gently tipped her head back, soaking her hair in the hot water. She took the soap from Jo and began washing her hair. The faint smell of lavender and rosemary wafted around Jo and filled her senses. She closed her eyes and leaned back, allowing Abigail to scrub and massage her scalp. As Abigail washed Jo's hair, she hummed a familiar tune, and Jo surrendered to her ministrations.

"We'll have you fixed up in no time," Abigail spoke quietly, as though not to disturb Jo.

Although she couldn't see any possible outcome to her current situation that was even tolerable, Jo would rest and take comfort from the rare generosity of this woman. She wasn't likely to reencounter its kind.

Chapter 4

Gideon - Age 8
Jo - Age 5

Gideon watched from across the knot of churchgoers as Jo stood impatiently tugging at her mother's skirt. She swayed back and forth like a jack-in-the-box on its spring. Mrs. Bradford bent down to hear Jo's request, smoothed Jo's coppery hair, and tucked a wayward strand behind the little girl's ear. With a pleasant smile, she gave a nod of her head and looked over the crowd to wave at Gideon, signaling that little Jo, three years younger, would now be in his charge for the afternoon.

Jo ran for him, squealing with a mischievous smile stretched across her freckled face.

"C'mon." She grasped him by the hand and dragged him out past the country church toward the creek.

Gideon scanned the small crowd to ensure his little brother was safely at Ma's side. He'd hate for the little guy to follow and get lost. Jimmy stood next to Ma as she spoke to Mrs. Bradford, his shy face buried in her skirt.

When Jo and Gideon had barely escaped the borders of the town, she began grasping at apron strings and tugging at skirts and petticoats, pulling them over her head.

"Jo, what are you doing?" Gideon whipped around to look behind them, and his heart gripped with panic that someone would see them. He let out a whistle of relief when he saw the pair of rolled-up britches under her skirt.

"We goin' fishing." Jo squealed again, flinging her dress behind her in sheer abandon.

Gideon caught the dress as it flew through the air and scrambled to pick up her stockings and boots scattered by the trail in her wake.

They reached their favorite spot, where the water cut into the bank, creating a deeper fishing hole than the main channel offered. Sunlight glinted off of the calm depths of the barely moving stream.

Gideon withdrew the coiled line from one pocket and a small jar from the other. He unwrapped the hook from its cotton wadding and held it between his teeth. Jo squirmed beside him, vibrating with anxious anticipation as he opened the small jar and produced a cricket. Her giggle bubbled up, extending its ripple out to him, causing him to chuckle as well. Jo's eyes were wide, her mouth twisting in concentration as she watched him slip the cricket onto the hook with care.

They crept over to a large, fallen white oak tree bordering the edge of the stream. Hiding behind the log, Gideon dangled the cricket over the water.

"Now, see here? You gotta trick 'em into thinking this'n is just another one of them bugs that be flyin' over the water." With light skips and quick jerks, Gideon tickled the shimmering surface with the bait, causing it to dance across the water.

They watched the trout weaving back and forth just out of reach under the glittering ripples.

"This was Wyatt Earp's favorite fishin' spot, you know," Gideon said importantly.

"Was not."

"Was so. Charlie Parker told me that his uncle Chet told him." Gideon tipped the broad brim of his straw hat back and leaned to one side, propping himself up on one elbow. "He caught a big'in right here in this very spot."

"A biggin? I ne'er even heard of a biggin. What's it look like?"

"Not a biggin, you ninny. A ... big ... one. It was a catfish this big." Gideon stretched out his arms and widened his eyes to magnify the effect.

Jo snorted. "You're pullin' my leg. They don't make 'em that big."

"No, I ain't. It was as big as you are. No foolin'!"

"Mama says Charlie Parker tells tall tales. You ought not to be listening to him."

"It ain't a tall tale. That catfish was fifty pounds at least." Gideon stood up, flustered that his story was being spoiled. Determined to impress on his little friend just how big the fish had been, he flung his arms wider than before, and the hook and line flew into the air.

"Dad-blame-it!" The hook snagged on a branch high in the air.

"I'll get it!" Jo immediately began climbing up the tall oak tree.

"Don't do that. You'll fall." Gideon looked around himself in a panic, trying to think of what to do. It was too late to stop her. The little possum was already out of his reach. She climbed out onto the limb the hook was caught on. It waved up and down over the water. "Jo, stop."

"Don't be silly, I got—"

A crack echoed over the water, and the branch broke free from the hundred-year-old tree trunk. Splash.

Gideon's heart clenched like a fist. Jo couldn't swim.

"Gideon!" The sound of thrashing in the water covered Jo's gurgling cries.

He flung himself into the water after her and gripped her tightly against himself. Her thrashing kept him from swimming straight for the bank. They bobbed under the surface and came up sputtering and gasping.

Hoping he could touch a toe to the bottom and steady them, Gideon straightened out a leg, resulting in an awkward stumble. *What—*

He planted the foot again, and mud squished between his bare toes as he stood straight out of the water which eddied around his hips. Jo clung to him tightly, squeezing her eyes shut.

"Put your foot down, ya loon."

She peeked up at him, one eye open, and released her grip. Even as small as she was, the water was only chest deep on her.

"Oh." She gave a sheepish grin and a giggle.

Gideon tried to remain stern and severe, but a snort fizzled out through his nose.

"Well, it's hot today. We should be able to dry off before anyone sees us." Gideon sheltered his eyes from the bright sun with one hand.

They climbed up onto the bank, laughing. When they looked up, Elaine, Jo's older sister, stood on the bank with a hand on her hip, eyes wide with triumph.

"You two are in so much trouble."

GIDEON TIGHTENED THE cinch of the mule's pack saddle and began tying down the two canvas bags filled with fresh elk meat that he had thoroughly cooled in the creek. He'd killed three elk in the past two weeks, two cows, and the bull he'd shot yesterday. One, Gideon had butchered and preserved with salt in the cellar dug into the mountainside behind the cabin. The other two he would be bringing down to Cripple Creek to sell. The cook at the Imperial Hotel would pay a pretty price if he could get it there quickly.

Hunting and trapping on a large scale in the Rockies had become a thing of the past. The early mountain men had over-trapped the beaver and lost interest. Most gold mining endeavors in Colorado had also played out, but Gideon found the mining boom in Cripple Creek had started later than the other mining towns in Colorado and was still thriving.

Living deep in the mountains, a full day's ride from the mining town nicknamed "The Paris of the West," Gideon could hunt and trap on a smaller scale, supplying the businesses of Cripple Creek with game meat and furs.

After tying down the packs on Jack, Gideon walked back to the cabin to close things up. He secured the oiled hides over the windows and latched the heavy wooden door with a leather strap. It would be secured from the elements, but if anyone needed shelter for the night, they would be welcome.

Before mounting, he gave Jack, his big black mule, a smart smack on the belly. "Come on now, suck it in." There was no time for shenanigans today.

Jack was faithful and steady but ornery as they came. He'd learned to take an enormous breath while being saddled, expanding his midsection by at least three inches. Once Gideon turned his back, Jack would relax, causing the cinch on the pack to loosen. Half a mile down the trail, the pack would begin tipping sideways, eventually slipping around his middle, dropping Jack's load below his belly.

Gideon had now developed the habit of loading him early and walking away. When it was time to leave, he would quickly tighten the cinch on the unsuspecting mule, and they could be on their way without further incident.

Jack gave a reluctant groan and relaxed. Gideon tightened the slack of the heavy panniers' cinch one more time.

He mounted his paint gelding, Sarge, and looked over the place he called home. This piece of ground was pretty enough to be considered hallowed.

Gideon had built the cabin against a hillside where quaking aspen trees mingled with the tall spruce that dominated the mountains' higher elevation above the house.

While most cabins in the mountains were only about six feet tall, Gideon built his roof another two feet higher, making it more comfortable for his large frame. He detested cramped spaces and wasn't about to live in one, even if it meant cutting more firewood to keep it warm.

He'd added a covered porch, complete with a handmade rocking bench he'd built from aspen wood, barked with a draw knife until it was smooth.

It was a beautiful home, and Gideon was proud of the workmanship he had accomplished, but he wasn't satisfied living here alone.

After leaving Kansas to find Pa, he'd settled down near Pikes Peak and began building the cabin. He'd planned to return to Kansas, marry Jo, and bring her to live in this haven he had made for them. When Gideon had written to tell Jo he was coming back for her, he'd received a letter from Ma that had brought him to his knees.

Jo was gone. Vanished. Just like Pa.

No one knew where she was or what had happened to her. She had disappeared six months after Gideon left for Colorado.

Now, he woke each day in the cabin he'd built for her, left only with a hollow ache in his chest. He loved his mountain lifestyle, but it wasn't the life he wanted. Not without her.

Gideon turned Sarge's head down the trail and clicked his tongue for Jack to keep up, glancing, one last time, at the cabin he had built for Jo. Everything was about to change. He'd made many trips up and down this mountain, but this time, he wouldn't return alone.

Gideon had grieved the loss of Jo long enough, though. Something tragic had befallen her, and after nearly three years, perhaps it was time to give God a chance to fill the hole in his heart.

He didn't like to admit he was lonely. Didn't like it one bit. But God said it wasn't good for man to be alone. After his own family had been torn apart when Pa left, Gideon's purpose became simple. Rebuild the family he'd lost. He wanted a wife and family to provide for and cherish, even if it meant putting his youthful dreams of a life with Jo behind him.

Everything had been settled with the pastor last month. On this trip back to town, he was going to bring home a wife. The town of Cripple Creek boomed with gold miners, cowboys, bankers, and laborers. The ratio of men to women was roughly five to one, so naturally, any well-bred young lady would be hitched the moment she was of marrying age. However, overpopulation, crowding, and poverty in eastern cities had left many young women back east looking for better circumstances.

One such young woman was due to arrive on the train this morning, and Pastor Walton agreed to introduce her to Gideon and arrange the match.

Gideon didn't fancy the idea of a city girl, and the prospect of marrying someone he hardly knew was daunting, but he reckoned that it was the only way for him to find a wife with the secluded life he lived.

Halfway down the mountain, Gideon reined his horse to a stop near a large boulder that caused an eddying pool near the grassy bank. It wouldn't do to show up in Cripple Creek, hoping to bring home a wife, smelling like a wild animal.

He loosely looped the reins of his horse around a branch and slipped off his moccasins. As he dipped a toe in the water to test how frigid his bath would be, a convulsive shiver ran over him.

It was going to be a cold one. Although marginally warmer than the first spring run-off, Colorado mountain creeks were always as cold as the year-round snowmelt they came from. It had been a big adjustment from the warmer streams he and Jo used to fish in back in Kansas.

He stripped off his buckskin shirt and leggings and stepped purposefully into the shallow water. The bones of his ankles ached from the cold, but he steadied himself, bracing one hand on the bank behind him. Drawing in a deep, fortifying breath, he plunged himself as thoroughly as he could.

It was like trying to baptize a cat. Involuntary muscle control took over, and Gideon shot right back up.

"WHOO! Dad-gum, that's cold!" His yodeling cry echoed off the cliff walls above.

Sarge threw his head at the explosion of water, and Jack let out a loud bray as if he found the whole thing hilarious.

"Laugh it up, ya old goat." Gideon gave Jack a narrow glare. Gathering his remaining determination, he forced himself to sit back down in the water and began scrubbing as quickly as possible.

After the brisk bath, he stepped out onto the grassy bank and dressed again. The wet skin on his arms clinging to the leather accentuated how much tighter his buckskin attire was now than it had been when he acquired it at a trading post when he arrived in Colorado. He'd left Kansas at twenty years old, and although he'd known hard work on the ranch, he still had some of the softness of youth left on his tall frame.

Now, after two years in the Rockies, Gideon had begun to harden with maturity, not unlike the logs he cut down for the cabin. Sawing each log to a specific length and barking them with a draw knife until they were smooth, stacking large rocks for the cellar walls, hiking up and down the steep slopes to hunt for the wild game; all of these things had made him into a man. It was hard work living on the mountain. He hoped his new bride would be up to the challenge.

Jo would have been up to it, that was certain. But that dream was in the past now, and it needed to be left there.

Chapter 5

The sound of melodic humming filled the kitchen as Abigail stood in front of the wood cookstove, removing soda farls from the griddle and arranging them on a silver serving dish. Every afternoon, she set out a tea service for the two ladies, and it gave Jo the false sensation of being a fine lady in a grand house.

Abigail was a beautiful woman and carried with her an air of purity and grace. Jo wished she could shake off her constant companion of shame and carry the same lightness this woman had.

Abigail was humming the same familiar tune Jo had heard often over the past few days.

"What song is that, Abigail?" Jo asked as she took her seat at the beautifully laid table.

"Hmm? Oh, it's my favorite hymn. 'Softly and Tenderly, Jesus is Calling,'" Abigail answered over her shoulder.

"Oh." Jo pursed her lips and nodded, looking away, ruffled at yet another reference to Jesus from her new friend. The topic of God set Jo on edge. She'd abandoned the picturesque idea of a loving Heavenly Father somewhere out there. If He did exist as she once had believed, He had long since turned his back on her.

"How soon before I can go back?" Jo asked.

"Oh Jo, please don't." Abigail whipped around to face Jo. "This is your chance to get out. You don't have to go back."

"I can't afford to stay any longer. I don't even know how I'm going to pay your husband for what he's done and the time I've been here so far."

"John and I have spoken about it, and you don't owe us anything. We want to help you get out of that life." Abigail smiled as if she were receiving a generous gift rather than offering one. She turned back and slid the cast iron pan to the cool side of the stove, replacing it with a large teakettle.

What a strange woman this was. What possessed her to treat Jo like a friend? Was she mad? Tears welled in Jo's eyes, and she closed them tight to stop the flow.

"I can't begin to thank you folks enough for what you've done, but it's too late for me," Jo insisted and shook her head. "Look at me, Abigail." Jo raised her voice and gestured to her scarred face. "I am marked for life, branded as a whore. Even if I could find a way to move on from here, move to a new town where no one knew me, what are my choices? Either I am honest about what I am, what I've done, and become an outcast, or I make up some story to explain this scar, pretending like none of this ever happened, making me a liar."

"I'm not only talking about moving to a new place, Jo. I'm talking about a completely fresh start, a chance at love and a family." Abigail pulled off the quilted oven mitts and set them on the counter.

Jo let out a short laugh. "A family? Even if I never turned a trick again, no one would ever marry me." Jo shook her head. "Have you taken a look at me lately?" The lump in Jo's throat was growing larger. "I don't *want* to go back there. But I have to. That's all there is to it." Jo slumped in her chair and picked at a tiny, loose thread on the lace tablecloth. Such a delicate thing, lace. It seemed so stable, one beautiful piece of artwork, but one good tug at the loosened thread, and it would all start to unravel.

"I don't know exactly what I'll do about my appearance. Maybe I can cover this up somehow." Jo firmly pressed her lips together and sighed. "But there's nothing else for me."

Jo peeked over her shoulder. Abigail stared out the kitchen window, wringing her apron in her hands. Why did she even care? The large grandfather clock against the back wall gave a groaning tick and let out a slow chime, marking the three o'clock hour.

"Are you in the habit of reading the Bible at all?" Abigail asked the question casually, leaning back against the counter.

Jo bristled. Abigail was going somewhere with this, and Jo wasn't looking forward to the trip. "Are most girls of my sort in the habit, do you think?" she asked sardonically, raising an auburn eyebrow.

"No, I don't suppose they are, but they should be," Abigail said without any trace of sarcasm or condemnation. She held out a hand to stifle the protest of indignation forming on Jo's lips. "I don't mean that you or they need the Bible more than others do, but you see, there're many stories in this book, true stories, mind you, every word. Throughout those stories, there is a common theme that would likely change your mind." She brought the tray of soda farls to the table and returned for the tea.

"I've read the Bible. I know the stories." Jo shrugged.

"Do you believe them?"

"I did once." Jo sighed. "But that was a long time ago, and He's long since forgotten about me. I've wandered too far and am lost to Him now."

"You're never lost to Him, Jo, not if you once knew Him as you say." Abigail wiped a tear from her cheek.

"As I said, Abigail, it's too late for me." Jo shook her head.

"It's never too late to change your path."

"With all due respect, you wouldn't know a thing about it." Jo bit her lip in irritation.

Abigail carried the tea tray to the table, taking her seat. "I think it's time,"—Abigail pulled in a deep breath and continued—"I think it's time to tell you my own story." She poured each of them a cup of tea and handed Jo the delicate china cup painted with daffodils. The amber-colored liquid swirled around the edge of Jo's cup as she stirred.

"Mind you, this story isn't something I've ever shared with—well—anyone." Abigail's hesitation lingered between them for a few moments. Only the clinking of a silver spoon against china and sugar grating under the crystal sugar bowl lid disturbed the silence.

"You have to understand ..." Abigail continued. "While I've found freedom from my past, many folks would not be as forgiving as my Savior. I need you to know the truth, but we have a good standing in this town, and if some of the more narrow-minded busybodies found out the whole story, our livelihood, John's business, could fail." Abigail pressed her lips tight.

Jo nodded slowly. She didn't understand what Abigail was talking about, but she did understand the need for discretion.

"Contrary to what you may think, I didn't always have this life you see here." Abigail's eyes took on an unfocused stare, entranced as if she were not seeing the lump of sugar dissolving in her cup but something else swirling in its depths. "I grew up in Denver. We didn't have much money. What little money my father earned, he drank away. He died of consumption when I was fourteen years old, and my mother was left destitute with six children." She hesitated, swirling the tea with her spoon in a rhythmic motion. "I was fourteen years old when my mother sold me into prostitution."

Jo dropped her spoon on the saucer with a clatter.

"You?" Jo mouthed the word in shock, and her grasp on the balance of the world as she knew it slipped.

"I was made to work in a brothel for three years, but that particular establishment catered to clients with a specific taste." She grimaced. "At seventeen, I was kicked out. I only knew one trade, so I began street-walking. Much like yourself, I was attacked by a wicked man bent on terrifying and brutalizing. It was winter. When he finished with me, he held my head under the freezing water of Cherry Creek. I almost drowned. He left me for dead, soaking wet in the bitterly cold elements." Abigail shivered before looking up to meet Jo's eyes.

"Oh, Abigail." Jo reached out and took Abigail's hand. This woman had known horrors even Jo hadn't faced. How was it possible that she seemed so proper, so untouched?

"A kind man found me that night and brought me to his friend, who was a doctor who recently graduated medical school." She smiled, but her gaze still lingered far off. "My Johnny cared for me and brought me back to life in more ways than one. He was a Christian man but different than any I'd encountered before. He didn't shun me for my occupation. He just showed compassion. There was a brightness about him that brought light to my darkest corners."

"How did you ... with what you'd been through, how could you ever trust a man, let alone marry one?" Jo had known love once, but she couldn't begin to imagine loving a man again. She was bound to go back to work at the brothel because she had no choice. But that wasn't love.

"By the time my injuries healed, we had developed a friendship of sorts. Something drew me to John. It didn't make any sense, I know. I should have had no use for, let alone trust in, any man. But John was always there. He helped me start a new life and a new job as a seamstress. It was a meager wage but free from the degradation I'd grown accustomed to. He arranged for me to stay with the pastor's family of the church we attended together and escorted me to and from work each day to ensure my safety. He knew, for much longer than I did, that we would be married one day. He chose to put my past behind and only to look forward, but it took me much longer to heal and to come around."

Jo sat in silence, stunned at this revelation. The beautiful, shining example of grace and virtue had once been a soiled dove like herself. She couldn't wrap her mind around it. The ugly shadow of sin and shame Jo was so sure would always be visible to the rest of the world was not evident in Abigail. It wasn't evident in the least. She was a radiant light, not some shadowy figure. Could it be that simple? Was it possible to start over?

"I can't—" Jo stammered, "I can't believe what you're telling me. I mean—well, I believe you, but I can't comprehend it, that's all."

"I think you should go talk to Pastor Walton," Abigail encouraged. "He knows all about my past, and he has been a great source of encouragement to me. Please, Jo. Please go talk to him before you make any decisions about going back."

Chapter 6

Gideon - Age 18
Jo - Age 15

Gideon wiped the sweat from his brow with a shirtsleeve and leaned across the top rail of the corral fence. Dust from the horse's hooves as it bucked and kicked around the far edge of the round pen clung to the moisture on his face. Jo walked casually inside, inspecting the fence here and there, seemingly ignoring the gelding's antics.

The horse kicking up all the dust was a bay gelding from a lot of rough broncs Mr. Bradford bought last week. The cowboys had been taking it in turn to break the broncs to ride. They'd since gone to drive the cows to the south range where there would be better pasture and water for the summer. Gideon was the only ranch hand who stayed behind. He'd been tasked to keep an eye on the stock remaining on the home section.

Jo walked over to the fence and leaned an elbow on the rail, facing Gideon. "Those boys have been breaking broncs all week. Whooping and hollering, waving their bandanas like a bunch of lunatics." She huffed and shook her head.

"And that's wrong because ...?" Gideon didn't see the problem with what the cowboys had been doing. It was what all cowboys did when it came to breaking in wild horses.

"Well, how would you like it if you'd been rounded up and moved from your home? Then were trapped in a confined space and had maniacs throw a rope around your neck, snub you down to a pole, put a saddle on you, and jump up on your back?" She widened her eyes at Gideon.

"I don't 'spose I'd like it much." He twisted his mouth in amusement and rubbed his chin.

She was growing more and more animated as she spoke.

"Then the cowboys ride them down into complete exhaustion. And when they're all done—"

The bay, who had begun to settle, threw his head and whinnied across the pen.

Jo paused, lowering her voice. "Sorry, boy." She continued in a quieter tone. "When the horse gives in, the idiots think they've done some great thing. But all they're left with is an animal with a broken will. It's savage."

Savage might be taking it a bit far, but it was pointless to argue with her when she got on a tangent about something.

"And what do you aim to do then?" Gideon narrowed his eyes at Jo in challenge.

"What if there's another way? The horse is a magnificent creature. You can see intelligence in their eyes." She watched the restless gelding trot back and forth. "What if, rather than breaking their spirit, you gained their trust? What if you ended up with a partner rather than a slave?" Her eyebrows lifted, and she turned, strolling back across the pen.

She moved in a gentle arc past the gelding's shoulder, then back to the center of the pen, all the while managing not to face the wild horse directly or to turn her back. Jo allowed the gelding to move around the edge of the corral at his own speed. After a few minutes, she faced him straight on, which made him move quicker as if he was being pushed away. Once he dropped his head, Jo turned slightly away again.

The gelding turned toward her for the first time, and Jo relaxed her posture even more, turning almost sideways. The gelding's eyes gentled, and he lowered his head, slowing his gait. Jo patted her chest, put a hand out toward the gelding, and called gently to him, almost crooning. His ears pricked forward momentarily.

Watching Jo in this element was captivating. She wasn't just a rough and tumble tomboy anymore. Even though she still wore trousers and a large brimmed hat with her hair braided back, there was a grace and a gentleness about her that drew him.

The gelding threw his head again and shook his black mane, raising his front hooves for a slight hop.

Jo stomped the dust, creating a cloud around her, and shook her head.

"Agh, none of that now." She spoke firmly and waved a hand, not wildly, but enough to make the horse back off a few steps.

Jo came back to the edge of the pen and met Gideon's gaze, confidently smiling. Her own eyes were warm and green as junipers.

His heart thudded a little louder in his chest as she approached. Could she hear it?

"So, what d'ya think?" Her words broke his trance. "Think I'm crazy?"

Gideon blinked, trying to clear the fog from his brain. Unable to meet her eye again, he looked past her, back to the horse. The bay was still restless across the pen, yet something was shifting in his behavior. There was a new clarity, a new connection in the horse's eyes as he looked at Jo. What was it? Curiosity?

Maybe Jo had a point. Anyone else would say she was crazy, but she might just be crazy enough to be right.

"Nah, not crazy. I think you might be onto somethin'," Gideon said.

Reaching into her pocket, Jo withdrew a few brown lumps of sugar. She popped one into her mouth and gave Gideon a wry grin. A grain of sugar clung to her bottom lip, and he had a wild desire to take her mouth with his and taste the sweetness. She licked the sugar from her lips and turned away again, softly singing "Red River Valley."

Keeping a side-eye on the wild creature, she casually wandered across the pen, singing to herself, investigating a pile of manure here, a fence rail there.

"Easy now, boy." Jo's tone was slow and soothing as honey as she moved about the pen.

She continued speaking of nothing, letting her soft words linger in the air as she moved toward the center of the pen. Her companion had calmed again, and, this time, his ears stayed forward. Jo reached into her trouser pocket and produced another lump of sugar. Holding it out with a relaxed, flat palm, Jo stood quite still, turned slightly away, head lowered, waiting.

The gelding gave a soft nicker and took a step forward, causing Gideon's heart to skip a beat. The crazy girl was doing it.

"That's it, you're alright," Jo crooned.

The horse took a few more steps, his head lowered, and stretched his long neck out, lipping the sugar from Jo's hand. She sent a triumphant smile over her shoulder. Gideon's heart soared.

There was no avoiding it any longer. He had to find a way to make sure this feisty filly was his for the keeping. But how? Every time he tried to say something that would take their relationship beyond friendship, the words stuck in his throat like he'd just stood in the middle of a stampede with his mouth open.

THE MUDDY STREETS BUSTLED with people and wagons being loaded with supplies. The loud rap of hammers rang out as builders put up the framework for new buildings. Men were shouting outside a saloon, and fallen women called out, their voices carrying over from Meyer Street. All of the busyness and noise after a month of quiet mountain solitude was jarring.

Gideon braced himself for a day in the booming mining town. He headed straight over to the Imperial Hotel to unload his bounty and settle with the cook for the meat.

He paced the street behind the hotel. Pastor Walton was expecting him. But now, Gideon questioned the entire arrangement. Was he ready for this? Was it the right decision? He had prayed for wisdom, but right now, he couldn't think straight. His head was spinning, and his mind was racing. Every time he tried to picture what his bride would look like, all he could see was apricot-colored wisps of hair blowing in the wind across a fair face, freckled by the sun. A pair of round, juniper green eyes brimmed with tears, staring back at him.

Jo, the last time he had seen her.

It was an image he cherished in the first month after his departure, and that haunted him since the day he learned of her disappearance.

He jerked off his wide-brimmed hat and ran his fingers through his hair as if he could comb the memory from his mind. Shaking off the distraction, he mounted Sarge once again and rode purposefully to the country church on the edge of town.

He hobbled his gelding and mule in a shady spot behind the church and sent up another plea for guidance. It took a moment for his eyes to adjust from the brilliant sunlight to the dimness inside. A woman was on a front pew, with her head bowed as she spoke to Pastor Walton. She wore a flowery hat with a long gauzy veil that hid her face from view.

Pastor Walton, who was speaking with her, handed her a brown leather Bible and rose to meet him at the back of the church. Gideon was anxious to see the young woman remove her veil, but to his surprise, she quickly stood and exited the church using a side door. His eyes followed her retreat and snapped back to the pastor.

"Was it something I said?" he asked in jest.

"Something you—" Pastor Walton's expression was one of distraction and concern. "Oh, no, she—no. I'm so sorry, Mr. Cross, but the woman you are here for hasn't arrived yet," he said as he shook Gideon's hand and patted him on the back. "There's been a gravel slide on the tracks, and the train from Cañon City has been delayed."

"Mm-hmm," Gideon grunted. He wasn't sure what to make of this development. Maybe this wasn't the woman he was supposed to marry after all.

"The train will arrive tomorrow, though. Never fear." The small, quiet man smiled at him. "Can you stay one night here in town?"

"Well, I had intended to make arrangements at the hotel for one night. Figured we could have you hitch us and be on our way tomorrow morning. It's a long ride back, you know."

"I see," Pastor Walton said with a knowing smile. "Well, the train should arrive at eight o'clock in the morning. It would still give you time to be on your way, but she may not be so all-fired anxious to get married and head off into the mountains right off the train."

"She wouldn't?" Gideon scratched his head. He could see no reason why someone wouldn't want to be on their way out of this town right off.

"No, Mr. Cross, I don't think so. Most ladies need a bit of courtin', you see, even if she has moved across the country to find a husband." He paused, allowing Gideon to take in the information. "In some cases, a marriage can be fixed right away, but then there's usually been some letters exchanged ahead of time. You and Miss Fletcher have had no correspondence of any kind. She's agreed to come to Cripple Creek and find a husband, yes. But being a family friend, she'd planned to stay with my wife and me while we helped find a match for her."

"With all due respect, Pastor Walton, I don't have time for all that courtin' business." Gideon frowned.

The pastor gave a half-smile. "Why don't you sleep on it? If she favors the match tomorrow, perhaps you can let her settle in here, with my wife and I, and come back to claim her next month."

Gideon took Sarge and Jack to the livery and paid to have them fed and kept overnight. The horse and mule trotted out to the corral where a handful of other horses were milling about.

"Any of 'em for sale?" Gideon strode to the fence to observe the other horses. By the sound of things, he might not be leaving with a wife tomorrow, but if this gal were agreeable, she would need a horse.

The white-haired liveryman, Horace, who had a slight tilt due to the peg that replaced his right leg, teetered over to stand next to Gideon.

"That gray over thar." Horace gestured with his chin to a tall, dappled gray gelding, currently having his head scratched by none other than the woman Gideon had seen at the church. She stood outside the corral, leaning against the top rail of the fence. She was entirely out of place in her fashionable dress and veil. She was dressed so strangely for someone who chose to spend their time with horses and seemed quite comfortable with the animals.

Gideon and the liveryman stood back in the shadow of the barn, apparently unnoticed by the woman. There was something highly unusual about her, and he couldn't help but watch her.

"The woman ... who is she?" He mentally rebuked himself for the idle gossip, but this mystery woman had so entranced him, he had spoken without thinking.

"Ah, that be a sportin' gal they call Copper Kate. One uh them fine, fancy girls in yonder Parlor House." Horace jerked a chin in the general direction of Meyer Street. "Word around town be that some rogue cut her up real bad." Shaking his head somberly, Horace continued, "Dang shame. She was one uh the purtiest gals I ever saw. Not that I was customer, mind, but she comes over here ta see the horses now and then. See that house back there down Meyer Street? That's the brothel where she works ... or worked." He gave a lopsided shrug. "Kate'd walk over here, and hep me curry and feed some days. I think maybe to forget ..." He trailed off, suggesting Gideon could reason out the rest.

"A fancy prostitute ... helped you with the horses?" Gideon asked incredulously. Again, he chided himself for not holding his tongue. What in tarnation had gotten into him today? He oughta be whipped for his carelessness.

"Watch yer step there, mister." Horace glared. "She ain't yer average streetwalker." He poked Gideon in the chest with a stubby finger. "Who are you to be castin' stones?" Gideon stepped back, not from the jab in his chest but from the stab to the heart from Horace's rebuke. He recognized the Bible reference immediately and was ashamed both for being party to gossip and judging the woman.

"Forgive me," Gideon implored. "And my mouth." He swiped a hand over his lips and shook his head.

After making plans to return for the horses in the morning, Gideon excused himself, feeling the need to crawl in a hole.

Ma told him that he'd had the gift of gab from the time he could first form a sentence. His mouth ran a mile a minute, and he'd loved the attention of being a storyteller or having news to share. But after gossip he'd brought home of a renewed mining boom on Colorado's Red Mountain had caused Pa to disappear, he'd vowed never to let his tongue run away with him again.

This situation was as good a reason as any why he had no business being in town longer than was necessary. There were far too many opportunities for him to slip into old habits and disgrace himself with a loose tongue.

Chapter 7

Jo turned back from the corral fence at the livery and started back toward the Thorntons' house. Her spirits and her steps were a little lighter than they had been earlier. She'd been apprehensive about visiting the preacher and was shocked to have received so much compassion from a man she'd expected to toss her out on her ear.

Could Abigail be right? She had found a clean and beautiful life. She had the love of a kind man, a home to tend, and she didn't seem to be carrying this heavy load Jo was carrying. Could Jo shuck this burden and have a fresh start after all?

Wearing one of Abigail's dresses and the concealing hat and veil, she had the benefit of blending into the crowd as she walked down the busy street. As much as she hated the fussy frills of hats and bonnets, the anonymity it provided her here had become a comfort since the attack.

Shouts of *fire* rang out, and a billow of black smoke rose from a building down the street. Panic traveled between the citizens of Cripple Creek like a lightning bolt through a herd of longhorn cattle. The town had been rebuilt over the last year after nearly all of it had burned to the ground. The threat of losing everything again caused chaos to break out in the street.

A man brushed past Jo as he ran down Bennet Avenue toward the firehouse. People poured out of the businesses onto the boardwalks. The loud clanging of a bell and the thunder of hooves had everyone on the crowded street scattering to clear a path for the fire wagon.

A child's cry rose above the chaos and noise. A small boy, ripped away from his parents in the press of people, stumbled into the road.

The fire wagon barreled down the street, sliding around the corner with mud flying from an erratically shaking wheel. Jo ran into the street to grab the child. The rushing horses spooked and shied as Jo jumped in their path and yanked the boy back before their hooves could trample him. She slipped in the mud and rolled, clutching the boy to her. There was a loud crack as the axle snapped and the large back wheel splashed into the muddy street.

Pulling the boy to her, she looked wildly around for the person who should be responsible for him. Surely there would be a panicked mother calling out for the boy, but the street was in chaos. The high-strung horses were squealing and stamping as men ran to assist the firemen with the wagon. Someone was shouting for water. With the fire wagon disabled, the rescue of its water tank would be postponed.

The child wailed and clutched Jo's skirts, tears streaking down his muddy face. Where was his mother?

Jo looked him over to make sure he wasn't injured and noticed a scrape down his chubby leg below his short-pants. What should she do? The sheriff was directing people and attempting to organize the pandemonium. She scooped the boy up into her arms and made her way to him.

"Excuse me, Sheriff?" Jo placed a tentative hand on the tall man's arm. She had never met him and was apprehensive about interrupting his concentration.

Glancing down at her distractedly, he gave a short, "Yes," in response.

"I can't find this boy's mother—" Jo hesitated, knowing no respectable woman would approve of Jo holding her child, much less being left responsible with him. "He's hurt. I'm going to take him to Doc Thornton's and get him taken care of. If you find his parents or anyone looking for him, will you please tell them where I've taken him?"

The sheriff gave a brief nod and went on pointing and shouting to other men.

Jo looked around one more time. No one in sight looked like a distraught parent. The boy's frantic crying had calmed now to an exhausted, hiccupping sob, and he laid his head on her chest as she walked to the Thorntons' house down the side street.

Once inside, Jo explained the situation to Abigail, who guided her to the examination room. Jo gently attempted to pull the boy away from her to deposit him on the table, but he clung tighter to her, burying his face in her neck. The gauzy veil attached to her hat was soaked with his tears and pinned down under his weight. She gently tried to peel his chubby fingers from her shirtfront, but it was no use.

"Sit down here, Jo. We don't need to frighten him any more than he already is." Abigail motioned Jo to a chair in the corner and left the room, presumably to find her husband.

Jo sat down and shifted the boy so John would have access to the abrasion on the child's knee. She leaned her head back against the cushion of the high-backed chair. The veil of her hat was caught beneath the boy's head as he pressed it into her chest, and she gently shifted him, removing the hat and veil. He didn't even look up but snuggled back against her and slipped a thumb into his mouth. She wrapped an arm around him and relished the heavy weight on her chest. Was Abigail right? Was this a possibility in her future? The endearing attachment of the boy lit a spark of hope deep within her.

Abigail's voice carried into the patient room from the front parlor.

"Yes, Mrs. Johnson, little Robert is safe and sound. Come this way."

Jo smiled for the boy's sake, but she was also reluctant to let go of the presence that warmed her heart.

"Mama!" The boy tearfully reached out, and Jo handed him over, smiling at the happy reunion.

"We didn't even know he'd slipped out." The woman's voice shook. "He was playing on the floor by the door of our shop when people started shouting about a fire." The woman's voice broke, and she squeezed her son tighter. "He must have slipped out behind us when we stepped onto the porch—I—I didn't even know he was gone at first." She buried her lips in the boy's wispy blond hair and kissed the top of his head.

Robert's sniffling eased, and he smiled and patted his mother's own, tear-streaked face.

"I am so grateful to you, Miss ...."

Jo cleared her throat. She had only ever gone by "Copper Kate" in this town, but the Thorntons and Pastor Walton were right. This could be her chance to move forward.

"Jo, Josephina Bradford." She stumbled over the introduction as she rose to her feet.

"My name's Johnson, ma'am. Martha Johnson." Martha bobbed her head.

Martha looked up to meet Jo's eyes, and a momentary flash of shock crossed her face. Little Robert's calm demeanor split into a frightened wail. Heat flooded Jo's neck as realization struck her like a stab to her heart. Their reaction could only be due to the sight of her scar.

It was a dreadful sight, which was why she always wore the veil. How stupid had she been to take it off when someone besides the Thorntons could see her?

"Excuse me." Jo turned and rushed down the hall to her room.

"Wait, Miss—" The woman called behind her, but Jo shut herself in, locking the door.

She pressed a hand against the ache in her chest and sank onto the blue and yellow patchwork quilt. The weight of the Bible Pastor Walton gave her caught under her as she sat down, and she yanked at it, pulling it free from the tangle of her skirt pocket.

She turned the leather-bound book over in her hands with an equal measure of inclination both to throw it out the window and to open it up and soak up the comfort Abigail, and the pastor insisted it offered.

She hadn't read a word of scripture since leaving her Kansas home and falling into the life of an outlaw and prostitute. In her childhood, she had found comfort in its stories and in "God's rescue plan," as her mother called it. She'd been anxious to know what her part in God's plan would be, but she'd chosen to turn her back on that plan, hadn't she?

The difference between Abigail's story and her own was that Abigail had been sold into prostitution with no understanding of a different option, and she'd never been told about the love of God. Abigail hadn't rejected God's word. She had been ignorant of it.

Jo wasn't ignorant. She'd had the benefit of a God-fearing family and had chosen to follow Christ as a young girl.

That was the difference.

Whether it began as Jo's choice or not, she had ultimately chosen to stay with Kane and the Blake Gang. It had been her choice to accept the lure of money and luxurious living when Pearl found her starving and invited her to live and work in the high-end brothel. Now she had to live the rest of her life with the consequences of her choice.

With a scar announcing her shame to the world, she would never be accepted in society and never be loved by a good man. She had lost her place in God's plan.

You have to go back. Jo took a deep breath and accepted the reality of her situation. There was nothing else left for her now.

Chapter 8

Gideon would have preferred to ride straight out of town, back to his usual aspen-stand a half-mile back, and sleep under the stars. But when he left the livery, the town was in chaos. A fire had broken out down the street. The fire wagon had been somehow detained, and Gideon had found himself hauling buckets of water to help put out the flames.

He was smeared with smoke and sweat and in need of a warm bath and maybe even a shave. And as much as he loathed spending the coin, he might oughta buy some new clothes, if not appropriate to a gentleman, at least to a civilized man. A new set of Sunday clothes wouldn't go amiss for the occasion, but there was nothing more comfortable and more suited to him than the supple leather shirt and leggings he'd grown accustomed to. When he returned to the mountain, he'd have to get to work on a new, better-fitting, buckskin tunic.

After outfitting himself properly, he headed back down the street to the Collins Hotel. He had no interest in the gambling and nightlife offered over on Meyer Street. He gave the hotel clerk a half eagle coin for the room, a bath, and a shave but refused the company of a woman who commonly attended a man in his bathing. Not that there wasn't any temptation in the offer, but giving in to that kind of allure was a snare he couldn't afford to stick his neck into.

Instead, he focused on the appeal of a meal cooked by someone who knew what they were doing rather than his usual fare of bear stew and hardtack.

The meal was worth every cent of the half dollar he had paid. He mopped up the last of the rich pheasant in cream sauce with a piece of sourdough and savored the last drop of genuine coffee he would have for some time.

A piano was playing at the far end of the room. Gideon leaned back, satisfied with deep contentment in his choice of entertainment this evening. Something about music spoke to his soul on a deeper level than most things in this world. Whether it was a favorite hymn or a ballad, it soothed him and calmed his spirit.

He could feel the piano's melody playing through his fingertips, moving over the imagined finger holes of his wooden flute with every note. On quiet, lonely evenings on the mountain, he would play the Indian flute, seeking to share some form of communication with the night.

He hoped and prayed this marriage was the right thing for him. In the first months of being in Colorado, his heartstrings had been tied to a girl in Kansas, even though they were hundreds of miles apart. She was the piece that would bring together the final picture of the family he wanted to rebuild. He missed her something fierce but had contentment in knowing he would have her back by his side soon. But when she had disappeared, the string snapped in two.

Jo was gone. Pa had absconded to seek his fortune in a silver mine. And with what Gideon found when he'd come to Colorado to look for Pa, Gideon surely could never face his mother and brother again. He was truly alone.

He had no one to care for and no one to share his life with. This young woman, on a train from Pittsburgh, was his chance to find companionship. A chance to heal the hole in his heart and give him a family again.

THE NEXT MORNING, GIDEON left the hotel in the new blue bib-front shirt he'd bought. He looked like a peacock. At least the denim jeans he purchased would be more durable than cotton trousers, even if they weren't as comfortable as his beloved buckskin leggings. But none of that mattered. Today was going to be a good day. After today, he would have a wife.

When he arrived at the church, the pastor's small trap was out front, hitched to an old black mare, head down, dozing in contentment in the morning sun. In the boot of the trap was a large trunk. This was it. She was here.

Gideon removed his hat inside the church, and Pastor Walton greeted him cheerfully and introduced him to Leah. She was a beautiful, raven-haired girl. She held out a few fingers of her delicate hand for him to shake and offered him a smile that didn't quite reach her eyes.

"How do you do, Leah, is it?" Gideon stammered.

"It is," she answered shortly but added, "I am well but tired. The train ride was just dreadful." She punctuated her statement with a pout that emphasized her full lips to their best effect.

"I'm sorry to hear that," he responded but didn't know how he should move forward at this point in the conversation. His mother had raised him to be respectful and polite, but he'd never before needed charm. In the uncomfortable moment of silence, she cocked her head to the side and eyed him critically from head to toe.

Never before had he felt so much like a horse at auction. Leah's eyes flashed with approval, and he nervously scratched his freshly shaved cheek.

"A-hem." Pastor Walton cleared his throat, and it drew Leah's gaze out of its perusal, for which Gideon was extremely grateful. "I've known Gideon for the past two years or so. He's a fine man and a hard worker." The character reference may have broken Leah's attention, but it did nothing more to ease the awkward tension.

"I'm sure he is," she said. "And what is it, might I ask, that you do for work?"

"I hunt and trap mostly. I also act as a guide when there is a need," Gideon said proudly.

She blinked and scrunched her forehead in a way that told him she had no idea what he was talking about.

"It's not a common profession anymore. Most trappers and mountain men left the territory years ago, but I suppose it's for the best. Gives me most of the mountain to myself."

"The mountain?" she asked. "But we're in the mountains now, aren't we? Why, there must be thousands of people living here."

His love for the mountains snapped him out of his nervous state, and he took her excitedly by the arm, not quite dragging, but encouraging her to follow him through the side door of the church. Once outside again, he breathed easier.

"Nah, this is only some little foothills here." He pointed to Pikes Peak, standing so grand and tall surrounded by smaller mountains. "That there's Pikes Peak, and below that is your new home," he announced before he had a chance to stop himself.

"Oh, indeed ...?" Her eyes widened as she looked up at the vast wilderness and back at the pastor.

"Gideon comes down to town about every month or so—at least in the finer months," Pastor Walton clarified. "The snow often makes travel too difficult in the winter months."

"I see ..." She trailed off.

"Why don't you two take some time to get better acquainted," suggested the pastor.

"Right, a walk." Gideon was suddenly terrified. He despised small talk. It would be a struggle to summon the polite manners his mother had raised him with after so many years avoiding such situations. "Would you ... care ... to go for a walk ... miss?"

"Leah," she said, looking at him like she was beginning to doubt his intelligence. "You might as well call me Leah. But Pastor Walton, aren't you going to act as a chaperon?"

"No need for that. You'll find things are quite different around these parts than you're accustomed to. You two go right on ahead."

Gideon placed a hand at the small of Leah's back, guiding her in the direction of Bennett Avenue. She was a sprite of a thing. His hand nearly covered the width of her back. He removed his hand and offered his elbow to her instead. She opened a frilly parasol, setting it over her right shoulder. He nearly jumped when she popped open the ruffled contraption, and he scowled at it unintentionally.

"The sun here is so intense," she commented and took his arm gingerly with her left hand. "I'll lose my complexion in a week if I'm not careful."

"Mhmm." Gideon gave a noncommittal grunt.

She prattled on and on about her life, but Gideon was too distracted by the lacy parasol that tickled his neck every time she turned her head to take in the sights.

Jo had never fancied all the fuss and frills, and he'd been grateful for that. She'd been perfect in her natural state. He kicked himself for not paying attention to Leah's running monologue and nodded, hoping to look adequately impressed by her parentage.

"Hmm," was all he managed.

"With all the eligible bachelors in Pittsburgh flocking to the gold rushes out west, it's been just dreadful." She had that pout to her mouth again. It *was* pretty if such a thing could be said about a sour expression, in all honesty. "Now my sisters and I have been spread out between friends and relatives all over. We might as well have been cast out to the wolves."

Was Gideon a wolf in this metaphor? He wasn't sure, but he must be, and the insinuation made him uncomfortable.

"I shot a wolf just last winter," he said, pleased to have finally come up with a response in the conversation. Leah's wide eyes and horrified expression told him perhaps it wasn't the correct response. He cleared his throat, but his search for words came up dry.

She accepted his barbaric anecdote with an uncertain smile and cast down her thick, black lashes. "As I was saying, my sisters and I are forced to seek husbands elsewhere. Pastor Walton has been a friend of my father's for years. When he mentioned this 'Paris of the West,' I knew right where I was bound."

"I see," said Gideon, although he did not see. This pampered life she came from was as foreign to him as the rugged wilderness must be to her. Coming to that realization helped to soften his opinion of her prim behavior. Hoping to ease her apprehension, he began telling her about the cabin he had built and the beauty of the home he would be taking her to. He told her how he hoped to put in glass windows next year and perhaps one day a wood cookstove so she wouldn't always have to use the hearth. "It's a mighty fine hearth, though," he told her quickly when he saw the expression of shock on her face. "There's a hook for the cook-pot and even shelves built into the side for your bread and pies and whatever else you'd like to bake."

"I don't know how to bake ..." She looked up at him as if he should have known such a thing. "I've never even boiled water for tea. Our housemaid did that." She sniffed. "I assumed in a town growing as rapidly as this—My husband would be able to provide the standard of living I'm accustomed to."

This revelation came as much of a shock to Gideon as his primitive cabin must have been to her. His pride in the home he had prepared diminished. What did he have to offer someone like this?

"It may not sound like much now, but I'm offering you my protection and a warm home. I'm not a violent man. You'll need never fear me." He sighed. It was all he had to offer, and he hoped she wasn't too disappointed.

He guided her around a puddle in the street, and she made a face of disgust. "For heaven's sake, is there no sidewalk in this forsaken place?" she snapped, and the softening of his opinion toward her wavered once more.

"This way." He led her toward the Rocky Mountain Mercantile so she could once again find dry footing.

As they reached the covered porch in front of the store, a gust of wind whipped her parasol up and to the right, startling a horse hitched a few feet away. The horse crow-hopped three feet in the air, and Leah, with a look of terror, sidestepped, slipping in the mud and landing hard in a puddle.

"Ugh!" she screeched.

Gideon stifled the laugh that absurdly threatened to overtake him, and he stretched out a hand.

"No, I can't—stop!" she wailed as he tried to help her up.

"What is it?" he asked, shocked at her vehement response.

"My ankle," she grimaced. "I think it's broken." Plump tears began to overflow her dark lashes as people gathered to see what the ruckus was all about.

"Alright," Gideon said softly. "Let's get you to a doctor." He deftly scooped up her petite form and looked around. He'd never had any need for a doctor here and wasn't sure where to go.

"This way, sir!" A man with slicked back, pale brown hair popped up like a prairie dog out of its hole and guided Gideon through the throng and down a side street to a pretty yellow cottage with white trim.

"This is it. Doc Thornton will see to her," the man said as he peered up over the edge of Gideon's arm at the heap of pink and purple frills. "Yes, I'm sure your beautiful wife will be just fine."

"Not my wife," Gideon said, impatient for the prairie dog to scurry off.

"Not your wife?" The persistent pest still hovered at the edge of Gideon's elbow. "Your sister then?"

"Not my wife. Not my sister." Gideon turned away, tapping the door with the toe of his boot. "She's new in town, just came in on the train today."

"Ah ... I see ..." The shorter man nodded and scampered off.

Gideon shifted Leah's weight to make her more comfortable. She looked up at him through glistening, teary eyes, apparently in awe of this display of masculine prowess. Maybe she wasn't so opposed to wolves after all.

A voice called from inside the house. "I'll get it, Abigail."

When the door opened, Gideon looked up from the pretty, pouting face resting on his chest and nearly dropped Leah on the porch.

"Jo." Gideon's heart leaped with joy at the sight of those round, juniper eyes, then plummeted to the center of the earth when his mind registered what it had first looked past.

An angry red line ran from her eyebrow down the length of her face and neck. Her soft, strawberry blonde waves were chopped short and shot up in spiky tendrils like a child's drawing of the sun.

How was this possible?

Chapter 9

Jo stood motionless, dumbstruck at the man before her. The handsome face she had long since tried to banish from her memory was standing in the doorway. She would've recognized that face anywhere, but the boy she knew was gone. A man stood before her now, cradling in his arms one of the most stunning women Jo had ever seen.

Unable to do anything but blink stupidly, Jo gaped at him, her mouth going slack. Abigail rushed over and brushed past Jo, jarring her out of her stupor.

"Come in, sir. Bring her in here." She ushered Gideon into the treatment room with the girl. "Put her here on the bed. What seems to be the problem?" Abigail asked.

He didn't appear to hear a word but turned and stared back at Jo, frozen in the front parlor. Slowly, Jo followed them in a trance and hovered in the hall outside the room.

"My ankle is broken!" The dark-haired beauty began to sob, clearly frustrated by her escort's sudden lack of interest.

"Dr. Thornton is making rounds just now, but he will be back shortly. In the meantime, why don't we remove your boot and take a look?" She glanced up at Gideon, who had once again regained consciousness at the shrill wail coming from the bed. "Is this your wife, sir?"

"My wife?" He blinked, appearing disoriented.

"If she's not your wife, perhaps you could step out of the room while I examine her leg?" Abigail asked.

"He's my fiancé."

A small, wounded sound escaped Jo, and Gideon whirled around.

"No!" he said. "I mean, well, not exactly. I, ah—" Gideon sputtered, looking back from Jo to the injured woman and back at Jo again. He took a hasty step toward Jo, his boot catching the leg of the wooden stool beside the bed, and he stumbled into the door jamb.

Abigail shooed him out of the room and closed the door behind him, clearly trying to quarantine the alleged "fiancée" before things could become any more complicated. Gideon and Jo stood in pregnant silence, staring.

"What ... happened?" Gideon asked shakily and then forcefully, "Where have you been?" Something sharp in his tone told Jo not only was the question rhetorical, it was an accusation.

Anger prickled up her spine. "Where have I been?" she shouted. "What do you care? You left me behind. You abandoned me!" All the desperation and hopelessness of the past three years threatened to overflow in tears.

Gideon stepped back, eyes wide with shock.

"Abandoned? I said I was coming back for you." His voice had the tone of an angry bear.

"You told me you didn't want me." Jo's voice cracked, and she cringed at this sign of weakness.

Abigail rushed into the room, shutting the door behind her.

"Sir, I must ask you to leave." She gestured a hand toward the other end of the parlor and the front door.

Gideon ducked his head, abashed. "Forgive me, ma'am. I mean no harm." He instantly softened his demeanor and lowered his voice.

"Are you okay, Jo? Is this man bothering you?" Abigail asked, looking back and forth between them with concern.

"I'm fine." Jo set her jaw and crossed her arms across her midsection. "So, congratulations are in order, I gather," she said with a slight jerk of her chin toward the closed door. "I wish you great joy." Her eyes stung as she stared him down, daring him to deny the truth.

"Jo, it's not—we haven't—" Gideon spoke in a fluster. "I don't even know her!"

"And yet you're marrying her?" Jo let out a rueful laugh, shaking her head at Gideon's attempt at denial. Her skin tingled as the heat of her emotion crept from her chest up to her face.

"I don't know. Jo, I thought you were ..." He huffed a heavy sigh. "Dadgummit, you've been gone for two and a half years."

"I've been gone? Gideon, you left Kansas. You left me."

The glossy brightness of his eyes softened the hardness of Jo's heart. It was clear her disappearance hurt him. How had he known how long she'd been gone? The certainty she'd steeled herself with all this time began to crack. Had she been wrong? Had he gone back for her?

"Gideon?" a simpering voice called from the other room. "Gideon, what's going on? Where are you?" At this reminder of the woman in the other room, heat flushed through Jo's entire body. She began building back the wall of her defenses that had crumbled at the sight of him.

"Don't let me keep you." Jo glared, eyes blazing, and walked resolutely to her room, slamming the door behind her.

She leaned back against the door and slid down into a puddle of calico fabric on the floor. Shaken and shaking, her mind began to race. How was this possible? How long had he been here? It hadn't occurred to her when she ended up in Cripple Creek that he might be here. His father's claim was on Red Mountain, wasn't it? That was across the state.

Her mind reeled as she recalled every word, every expression. Gideon had said she had been gone two and a half years. Had he spoken to her family? What harm had she done to them by running away? What did they think had become of her?

Gideon looked like he'd seen a ghost. Is that what everyone thought? That she'd been killed?

Her head fell back against the door behind her with a solid thump. If only she had been, it would have been so much better. She pulled herself up onto the bed and buried her face in the smooth fabric of the pillow, a steady stream of tears watering the embroidered forget-me-nots along the open edge of the pillowcase.

In the past two weeks, she had refused to allow herself to cry. She had compartmentalized her fear and despair, blinking away the moist advances of tears when they would rise to the surface. With the painful cut across her eye and the deeper wound of her soul, she had been afraid to let go. Now, having been pushed over the precipice of her inner fortress, she wept with deep, painful sobs that racked her body and caused her throat to ache.

In silent surrender, she gave herself over to it. Grief over the loss of the man she had loved, over the life she had wanted, and the girl she had been. Most of all, she grieved the innocence she had lost.

GIDEON STOOD IN THE front parlor, reeling from the revelation that Jo was right here in the same town, the same house for that matter. It was Jo, alive and in the flesh. Oh, but what a state of her beautiful flesh. What had happened to her?

The woman in the veil. At the church. At the livery. What had the liveryman said? The scarred ... prostitute?

No, it couldn't be, couldn't possibly be. Jo would never have—how could she ever have ...? But the liveryman had called her by another name, Kate. Could he be wrong in thinking she was the same woman he had seen yesterday?

"Sir." Abigail gently shook his arm, then took a few steps back, a wary look in her eyes. "Sir, your fiancée ... the young woman, that is, is asking for you."

Gideon tried to shake off the shock that turned him to stone. Heaving against the heavy pull of his distraction, he forced his mind to focus on the words being spoken to him.

His fiancée. *Oh, Lord, no. Please help me.*

Leah must be confused about his strange behavior. What was he supposed to do about her? How could he possibly marry her now? After all this time, Jo was alive! Alive. But what kind of a life had she been living, and why? Could she truly be a prostitute?

Gideon turned from the closed door where the love of his life had once again disappeared. He must do the next right thing. He returned to the patient room to find Leah pouting.

"Where did you go, Gideon? Who was that woman?"

Gideon sat down on the wooden stool by the bed and ran a calloused hand over his face as though he could scrub away all the chaos in his mind.

"Someone I used to know."

Jo never came out from behind her closed door, and Gideon stayed with Leah. It wouldn't have been right to ignore her, no matter that a stick of dynamite had just been thrown into his path.

The doctor's wife brought in a tea tray and placed it on the bedside table next to Leah. A middle-aged man followed her in, putting on a pair of spectacles.

"Dr. Thornton." He introduced himself and gave Gideon a firm handshake.

"Gideon," Gideon mumbled as he surrendered the chair and excused himself to give Leah some privacy.

Abigail escorted him to a sitting room and offered him a seat and a cup of strong black tea.

"For the shock," she quipped as she handed him a fragile cup with flowers painted on it. The tiny cup seemed absurd in his large, rough hands, but he gratefully swallowed the dark liquid.

"So you know *our* Jo, then?" She cocked an almost invisible, blonde eyebrow at him. She was searching his face but searching for what, he didn't know. He nodded, his head bent in concentration. Then it came to him what she had said—Jo, not Kate. So Jo must be closer to these people than just any doctor-patient relationship.

"*My* Jo," he said pointedly and met her eyes. He held her questioning gaze and imbued all the feeling he had for Jo into their locked, silent exchange. He wouldn't say more. Who knew who these people were or if they would go around spreading gossip?

After the doctor checked Leah's ankle and confirmed it wasn't broken, only twisted, Gideon asked if he might borrow a wagon to give her a ride to the pastor's home.

Gideon hitched the Thorntons' pony cart to the shaggy white pony and gingerly lifted her onto the seat. He drove without a single word beyond the gee and haw necessary to guide the clip-clopping pony to the little cottage behind the church.

Pastor Walton met him at the gate with a concerned gaze as Gideon helped Leah to the front door.

"Will you stay?" he asked as Gideon deposited the petulant Leah onto a sofa in the parlor.

"Thanks, but no. I need to return doc's cart and attend to some business."

The pastor gave him a curious tilt of the head, suggesting he sensed something was amiss.

"Have you and the young lady come to an agreement?" Pastor Walton asked when they were back in the yard. "Will there be a marriage in the morning, or have you decided on a longer engagement?"

Gideon shook his head. What could he say? What should he do?

"Pray for me, Pastor. I don't know—I just don't know." He should offer more information but couldn't bring himself to continue.

He didn't often share his troubles, but he'd developed a level of honesty and trust with the pastor over the past few years. Still, this time the words wouldn't come. This was too big, too personal to open up about.

"I'll do that." Pastor Walton patted Gideon on the shoulder.

Gideon nodded his thanks and excused himself without another word. Mounting the bench seat with a hefty creak of the pony cart, he drove back into town.

Back at Doc Thornton's house, Gideon drove around to the small lean-to barn out back. He unhitched the pony, attaching a lead rope to the halter in place of the reins, and tied him to the hitching post.

Gideon took the time to put all the harness pieces away clean and oiled and set to currying the short, shaggy pony from poll to fetlock. When he'd finished grooming, he scratched the pony's head underneath the thick forelock and heaved a deep sigh.

"Not yet," he told the little gelding. "I ain't ready yet." He started the currying process all over again with increasing vigor until the pony shivered and stamped, signaling his impatience to be loosed into the small paddock.

Releasing the pony and the only distraction left to him, he strode purposefully back to the front porch. He paused, muscles tense, as he lifted a hand to knock on the door.

John Thornton himself opened the door this time. "Mr. Cross?"

"Doc." Gideon nodded. "I want to thank you for the use of your cart. I've curried the little fella and put him back in the pasture."

"Thank you, sir. Please, call me John." He reached a hand out to shake Gideon's.

"I wondered if Jo might still be here." Gideon choked the words out. The last thing he wanted was to prattle on with strangers, but the protective way John braced his arm across the doorway told Gideon he'd best be polite. "Thought she might be willing to take a walk."

John looked up into Gideon's face skeptically but with no sign of intimidation. Unusual for most men, due to Gideon's imposing size.

"Wait here." John nodded and closed the door again.

Waiting on the porch for an answer, Gideon leaned against the whitewashed porch railing and prayed once more for God's wisdom.

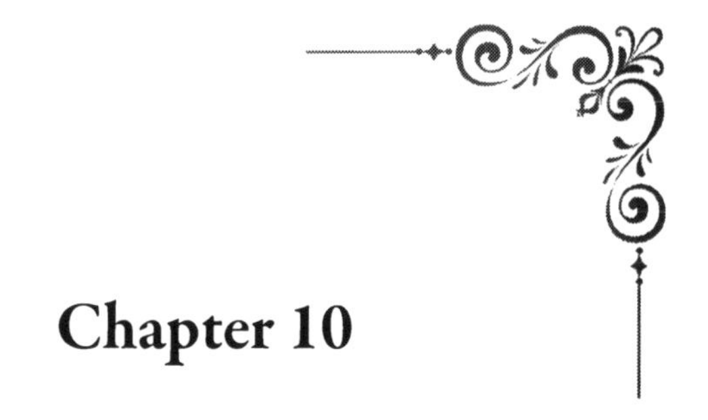

Chapter 10

Jo rested a hand on the doorknob, filled with dread. What would Gideon be thinking after their meeting earlier in the day? Had he reasoned out the kind of life she'd been living by the scabbing scar across her face?

In the first months after Gideon left, missing him had filled her mind and drowned her in longing. When she'd found herself in the clutches of an outlaw gang, she became determined to force out every thought of him and shut out all hope. Putting him out of her mind was the only way to survive. But she couldn't shut him out anymore, and the crushing wave of emotion battered her against the sharp edges of her self-protection.

She drew in a steadying breath. She would not give in to the sick feeling burning in her chest. She straightened her back, adjusted the veil that covered her face, and stepped out onto the porch.

Contrary to what she feared, when Gideon turned to face her, there was no reproach. He met her with a wavering smile and glassy eyes.

"Jo." He took her hand, gripped it as though she might slip away, and a part of her wanted to do just that.

The electric current of their familiarity shot through their connection and up her arm. She fought the urge to jerk her hand back.

"Gideon, I—" She faltered and shook her head. What could she possibly say?

He crushed her hand into the crook of his arm as if she would vanish into thin air if he didn't have a firm grip on her and escorted her down the porch steps.

Neither spoke for a long while as they walked down the street. The sun had risen high overhead, and the crisp morning had faded into a warm fall day.

Jo's hands prickled with the urge to remove the ridiculous hat she wore and soak up the glorious sunshine. For the past year, she hadn't been allowed to leave the parlor house without a proper hat to protect her fair skin from the elements. But after the reaction she'd gotten from Mrs. Johnson and her son, she didn't want to face that again here on the street.

"Let's get out of here for a little while," Gideon broke the silence with an encouraging wink, turning toward the livery. They retrieved Gideon's paint gelding, Sarge, from Horace. The familiar sight of Gideon's faithful gelding steadied Jo's nerves.

Gideon allowed her to mount the saddle first, and she sucked in a shallow breath through gritted teeth from the strain on her cracked ribs. She tried not to show her discomfort. Painful as it may be, she desperately wanted to escape the smothering oppression of the busy mining town.

She removed the hat with its towering plumes to allow Gideon to see over her shoulder. A cool breeze grazed across the back of her neck. She pulled at her collar, highly aware of her shamefully cropped hair. Despite Abigail's attempt to trim and tame the wild locks, each time she removed the hat, her hair seemed to stand out in all directions in defiance of her endeavors to smooth over its unruliness and her shame.

They rode out of town through rolling meadows lined by ponderosa pines and freckled with red Indian paintbrush and blue bell flowers.

His breath warmed her skin as his arm reached around her to guide the horse. She was uneasy and stiff, but the farther they rode from town, the more relaxed she became. Gideon had always been her anchor. Despite her anger for how their youthful attachment had ended, she certainly didn't need to fear him.

After they'd ridden for some time in silence, Gideon leaned his head close, his breath tickling her ear. "Jo, what happened to you?"

She didn't want to talk about it. Didn't want to admit to all her failures. Yet, here they were, alone and without distraction. Answering the question was unavoidable. She took a resigned breath and started at the beginning.

"When you left to search for your father," she started, "I was sure I'd lost you."

"I told you I was coming back," Gideon interjected gruffly.

"You want me to tell you or not?" Jo snapped.

"Hmph."

"You told me you didn't want me to come, and you rode away," she explained.

"I—"

"Shush," she interrupted, waving a hand over her shoulder to stop him. "That's what I heard and what I believed. If that wasn't your intention, then you did a mighty poor job of expressing yourself otherwise."

The rumble vibrating through her from his chest expressed his protest, but he otherwise remained quiet.

"I received one letter informing me you had found your father's claim and a rambling journal entry of your father's about a sizable cache of silver. After that, I had no word from you." She straightened in the saddle, leaning forward slightly to accommodate her cracked rib. "And then nothing. For six months, I never heard another word." Her tone was heavy with accusation.

Gideon turned the horse up a short, steep trail leading to a plateau overlooking the valley. When they reached the top, he slid down, reaching up to lift her from the saddle. She gasped in pain when he put his hands around her sides. He released his grip and stepped back with a concerned look in his soft, brown eyes. She dismounted warily. Dragging in a slow breath, she turned to look out over the town, nestled in the expansive valley below them.

Jo sat down in the tall ryegrass and leaned back, resting her weight on one hand, stretching out to relieve the pain in her side. The intense, high elevation sun prickled the skin of her nose and cheeks, and she turned her face upward, soaking it all in. This moment of freedom was bliss. Why ruin it with the truth of the rest of her story? Could she just end it here?

No. Gideon was not going to let it go at that.

"You were gone. And with no word from you, Pa agreed you must've chosen to stay in Colorado. He wanted me to stay and marry that wheat farmer's son, Tom Barlow. It would've been a perfect partnership; cattle and wheat in one family, see?" She ran her hand along the seedy tops of the grass and continued. "I had no interest in the arrangement. No interest in Tom. I didn't want to be a rich man's wife, riding around in a hansom cab, parasol at the ready," she said with sarcasm and a snort. "Can you just picture it? Fancy hats and puffed sleeves, servants and high society?" She let out a short laugh of irony, "I always knew those stiff dresses of satin and lace would make a prison for me ... and so they did." Her jaw tightened as she clenched her teeth.

"A wheat farm and cattle ranch doesn't sound like high society to me." Gideon shrugged a shoulder.

"The Barlows don't do their own farming. They only reap the profits of others' hard work. Not my kind of farming." She closed an eye against the bright sun and peered up at him, waiting for some sign of understanding.

When he nodded, she continued. "I didn't want to go through with it, but Pa was insistent. He wanted me settled, wanted me to move on with my life. It was a week before the wedding, and I—I couldn't go through with it. Maybe it was irrational. Maybe I should've spoken to Pa again, but I wanted so badly to have what you had. To live a life of adventure and freedom." She sighed and shook her head. "I didn't stop to think what it would do to my folks ... I just left." She stared down at the seed head she was picking apart in her lap.

"And then ...?" Gideon prodded when she didn't continue.

Jo shook her head. "And then I found myself working in a mining-town brothel," she answered abruptly, brushing the grass seeds from her skirt. With painful effort, she stood and stalked away from him.

How could she tell him the rest? She'd been devastated when she hadn't been enough to keep Gideon from leaving. Heartbroken and foolish, she'd fled in the night and headed for Colorado, deciding to live her own adventure.

Within two weeks, she'd found herself the captive of an outlaw gang who had robbed the stage she was on. Kane had left her with only one option for survival, and she'd taken it. The ruin of her innocence and reputation was the price of her safety.

She didn't even want to think about what a fool she'd been, much less tell Gideon about it.

"What about you?" She turned the focus onto Gideon and crossed her arms, avoiding the rest of her own tarnished story. "This morning, you made it sound as if you knew I'd been gone from home all this time. How did you know that?"

"I did send you another letter to tell you I would be coming back, but instead of a letter from you, I got one from Ma." Gideon still sat in the grass, his head resting on his knees. He raised his eyes to meet hers now, imploring, "How could you think—think I abandoned you?" Gideon's voice shook. "You were my whole heart. You were everything to me, and then you were just gone. Dead for all I knew."

"Why? Why did you wait so long?" Jo's pulse quickened as something in his story didn't seem to add up. "You did want a new life without me. Why else would you have waited so long to write?"

Gideon buried his face in his hands as if trying to block some painful memory. He stood and paced away from her. "I needed time. Why didn't *you* wait? If you would've waited for me, we would be living in these mountains together. You would be my wife." He jerked the hat off of his head and ran his fingers through the thick chestnut waves. "None of the rest of this would have happened." He waved a hand, encompassing her scar.

The reality of his statement knocked her off balance, distracting her from her fury. She took a step back, reeling from the harsh truth of his words. It was her fault. If she hadn't been so impatient, would she ever have ended up like this?

She'd been convinced she hadn't been enough to keep him around. And now, with silver to pave his way, she was sure he would've gone and found some fine, fancy lady to be his wife—someone more like her sister.

Jo closed her eyes and rubbed the bridge of her nose. *You would be my wife*. His words painted a painful picture of what could have been. She could see herself standing barefoot in a mountain meadow with her long hair loose down her back and Gideon rolling around in the grass with a beautiful, copper-haired child. Her eyes brimmed with tears as she mourned the loss of a life she would never have.

Gideon stopped pacing and reached out, pulling her to his chest, wrapping his arms around her in a protective embrace. She sobbed into the smooth blue cotton of his bibbed shirt, the rhythmic thumping of his heart steadying her.

When her tears slowed, she pulled away slightly and looked up into the eyes of the man she had once loved. While the warmth in them was the same, the man before her had changed. His face had lost all its boyish charm. It now appeared to be chiseled from stone and bronzed by the sun. The arm beneath her hand was as smooth and hard as the trunk of an aspen tree. What experiences had he been through during their estrangement to make such a man of him? For that matter, how must she look to him?

They didn't know each other at all anymore, did they?

Gideon looked deeply into her eyes. The intensity of their connection blazed in her chest. His arms were still wrapped behind her back, supporting her. His touch scorched like fire through the fabric of her dress.

She had to gain some distance. This wasn't right. None of it was right. She was a fool to follow any man out into the hills like this. She may have known Gideon once, but she'd seen the ugly truth of what men wanted.

She braced her hands against his chest, pushing away. For a fraction of a second, there was a tension in his arms as he resisted her escape. Was he holding on to her? What was he going to do to her?

Panic shot through her veins and combusted, exploding fire in her chest. She wrenched her arms free of his hands, her heart pounding like an ancient drum. *You fool, he's just like all the rest.*

"DON'T!" JO SHOUTED, backing away and crossing her arms protectively around her midsection. She squeezed her eyes shut tightly and shook like a hunted cottontail. At that moment, she looked so small and vulnerable.

Gideon wanted to wrap her in his arms and comfort her, but, clearly, that would only make things worse. He scrubbed his face.

"I didn't mean to ... I wasn't going to ..." He sighed, "Jo, would you look at me?" The frustration in his voice wasn't helpful, but he couldn't seem to temper it. She reluctantly met his eyes. "I'd never hurt you. I had no indecent intentions." He spoke slowly and calmly now. "I'm sorry."

"You can't change what's happened, Gideon." Her voice cracked and shook. "We can't just go back in time. It's too late for us now."

"It's not too late," he countered and took a tentative step toward her.

"Gideon, it can never be the same between us again." She held out a hand in front of her, maintaining the distance between them. "I am fallen and soiled, and you are engaged to be married." Her voice was a little stronger now. She looked deep into his eyes, challenging.

No, I'm not, he wanted to say, but there was truth in her words. Although he didn't want to admit it, he had given his promise of provision and protection to someone else, and that knowledge was like a stab to his own heart. He shook his head, but he could offer no argument. What in tarnation had possessed him to such a foolish measure?

He turned and stalked a few paces away, taking hold of the reins on Sarge's bridle that were loosely draped over an aspen branch. Staring down at the smooth, hardened strips of leather in his hands, he prayed for an answer to this impossible situation.

Gideon was a man of his word, but hadn't he given his word to Jo first? What was a man supposed to do when the woman he loved came back from the dead? Her words came back to him, and he recalled what she had said about herself.

"You are not soiled, not in my eyes."

She looked back at him with incredulity. "I'm soiled beyond recognition, Gideon," she said as she walked over to him. "Look at me. This scar brands me for what I am." She gestured to the red line splitting her lovely face in two. "How could you ever look at me without seeing what I've become?"

The sun was beginning to lower in the sky, and its last rays of brilliance shone on her right side, illuminating the undamaged side of her face. For one moment, all he could see was an exquisite woman, alone, afraid, and in need of rescuing.

"I don't know what brought you to this, but I know it isn't who you are." He reached out a calloused hand and ran his thumb alongside the wound, down her eyelid and cheek to the corner of her mouth. She shuddered and pulled away.

Gideon clenched his hand into a fist and stepped back. "We'd better get going, or it will look mighty improper when we come riding back into town after sunset."

"Ha." A sarcastic laugh escaped Jo, and her voice broke. "People don't tend to expect proper etiquette from the likes of me."

Gideon stepped back and allowed her to mount, then swung up behind the saddle. He turned his horse's head down the mountain and cherished the nearness of her every minute as they rode back to town without another word.

What now, Lord?

Chapter 11

That night offered no rest for Gideon, and he tossed and turned in the hotel bed. His mind was an eddy of swirling questions. So many things were still unanswered about Jo's past.

Even if Leah wasn't in the picture, could he set aside the knowledge of what Jo's life had been these past few years? What did it matter, though? He had promised himself to Leah. He couldn't back out on someone who'd come across the country with no money and no other prospects. He couldn't abandon her.

Why God, why reveal Jo to him now, after all this time? He was so angry. Angry with God, with Jo, and himself for his impatience to fill the gap in his heart.

Before he knew it, he was out of bed and pacing the small room. The walls were too close, and the air was stifling. He had to get out of there. He strode to the hotel room's second-story window. A thin line of sunlight cracked above the mountains, shadowing the peaks in purple. He dressed quickly and slung his saddlebag over his shoulder. He couldn't stay cooped up in this place any longer.

Once outside, he could breathe again. It wasn't the deep healing breath of mountain air, but there at least seemed to be more of it. He looked left and right, gaining his bearings in the booming town. To his left was Bennett Avenue and the way home. But on that path was also the church and Pastor Walton's home where Leah, no doubt, was awaiting her groom or "fiancé," as she'd called him.

To his right was Meyer Street. In a fire the previous year, the town had been devastated. Only eight or ten structures had remained standing. The people of Cripple Creek had rallied and rebuilt quickly, putting much planning and consideration into practice. All the brothels, cribs, saloons, and gambling houses were moved back onto Meyer Street, where the unseemly activities would be separated from the more respectable businesses in town. That way, the genteel ladies and children could move about town comfortably without being exposed to the perverse reality of what went on there.

In the early morning half-light, Gideon could see men stumbling out of clapboard houses and ramshackle cottages, pulling on suspender straps and buttoning shirts, bottles of liquor in their hands.

A female voice shouted, "I don't know where you're going, man, but you can't stay here." A woman sent a man stumbling off the front stoop of a whitewashed, two-story house with a sign that read The Old Homestead Parlour House.

This was where Jo had been. For how long? How many times had he been in town, been right here? The weight of the knowledge and the senselessness of it all was too much for him to bear. He took a step, stopped, hesitated, then turned to the left and headed purposefully toward the church.

Walking down the street, he prayed for God's guidance in this storm. He looked up to the mountains that were his solace in times of disturbance, and he recalled the prayer he had offered two days ago. *Put in my path who you have for me.*

Who had God placed in his path after all? Leah or Jo?

The walk was long and cleansing. When Gideon arrived at Pastor Walton's home, the sun had risen above the treetops. While the air was brisk, the blue sky and early morning sunshine had done much to be a balm to his spirit.

He remained conflicted but had confidence that while he didn't have the answer, the Lord would bring him through.

He knocked on the whitewashed door, pulling in and slowly releasing a breath. When the pastor's wife reached the door, Gideon sent up one more prayer for clear guidance.

Mrs. Walton escorted him into a small sitting room. A tiny round table and two velvet-covered chairs stood by the front window, and a couch with a curved back and ornate framework of carved wood stood against one wall. There were lamps with stained glass lampshades, potted plants, and little china figures on every surface.

It was a comfortable home for them, he was sure, but it only accentuated Gideon's size, causing him to feel very large and out of place. If he turned around too quickly, a cascade of trinkets would tumble down, sending fragile shards of porcelain flying in all directions.

The pastor came in after a few minutes, followed by his wife, who carried a tea tray with four tiny cups and saucers. Gideon longed for his rustic cabin in the mountains with tall doorways, high ceilings, and large tin cups. It had been years since he had spent so much time in a town, and his surroundings seemed to be closing in.

"Good morning, Gideon," the pastor said, somewhat hesitantly as he checked the time on a silver pocket watch. "I trust you slept well."

"Mhmm," Gideon responded, not wanting to explain his lack of sleep. "Is Leah here?"

"Oh, Leah? Well, yes. I believe she will be here any minute now." The pastor fiddled with the watch, glancing out the window and back at the hall.

Just then, Leah came swishing into the room in a pale blue dress with puffy shoulders and an impossibly high collar. He pulled at his own collar, which was tight, as though slowly strangling him. He loosened the top button of his shirt and cleared his throat.

Things were so unsettled yesterday. She might be anticipating a wedding.

"Ah, Miss Fletcher, would you care to sit down?" Pastor Walton seemed to be relieved to have another person in the room. Something was off about the man. He'd never been uncomfortable with Gideon before.

"Thank you, Pastor." Leah nodded gracefully and glided over to one of the delicate chairs at the tiny table.

Pastor Walton motioned to the other chair for Gideon to sit down, but Gideon was sure if he sat down on the thing, it would shatter into kindling. Instead, he took a seat on the couch and ran his hands over his thighs, smoothing the crisp denim and longing for the buckskin leggings he'd grown accustomed to.

Sitting down in one of the velvet chairs, the pastor spoke. "It seems we should all have a little chat." He appeared to have gathered his wits once they were able to get things started. "Leah tells me you ran into a … friend at Dr. Thornton's house yesterday."

"I did," Gideon answered slowly, glancing at Leah, who sat straight in her chair, her slightly upturned nose a fraction higher than it had been before.

"The moment he saw that woman, he abandoned me," Leah said with a huff. The pout was back. Gideon was beginning to realize this was a habitual expression for her.

"And how is it you know Miss Bradford?" asked the pastor.

Gideon's dark eyebrows rose at his use of Jo's surname, and then the image of the woman in the hat and veil at the front of the church brought everything together and understanding set in.

"Miss Bradford," Gideon told the pastor, "was a close family friend when I was a young man in Kansas. I had not seen her in years. In fact, I had long since thought her to be deceased."

Understanding registered on the pastor's face, and he nodded.

"Ah, I see. What a curious stroke of providence that you were able to cross paths again," he said with a flicker of a wink and leaned back in his chair, more relaxed now.

Gideon was more baffled than ever, "Providence?"

"Well, while you chose to disappear for the rest of the day, I had a visitor." Leah turned the conversation in her direction with a satisfied smile.

"Oh?" Sensing the pastor's amusement, Gideon was ready to find out where this was all going.

"Indeed. A concerned gentleman who witnessed my injury inquired of Dr. Thornton where I was staying and came to call on me yesterday afternoon." Leah paused dramatically, relishing, Gideon assumed, in what she expected to be his indignation.

"How nice for you," he said unconcerned.

She bristled a bit and set her shoulders back. "His name is Stanley Thompson, and he's a banker. When he learned my need of a husband, he offered a marriage agreement." She leveled a challenging gaze at him.

Gideon's jaw dropped. He wasn't surprised that someone would propose marriage. She was a beautiful woman, and women were scarce these days. His surprise was that God's hand was so swift and direct in Gideon's time of need.

There was a knock at the door, and the pastor's wife ushered in and introduced Mr. Stanley Thompson, the prairie dog from yesterday.

Gideon let out a loud whoop of laughter and shook the man's hand heartily. "Congratulations, Mr. Thompson!" He ought to have been insulted, but this new development answered the questions that had kept him up all night with worry. "Best wishes," he told Leah. "Pastor, I do believe I will take my leave now, but I plan to call again later today. Would you mind if I stop back in?"

"That would be fine," the pastor said with a knowing smile. "Just fine."

Gideon collected his hat and rushed out the door. The weight of the world lifted from his shoulders.

UPON ARRIVING AT THE livery, Gideon's heart was light. God had brought Jo back to him. Whatever had happened in the past, he and Jo would work through it, though it wouldn't be easy. Hardship or no, he would be taking Jo back with him to the mountain as his wife. The swift resolution to the complication of his arranged marriage gave him a peace that God's hand was in this, and he would trust in that, come what may.

Gideon settled with Horace for the feed and board of his horse and mule and purchased the tall dapple gray for Jo, as well as the saddle and bridle she would need. The irony was not lost on him that he was buying a horse for the very woman he had been so judgmental of that first night in town, and it shamed him.

He rode back to the Thorntons' house, the mule and gray gelding strung behind him. He knocked on the door, anxious to find Jo and take her away from this town.

"Doc—John," Gideon began when John answered the door, "I need to see Jo again."

"I'm sorry, Mr. Cross. Miss Bradford is gone." Furrowed lines between tired eyes aged the man something terrible.

"Gone?"

"She left just a few minutes ago for the parlor house. We tried to convince her to stay, but she was insistent that she had no choice but to go back."

"Go back?" Gideon repeated the words to himself, then threw them back at John. "Go back? What the Sam Hill for?"

"To work."

Heat burned in Gideon's neck and face. "Work? You mean to tell me she's going back to that hell? How could you? How could you let her go?"

"Mr. Cross, we tried," Abigail said, coming to his side and resting a hand on his arm in a calming gesture. "Jo knows she has a safe place with us here, but she's convinced it's impossible for her to do anything else."

"And what about us? We weren't done sorting things out." Gideon was pacing the wooden planks of the front porch, his heart pounding like a war drum.

"She said you were marrying Leah ..." Abigail's voice trailed off, waiting for Gideon to explain.

"Well, I'm not!" he said in a huff. "When did she leave?"

"Not five minutes ago."

Gideon rushed out the door and squinted toward Meyer Street. He could see a woman walking a few hundred yards ahead, and he leaped to the saddle, spurring Sarge into a full run.

Sliding to a stop beside her, Gideon swung down from his horse in a cloud of dust and grabbed Jo by a calico sleeve. "Jo, what are you doing?"

Jo jerked her arm from him and stumbled back, a hand braced protectively over her face.

His heart clenched. He hadn't meant to frighten her.

"I should ask you the same, Gideon Cross." Jo spat the words at him.

"What do you mean by going back to that foul place?" He tried to temper his tone despite the heat rising in his chest.

"The only thing I *can* do. What else is there for me?" She kept her eyes on the ground and fiddled with the lace edge of her sleeve.

"What—what else?" he stuttered. "Me, Jo, standing right in front of you. You. Have. Me."

"Gideon, be reasonable." Her voice thickened. "I may not know where you've been the past three years or what your story is with that raven-haired filly, but I'll not stand in your way."

"I am not going to marry her."

"I won't be the one to keep you from your word. If I know anything about you, I know how important it is to you that you keep your word." She looked up at him, her eyes dull and vacant.

"Then why won't you listen to a word I say?" Gideon spoke through clenched teeth.

"Nothing you can say will change my mind." She took a step back, looking like she'd bolt at the first chance to get away.

"I mean to marry you today and take you away from this place." He instinctively took hold of her hand and pulled her toward himself, gently this time.

She tensed and pulled her fingers from his grasp. "You may think you have to rescue me, but I won't ruin your life like I've ruined mine."

"Will you let me be the judge of what will ruin my own life?" Gideon punctuated each word.

"A spoiled piece of fruit doesn't improve by being put with good fruit. It ruins the whole bushel." Jo's voice wavered, but her resolve did not. "We're done talking about this." There was a growing edge of intensity in her voice, and she held her hands up, palms out to keep him from touching her again.

"No, we're not done talking about this." The tightness in his chest radiated into his jaw. She was always stubborn, but this was unbelievable.

Clasping her hands together in front of her so hard her knuckles showed white, she shook her head and pushed past him. He turned after her, feeling like a fool for following her.

"Jo, would you stop and listen to me?" Gideon's voice was rising again.

"No, you listen to me." She whirled around, glaring up at him now. "You would always know ... my debasement. And—" Her voice wavered, and angry tears welled against auburn lashes. "I'll never forgive you for leaving me behind."

"For ... what? I didn't leave you behind! I didn't abandon you." He drew in a deep breath and released it slowly, trying to calm himself. The breath didn't help. His chest tightened, and his temper shortened.

"How many times do I have to tell you?" He gestured with a wave of his hand, sending Sarge's head flying as the horse responded to Gideon's tension. The tall paint gelding began side-stepping and pulling away, stamping his hooves.

"It's your fault I am here. You cared more about that silver than you did about me or you would have said something. You would've come back for me." Her voice was becoming raspy with strain and desperation.

"How can you say that? I did write to you. You were just too impatient to wait for me." The crowd was drawing in closer now, whispering, and Gideon lowered his voice. "And now we're both stuck with the consequences."

He didn't see her hand raised, but the stinging crack across his cheek caused his head to thrum. She was no dainty, fairy princess, this one. Never had been. But the throbbing in his head warned him there was something even fiercer about her than he'd ever seen before.

"Get out of town and get out of my life," she hissed through clenched teeth. "I don't need rescuing." She gathered her blue skirt with a shaky hand and resolutely turned her back on him, marching toward Meyer Street without a backward glance.

Chapter 12

Jo - Age 17

Gideon - Age 20

Jo stood at the hitching post, gripping the tall paint gelding's reins as if she could stop Gideon from leaving.

"Take me with you." Jo's whisper was desperate. She'd meant it as a statement, but it wavered shakily on the edge of a plea.

"You know I can't." Gideon sighed. "Ain't safe. You're too young," he snapped, jerking the hat from his head and running a hand through his chestnut waves.

"I'm seventeen years old, Gideon, and I know my own mind." Her voice was rising now. She straightened her back and lifted her chin.

"Ha." Gideon tightened the cinch and lowered the stirrup.

"You think I don't?"

"No, you ninny, I mean Colorado is wild and unsettled and ain't no place for a lady so young and fragile."

"Fragile?" Her shriek was a warning he ought to heed, but she knew he wouldn't.

"Like one a them wild roses down by the creek. You got some thorns alright, but yer just as fragile as them tender pink petals that scatter in the wind." His voice wavered.

Jo snorted a puff of air that would rival Sarge and rolled her eyes. "Hogwash. That's not true, and you know it."

Gideon let out a long sigh and pulled on the bridge of his nose. "You're not fragile. That's not what I really meant."

"Then what?"

"It is rough country, Jo."

"I can out-ride any of these cowboys." Jo's grip tightened on the hardened leather reins.

"I ain't talkin' about riding. Colorado is still wild, and mining towns are full of rough characters. I've got to concentrate on finding Pa. I can't do that if I'm always worried about keeping you safe."

"You don't ... want me to come." It was a statement rather than a question, but she desperately waited for an answer.

"No, I don't want you to come." He gritted his teeth. "You'd just get yerself into trouble."

"Then go!" She tossed the reins toward him and shoved his broad chest with both hands. Gideon dropped the felt hat in his hand and grabbed her by both arms, holding her captive.

"I'm coming back, Jo." He gave her a little shake. "Once I find out what happened to Pa, I'll find a place and make a good start for us. I'm coming back to get you."

"Like your pa came back for you?" Her words were sharp, and she tasted the bitterness of them on her tongue. She chewed on the inside of her lower lip and looked down, regretting the snide remark.

"What about your ma? She depends on you." Jo's eyes prickled with unshed tears.

"She's got Jimmy to take care of her. She'll be fine." Gideon's grip on her arms loosened, and his rough, work-worn thumb grazed over the lip she had pinched between her teeth. His eyes shone with fear and anger as he slid his fingers around the back of her neck and bent his head. With the lightest touch of his lips, he stopped her heart.

So, this was goodbye.

All the world stood still. The warmth of Gideon's body, so close to hers, and his steadying touch gave Jo the security she needed. If he left for Colorado, that security would be gone.

"Don't go," she whispered one more time.

Sighing, he rested his forehead on hers. He pressed something cool and smooth into the palm of her hand, and suddenly, he was gone. Leaving her exposed and alone.

He picked up his hat from the ground, took two quick strides toward his horse, and in one swift motion, swung up into the saddle. Tipping his hat, he rode off into the crisp morning air without another word.

She watched him ride away until his silhouette vanished. She looked down and opened her hand. The object he had left with her was his pa's compass. Why he chose to leave it with her was beyond her. The tarnished thing hadn't worked in years.

Hands shaking, she had clenched it so tight the clasp cut into the palm of her hand. The metal was slick and wet from her blood. She looked up again and faced the empty horizon.

A bitter, cold, Kansas wind swirled up around her, whipping her skirt and settling in her heart.

JO ARRIVED AT THE PARLOR house with nothing but the veiled hat and dress Abigail gave her and the Bible, given to her by the pastor. She had no real interest in the old book with its worn leather binding, but Abigail had insisted she take it.

"This book is God's love letter to you. Whether you want it or not, keep it close. When all light has gone out in this world, it will light your path." Abigail had pressed the book into Jo's unwilling hand. Reading the pages of a book wouldn't offer any real help in a time of need, but Abigail was so kind, Jo didn't want to hurt her new friend by refusing it.

When Jo rapped on the heavy door, the butler answered, looking down his long, hooked nose at her. In Abigail's clothes and the veiled hat, which she had made a habit of wearing since her attack, she must have looked out of place on the doorstep of a brothel.

"Why, Bernard, aren't you happy to see me?" She smirked sardonically, knowing the aristocratic butler never looked happy to see anyone. She tilted her face up, allowing him to see her under the brim of the hat.

"Oh, it's you," the butler said with a shake of his head and turned on his heel, abandoning his post, disappearing to the back of the house.

Jo stepped inside and closed the door behind her. Once inside the brothel, she breathed a sigh of resignation. It was not home, but for the last year, it had been her hiding place. She pulled back the lacy curtain from the window facing the street, and like every time she had peeked out over the last year, a sickening ball of dread turned in her stomach.

Would he be there this time? Would Kane find her with all the gossip that had undoubtedly been swirling around the area about her attack? Something was different now, though. The churning ball of dread in her stomach had doubled in size. There wasn't just one man to fear anymore. There were two—one who scarred her face and one who'd tarnished her soul.

"Kate?" Hazel's voice startled Jo, and she whipped around. Over the past few weeks, she had grown accustomed once more to being called by her true name, and the use of her alias was disorienting. Hazel's face held a wary expectation in the dim light.

"Take off the hat," the madam said abruptly.

A jolt of apprehension shot up Jo's spine. She'd covered her scar with rice powder and paste before leaving Abigail's house. It had been nauseating, spending so much time in the mirror, trying to cover up the wreckage.

After doing her best to conceal the scar, she coiffed her hair with dozens of pins, tucking wayward strands into a mock version of the current style with a short row of wavy bangs combed down across her forehead. She prayed her efforts would stay in place as she removed the hat this time. It might not be convincing enough to meet Hazel's approval, but she hoped it would, at the least, soften her initial reaction.

Sighing, she removed the hat and veil.

"You were right, Bernard," the woman spoke to the butler over her shoulder. "This won't do at all."

Jo placed a steadying hand on the floral chair back beside her. "I know the hair isn't perfect, but it will grow back quickly." Jo tried to fill her voice with the confidence she didn't feel. "And I thought maybe I could use one of Pearl's old hairpieces in the meantime."

"It's not the hair I'm concerned with." Hazel swiped a hand down the side of Jo's face scraping away the thick layer of rice powder and sending a blazing line of pain down the length of her barely healing scar. "It's that ugly face," Hazel sneered.

Jo's shoulders slumped, and she choked back the sob that welled up in her chest.

"This is the finest parlor house in Colorado. You think I could use you now?"

"But—"

"Get your things and get out."

"But—I've nowhere to go!" Jo pleaded. "How could you send me away? You caused this!" Her desperation peaked. Panic and anger coursed through her in ebbing waves that unsteadied her. She gripped the chair tighter.

"I caused this?" Hazel's eyes widened in false shock.

"You let that man in here. I watched you take the bribe and waltz him through the door. Pearl would never have endangered us like that when she was the madam."

"I did no such thing. You filthy liar." Hazel's teeth pulled back like a rabid dog. "You have one hour to get out of here. I never want to see that hideous, scarred face of yours again."

Jo struggled to swallow past the lump in her throat. Where could she go? She wouldn't have come here if there had been any other choice. She'd hoped the paste and powder would cover the scar and refused to believe that this would be the result of her attempt to return to the brothel. What was left for her to do now?

She gripped the hat, tempted to tear the veil in two. Hazel hadn't paid her yet for her last week's work before the attack. That might be enough to get her as far as Denver, where she could try to start a new life, but after the cost of a train ticket, she'd have nothing else. She'd be just as destitute as she'd been when she accepted Pearl's offer and come to the parlor house. The shame of going home was something her heart couldn't bear right now, though. She had to find a way to start over somewhere else.

Jo trudged up the stairs to her old room. How had she reached a place where *not* working at the brothel was a crushing blow? Only a few weeks ago, she was desperate to find her way out.

She crumpled to the wood plank floor and opened the trunk containing the few things she owned. She had one purple satin and taffeta dress. The other high-fashion dress had been ruined the night of her attack. There was an ornate hair comb, a bottle of Ambre perfume, and a makeup kit containing rice powder, rouge, lip stain, and a charcoal eye pencil. She could sell the dress to one of the other girls here, but should she take some things with her?

As she sifted through the trunk, her hand grazed something else, something soft and homey. Her mother's woolen reticule, with its rust-brown homespun, looked worn and faded against the bright colors and rich fabrics in the trunk, and yet, the touch of it filled her heart with so much love and homesickness it overwhelmed her. She loosened the drawstring and looked at its contents for the first time in a year. All that was there were a few worn pieces of paper and a shiny silver disk. She lifted out the compass and ran her thumb over the cool, smooth metal case. The small, half-moon shaped scar in the palm of her hand matched perfectly underneath the clasp. She closed her grip around the compass and squeezed her eyes tight.

A loud knock on the bedroom door snapped her out of her reminiscence, and she dropped the compass and reticule back into the trunk.

"Yes?" Her voice wavered. Hazel walked in and stared down her slightly crooked nose at Jo.

"I've come to settle the matter of your debt."

"My debt?" Jo's eyes widened. "You mean my wages ..."

"Pfft." Hazel snorted unattractively. "You ain't got no wages comin' to you, girl."

"You still owe me for my last week's work."

"I don't owe you a bloomin' thing, you hoity-toity wench! Had to throw out a good oriental rug from this room, you know, ruined it with all that blood." She shivered in disgust.

Jo sat dumbfounded, blinking the stinging sensation from her eyes as she tried to make sense of this revelation.

"You can't be serious." A cold heaviness settled in her chest, "Hazel, what am I supposed to do without that money? Where am I supposed to go?"

"To the hog pens for all I care," Hazel snapped. "I'll let the debt for room and board this month slide if you get out today so I can get a new girl in here by tomorrow." She swirled out of the room and slammed the door. Jo put her hands out flat on the floor to steady herself, a cold wave of nausea building up inside her as the room began to tilt.

Chapter 13

Jo gathered her wits and a few of her things into a carpet-bag she acquired from one of the other girls. When she had arrived in Cripple Creek, she had nothing in her possession but her mother's woolen reticule, which she wore tied about her waist under her skirt as a pocket.

She exchanged a bottle of perfume for the carpet bag. It was a terrible trade if the value of the perfume mattered, but, of course, it didn't. Hazel took the purple dress as payment for the business's loss due to having had one less girl the past few weeks. Jo now only had the dress she wore, her mother's reticule, some makeup to cover her scar, and a Bible she didn't want.

She descended the short flight of stairs into the sitting room, and Hap, seeing her, jumped up from his stool at the small bar. "Kate!" he exclaimed. A look of relief turned to horror on his big, pudding face. "Oh, Kate," he repeated. He slid back onto his stool, now mournful. "I'm so sorry." His eyes were downcast, and he hung his head. Jo could see the pain etched across his face as clearly as her scar must be.

"It's not your fault, Hap." She laid a gentle hand on his burly shoulder.

"It is my fault! I—I wasn't there. I was supposed to be there." Plump, glistening tears were floating along his lower lash line and threatening to break over.

"I don't blame you, Hap." Jo squeezed his shoulder and sat down on the stool next to his. "I do wonder, though, what did happen?"

Hap squeezed his eyes tightly shut and hammered the heel of his hand against his forehead repeatedly. "Stupid, stupid Hap!" he muttered under his breath.

"Stop, Hap! You stop that right now." She wrapped her hand around his and tugged it away. He sighed and hung his head again, slumped over with his forearms resting on his knees.

"That bad man," he said after a long pause, "he bought me a mule skinner."

The pins in Jo's hair pulled as her eyes widened. "I've never seen you take a drink in all the time I've been here. I didn't think you drank liquor at all," she said with surprise.

"I don't! I don't anymore—I hadn't—I hadn't in a long time." He now lifted his hand, still clutched in Jo's, and pressed it against his head. "No good comes from the filthy stuff." Hap sniffed and turned to face the bar. "But he slid that drink in front of me, and oh, my, I could smell the blackberry and whiskey ... He said I looked mighty thirsty and hadn't I oughta be able to enjoy myself, too, watchin' everyone else enjoy themselves. After all these years, I guess it don't agree with me though, 'cause I got powerful sick. Felt like there were rattlesnakes in my belly, just a writhin', and a wrigglin'. I didn't have any choice but to run out back to heave it all up. Beggin' your pardon, ma'am."

Jo waved a hand at him, dismissing the uncouth nature of his story.

"When I was turning to go back inside, I saw that fancy man a runnin' down the alley, fit to split the leather from his boot soles. I came back inside and saw you was a missin'. That's when I went to your room and—" Now the tears cascaded freely down his cheeks, and he pressed his palms over his eyes as if he could blot out the memory.

"Thank you, Hap, for helping me. None of this was your fault. It sounds to me like he put something in your drink to make you sick. To get you out of the way." Jo straightened on her stool to go. "Did anything ever come from ... all this?" She gestured to her face. "Did anyone ever find the man?"

"I tried to track him, but this town is so busy anymore. I couldn't find hide nor hair of him." The big shoulders shrugged. "If I ever do, he won't be botherin' you no more. I'll make sure he never steps foot in this house again." Hap nodded firmly. Jo stood from her stool and picked up her carpetbag.

"Thanks, Hap, but I won't be in this house anymore. Let's just hope he's not still out there."

"Won't be here ...?" The big man looked at her bag and scrunched his lips while he slowly connected the facts. "You don't mean ... Miss Hazel is making you leave?" Color began to fill his open collar and creep toward his jawline. He stood quickly, looking around the room for the madam.

"It's alright. I'll be alright." Jo touched his arm in reassurance.

"She can't do that! Where will you go? How will I look out for you?"

"You stay here and do your job. You can't afford to lose it."

"But ..."

"There's no one out there looking to hurt me anymore. Don't you worry." She lied to her friend, but she couldn't lie to herself. He *was* still out there. They both were. Both Kane and Mr. Carver were out there, somewhere.

JO LEFT THE BROTHEL with nowhere to go. She made her way down the street, heading in the direction of the train depot. The heavy monsoon rains of August had now passed, and the dry, high desert air had hardened the wagon wheel ruts and hoof prints into ridges that made the footing precarious. One wrong step could land her a broken ankle. She deliberately placed a foot here and there, like playing an unsteady game of hopscotch. The meager weight of coins bounced against her thigh. With so little coin, what options were left to her now?

Without the protection of the high-end brothel and their supposed selective criteria to hide behind, Jo must leave town, and she must do it quickly. She hadn't made it far from Kane and his outlaw gang when she had escaped them near Colorado Springs. She'd known she was taking a risk by settling somewhere so close to their territory, but Pearl had found her in distress and offered her protection, food, a warm bed, and a sizable income.

Jo couldn't have made it far without money, a horse, or any resources at all. Being alone on the run left her vulnerable and conspicuous. She had already sunk so low as an outlaw. Acting as a courtesan in a place like the parlor house hadn't seemed as vile as it once would have. She told herself it was only temporary when her moral core had raised its objection.

Jo looked up from the frozen ruts in the road to find herself in the heart of crib row, the notorious Tenderloin District. She locked eyes briefly with a scantily clad woman who leaned against a porch railing, rolling a cigarette. Swallowing an uncomfortable lump in her throat, Jo averted her eyes.

Crib Row was comprised of a row of shacks at the end of Meyer Street, near the railway station. Poorly constructed, clapboard rooms with adjoining walls lined the street, offering a bed and a body, nothing more. The women were shabby, disheveled, and unkempt.

The combined stench of unwashed bodies and a nearby hog pen lay thick in the air, and Jo's stomach churned. She choked back the bitter tang that crept up her throat. She had never considered herself proper or refined, but even she had to turn her head to avoid the shocking surroundings. Covering her nose and mouth with the lace-edged handkerchief, she quickened her pace to reach the railway station a few blocks down.

Once safely inside the Florence and Cripple Creek railway station, she released the breath she'd been holding and tapped the bell on the counter. A small, white-haired man approached and peered over the tall counter.

"Where to then, miss?"

"Oh." She hesitated and cleared her throat, unsure what to say. "Well, I'm not traveling just yet." Jo bit her lip in contemplation. "I only need to know how much a ticket will cost when I am ready to go."

"And where is it you mean to go?" The diminutive man with the drooping mustache licked the tip of a finger and tapped it against the pages in front of him, ready to flip to the appropriate page.

"Well, now ..." She shuffled her feet and patted the reticule under her skirt. "I'm not sure." Where could she go? She frantically weighed her options and limitations. She could surrender her pride and go straight back home to Kansas, but facing the pain she had caused her family seemed far too great of a mountain to climb.

The cost of a train ticket to Dodge would be well outside her reach even after months of working. She wouldn't be able to come up with that kind of money. She slumped as regret weighed heavily on her chest. She didn't need the clerk to tell her that. She knew its cost all too well.

"Ahem." The stuffy little train station clerk was growing impatient with her lack of answers, even though there was no one in line waiting behind her.

"Denver," she said.

It wasn't ideal. Jo would have to travel straight through the Blake Gang's territory, who focused their attention on the gold flowing out of Cripple Creek by stage. But what were the odds she would encounter them if she were on the train? Once she reached Denver, she would be able to fade into the crowd, anonymous.

"Seven dollars to Denver." He sniffed and slammed his book shut, confident she didn't have the cash.

On the boardwalk in front of the station, she slid onto a wooden bench and heaved a hopeless, heavy sigh, burying her head in her hands.

When she'd left Kansas, she'd fled her parents' home in the moonlight, with enough money to buy her first-class ticket from Dodge City to Denver and still have enough money to live on while she built herself a new life. Yet, within two weeks, the generous inheritance her father had given her a few days before her impending marriage was all gone. A handsome devil with blue eyes had taken it, and so much more.

Jo rubbed the bridge of her nose between two fingers. She needed to make money, and a lot of it, before she could even consider moving on. The cold reality of what she would need to do to earn that money filled her veins with ice.

The chill settled in her stomach, surging in cold waves of nausea. She hadn't realized how badly she wanted to be free from her life of prostitution until she faced the reality of going back to it. Even worse, this time, it would be without the false glamour and protection of the high-end parlor house.

She lifted her eyes from the protective blindness of her clammy hands and faced her inevitable future. Ramshackle, clapboard shacks, walled canvas tents, and crumbling cottages lined the street in front of her. Their darkened doorways gaped like open sepulchers, with pale faces peering out, waiting for her to take her place among them.

Chapter 14

Gideon jabbed a pitchfork full of hay and manure from the stall floor and shook it off into the wheelbarrow behind him. He had wasted precious time with the fruitless trip to town, and there was much to be done before winter.

He also needed to get to Pueblo and make sure all was well there, and he had to make one last effort to speak to Jo. He couldn't leave her there. Even if she didn't want to marry him, he had to at least get her back to her folks. Jo was alive. Not just alive, but half a day's ride down the mountain, and doing what?

Gideon spat out the bitter tang of hay and dust. The usual sense of warmth and the sweet smell of hay, ever-present in the barn, sat hot and heavy in his lungs.

He removed his hat and wiped a wrist across his sweaty brow. The air was thick, and the barn walls were closed in. His temples pounded like his head would explode. It wasn't a particularly hot day, but the boiling in his blood threatened to burn him to the ground.

He stabbed the pitchfork into the dirt floor and stumbled out of the tight space of the stall. He leaned against the stock tank at the corral edge and dipped his head in the cold water he hauled up from the creek earlier that day. He surfaced with a gasping breath, and the crisp mountain air cleared his senses, allowing the humming in his head to subside.

He looked up into the cloudless sky and whispered the same furious, "Why God?" that had been the only utterance of his heart since coming home. Why would God choose to bring them back into each other's paths if this was how it was all going to end?

Replacing his hat, Gideon pushed the wheelbarrow over to the area he'd been cultivating for a future garden plot. He spread the hay and manure over the space, though it was a pointless effort now.

He'd started the plot as a kitchen garden, but now, without a wife to plant carrots and cabbages, what was the point? He didn't need the extra hassle for himself. He knew enough about the edible plants of these mountains to sustain himself. What did a man need, aside from a strip of dried meat and some lamb's quarter harvested from the creek bank?

For that matter, what good was the company of a wife anyway if all it meant was more work to grow fancy vegetables?

How could he have been so foolish? A wife? The idea was absurd. A woman would only end up cluttering every surface of the house with fragile trinkets and complicate his simple life.

Not only that, but he had the chance at two women in as many days and failed to acquire either one. This was what came of opening up to the pastor about his desire for companionship.

Weakness. That's what it had been. Was he so weak he needed a wife? He'd built this property up all on his own. Built the cabin, the barn, cleared trees, and made a mighty fine homestead. Mighty fine in his own eyes, anyway. To a wife, this place would never be sufficient. Leah had made that clear with the shock written all over her face when he'd described the one-room cabin with its primitive hearth.

He should have been stronger. What kind of a mountain man wanted a wife anyway?

He turned his attention from the pointless kitchen garden to fleshing the elk hides hanging on the side of the cabin. He had done a quick job of it before his trip to Cripple Creek but had left for town quickly so that the meat he was planning to sell wouldn't turn. Now, he would take the extra time to remove every bit of flesh from the hide as the first step in making leather for a new set of buckskins.

Gideon removed one of the elk hides from the cabin's shaded north wall, draped it over the upright beam braced in the fork of an aspen tree, and began the detailed work. No soft tissue could be left behind, or the hide would spoil and become useless.

The mindless task of fleshing the hides allowed the rhythmic scraping to soothe his troubled mind. Lost in his work, he didn't hear the padded footsteps of a beast rushing toward him.

Without warning, Gideon was knocked flat from his crouched position near the end of the beam. A rumbling growl and a tumbling of black fur engulfed him, pinning him to the ground by heavy paws. In a dead-lock stare with a pair of spectral, yellow eyes a few inches from his own, he was held motionless.

A sharp whistle rang out from behind him, and the beast's long, wet tongue bathed him from chin to hairline. Groaning as he waited for his bellows to mend, he rolled to one side and peered across the yard, one eye squinted against the sun. A long, lean figure, clad in buckskin, formed in his vision, and the monstrous beast took her place at her master's side.

"She missed you ... I think." The lanky young man walked forward, chuckling at Gideon's disheveled appearance. Gideon rose to his knees and welcomed the shaggy black wolf-dog against his chest as she came barreling back to him.

"And why wouldn't she, Clay?" Gideon teased. "All the ladies clamor for me." Gideon quirked an eyebrow to show his jest, sensing his smile hadn't quite reached his eyes. It must have been his first attempt at one in the past few days.

"That so, greenhorn?" Clay scanned the homestead. "Something tells me you are still alone." He gestured toward the cabin with a jerk of his chin. Gideon glanced back over his shoulder to the corral where Jack dozed lazily in the shade, and Sarge was nipping at the neck of the new gray gelding.

"That gelding carried no one back here. His prints were much too light to be carrying a rider." Clay smirked and waggled both eyebrows, mocking Gideon's challenge.

"Hmph," was Gideon's only response as he lifted his hat from the ground and dusted it against his breeches. Gideon turned away, hiding the smile tugging at the corner of his mouth.

The kid was sharper than Gideon's bowie knife. Shading his eyes with the broad brim in his hand to check the angle of the sun against the cliff-side, Gideon offered an olive branch. "Bout dinnertime, I reckon. Come and have a bite, then."

A toothy white grin split the bronze face of Gideon's visitor, and they trekked companionably up to the cabin.

"So, did you run her off?" Clay pestered Gideon as he took a seat at the table, scanning the empty cabin with hawk-like eyes. Gideon mentally scolded himself for voicing the fact he would be bringing a wife back to the mountain. He'd needed Clay to keep an eye on things while he was gone and mentioned the additional purpose of his errand, having thought everything was settled.

"I suppose," Gideon mumbled, cutting a few slices of corned elk meat and set it to soak in a pail of cool water to rinse the salt. "Coffee?"

Clay nodded, and Gideon returned to the hearth and added a handful of dried horse apples to the smoldering ashes of his morning fire.

The weather was cool, and a small fire, even at mid-day, was enjoyable. A month ago, he would have made do with cold coffee to avoid heating the cabin or using up his firewood for the noonday meal.

"Well, will there be a Mrs. Cross on the mountain soon then?" Clay asked persistently, pushing back the forelock of molasses-colored hair that was continually falling into his eyes.

"I suppose not." Gideon gritted his teeth and suppressed the urge to dot the lad on the head with the fire poker in his hand. "Is your grandmother well?" he asked, determined to change the subject.

"She is well." Clay smiled and shrugged, accepting the change of topic and his defeat in this game of banter. "Winter will be difficult for her, though. I do not think she will stray from the fireside at all when the snow falls."

Clay and his Ute grandmother, Florence, were Gideon's nearest neighbors and had been a reliable, quiet presence on the mountain. They had lived in the foothills of Pikes Peak far longer than Gideon had.

Florence had married a mountain man who trapped in the area fifty years prior. She'd grown to love the man she had been given to and chose to stay with him even after her people were forced out of their lands. After her husband had been killed by a grizzly, and her son and daughter-in-law had been lost to sickness when Clay was a boy, she raised him alone here on her mountain.

To Gideon's surprise, she and her grandson had been kind and welcoming, teaching him how to survive in the Rocky Mountains.

"You'll tell me if you need anything this winter, won't you?" Gideon asked.

Setting down their plates of cold meat and bannocks, he offered a prayer, thanking God for their meal. He also privately offered thanks for Florence and her grandson, Clay. As much as Gideon tried to separate himself from others, his mountain neighbors were most likely the only reason Gideon survived his first year on the mountain.

Chapter 15

Jo set the worn carpetbag on the sagging mattress and took in the state of the dim, dingy room. She took out her mother's reticule and retrieved her last gold dollar to pay the snaggle-toothed woman for the week's rent.

The woman slammed the door behind her, rattling the thin walls of the crib-house. Jo fingered through the contents of the reticule. Ten cents, a broken compass, and the scribbled journal entry Gideon had sent her before she'd left Kansas. It pained Jo to let go of all but her last ten cents for this pitiful purpose, but there was no help for it. She had to get out of town, and there was no alternative for how she'd have to make the money needed to buy a train ticket.

A stage fare would be half the cost, but with the Blake Gang's harassment of the local stage lines, that was not something she was willing to risk. Her escape had been a precarious one, and she had no doubt if Kane found her, he'd kill her for running off as she had.

Jo lifted out the journal page, scanning the nearly illegible scrawling. This page was the reason she'd been forced to break ties with the gang and run in the first place.

She had snuck out of camp early one morning in the flat, gray light of dawn after a night of Kane's drunken rampaging. He'd found the journal page Gideon had sent her before she left Kansas and had beaten her senseless when she didn't tell him where the silver was. She'd begged and pleaded with him to see reason.

She knew nothing more than he did. The journal page was barely legible, much less understandable, but Kane was blinded by mistrust, and it had been all her fault. She'd hated how betrayed he felt upon finding a letter from another man in her possession and scolded herself for being a foolish child and keeping such a memento.

Hadn't Kane risked everything by allowing Jo to live when the others in the gang might have killed or harmed her? Hadn't he always looked out for her welfare? And this was her repayment of all he'd done for her.

She had good reason to be terrified by his violent rantings. Gold and silver were what he valued most, and if he believed she was hiding something from him, she was in real danger. She had nothing to offer him in supplication for her safety, and there was no choice but to flee for her life.

As the year away from the handsome Irishman had passed, she had gained enough clarity to see her relationship with Kane had been one of abusive coercion, not one of real love. But she had never shaken the crippling fear of his savage temper.

Jo replaced the page and untied her hat and veil, dropping them onto the rumpled quilt next to her bag. Her cold hands shook as she attempted to light the oil lamp on the bedside table.

The night had grown late, and her feet ached from walking all day in uncomfortable high-heeled boots. She just wanted to lie down. She looked over the dingy quilt and sagging mattress. Peeling back the covers, the stench of unwashed bodies assaulted her senses. If she would've eaten that day, she would've retched. Unsure if the crawling sensation up her arm was from actual pests or only the sharpened reality of tomorrow's fate, she dropped the blanket and shivered.

She couldn't bring herself to lie on that bed. Instead, she blew out the lamp, wrapped herself snuggly in her wool cape, and curled up on the floor with only a carpetbag for a pillow.

JO SHIVERED AWAKE ON the cold floor of the crib house. Her neck ached from the awkward angle she slept in, and her stomach was hollow and queasy. In her haste to leave Abigail's house, she hadn't eaten. She'd better toughen up if she was going to survive this new life.

Laughter somewhere nearby hovered in the background. Still sitting on the dirty floor, she unbuttoned the boots she had failed to take off the night before. Pulling off the shoes and stockings, she wiggled her toes in relief. She didn't care what the day held for her. She couldn't bear to put those awful things back on her feet.

A sound like the chatter of magpies and another chorus of cackling laughter came from behind her crib house room. She walked out the back door to find a dirt lot with several wash kettles hung over small fires. A group of five women, in assorted shapes and sizes, turned and stared her way. An uncomfortable silence fell as the clamor faded.

"Good morning?" Jo shaded her eyes from the intense sun. Exhaustion must've gotten the better of her, and she must've slept into mid-morning.

"Well now, if it isn't the Princess of Prostitution," a heavyset woman with dark hair and a large mole on her chin boomed with a low voice. The women's laughter had subsided to a subterranean rumble of cruel mockery, side-long glances, and smirks to one another.

"Is that a crown on her head?" a knock-kneed blonde added. "I thought it was a tumbleweed."

Jo hadn't prepared herself for the kind of bitter reception she might meet here. She had looked down on the haggard, hard-looking women on this end of Meyer Street, but their reciprocation of animosity was unexpected.

"What happened to your face there, love?" the first woman spoke again. "Cut yerself on your tumble through the looking glass, did ya?"

The whole flock of women broke into uproarious laughter. Jo winced at the sharp tone of their mockery and wrapped her wool cape around her, though there was no real chill in the air. Looking glass indeed, and my, how far she had fallen. Resorting to prostitution had been a grievous mistake in itself. She had sunk so low even the fallen women of Crib Row looked down on her.

Jo sought to rebuff their slander, but humiliation crippled her ability to speak. She struggled to swallow the lump in her throat and turned to find refuge in her room, slamming the door behind her. The thin walls vibrated with its force.

She peeled the bedding off of the lumpy, sagging mattress and piled it against the back door. Although men could come around at any time, she would wait until evening to open her door. She would have to wash the grimy sheets, and for them to dry before evening, she would have to get the job done soon.

She sat down on the bare mattress and leaned back against the whitewashed wall. As she tried to regain her composure and bolster her courage to face the flock of magpies again, someone entered the room next to hers, the feminine voices becoming clear enough to discern through the paper-thin walls.

"What did happen to that girl?" the voice of a young woman asked.

"Hadn't you heard?" It sounded like the knock-kneed blonde was her companion. "She was one a them high-falutin fancy girls over at the parlor house up the street. Got herself set upon by that fiend what they been talkin' about all over town."

"A fiend?" The younger voice wavered.

"They say he's been cuttin' up high-class whores from here to Denver. Nobody knows who he is or where he's gonna turn up next, but he's makin' a right mess a things. See, usually, he just cuts a girl up, makes her ugly. Marks her, don't ya know?" The self-satisfied tone in her voice betrayed her enjoyment of the juicy gossip. "But a few days ago, I had a newspaperman in my bed, and he said a girl was killed in Cañon City just last week."

"Killed?" The young voice came in a hushed tone.

"Slit her from navel to gizzard is what I heard. They been callin' him the Colorado Carver."

Jo drew up her knees against her chest and covered her ears with trembling, clammy hands. *He's done with you. He has no reason to come back.* Telling herself that didn't matter. The knowledge alone that he was out there, an ominous presence lurking in the shadows—

A tap on her back door sent a thrill of panic through her raw nerves, and she jumped. A tall woman with dark hair and a black eye stepped inside.

"Alright then?" The woman cocked her head and a boldly darkened eyebrow as she evaluated Jo's defensive posture on the bed.

"Do you care?" Jo pushed her hands flat against the tops of her thighs, willing the rigor mortis of fear to release and allow her to uncurl.

"Oh, don't be lettin' all that nonsense out there bother you. We was just havin' a bit of fun." She stepped over the quilt on the floor.

"Fun?" Jo huffed and shook her head.

"Name's Myra. Course, they call me Sister Mary." She cautiously took a few more steps into the room, watching Jo as if she were a stick of dynamite. "Feelin' a bit nervous, are you?" Myra asked, preening in the bureau mirror, tucking a flighty strand of pin-straight, dark hair back into its intended top knot.

"It's not my first time," Jo answered with sarcasm, straightening her legs out on the bed and folding her arms tightly across her chest.

"Maybe not, but it'll be yer first time on this end of the street now, won't it?" Myra sat on the edge of the bed, leaning over on one elbow, lowering her voice conspiratorially. "It ain't the same thing, now is it, darlin'?"

Jo didn't answer. Myra's confirmation that this life would be something entirely different hardened in her stomach.

"Look, you probably only had, what—one fella a night before, right?" Myra cocked her head, waiting for some indication Jo was following. When Jo gave a slight shrug, Myra continued. "Here, if you want to survive ... let alone make enough money to keep by, you work day and night. Could be ten, could be a hundred a day." Myra delivered this last revelation with raised eyebrows and widened eyes.

Images of what she was facing raced through Jo's mind, and her stomach tightened into lead. She shivered convulsively and drew her knees up protectively against her chest again.

Myra withdrew a small flask from her pocket. The tarnished silver flask beckoned to Jo. Oh, how she missed the numbing effect a little whiskey or brandy could provide. She reached instinctively for it.

"Ah-ah," Myra scolded like a school teacher lining out a student. "This isn't just any elixir we have here." She opened the flask and waved it under her nose, breathing in its essence. "This here will get you through, sure enough." She passed the flask to Jo, who likewise inhaled in the aroma. Something sweet, spicy, and slightly herbal lingered over the usual sharpness of whiskey.

"Laudanum?" Jo handed the flask back.

"It'll cure what ails ya." Myra tightened down the lid and tossed it back to Jo. "You're gonna need somethin' stronger than yer sparkling personality if yer gonna make it through the night." She leaned back and gave Jo a sideways look. "I'll sell ya the bottle cheap, seein' as it's yer first night on the row."

Jo weighed the flask in one hand and nodded her agreement. She gave Myra the ten-cent piece that was the only money she had left and clung desperately to the promise of oblivion offered in its amber depths.

Chapter 16

Gideon - Age 14
Jo - Age 11

The bright summer sun radiated through Gideon's shirtsleeves as he rested his forearms on his knees. He sat comfortably beside Jo on top of a large mound of hay in the wagon parked behind the barn. He would need to get all this hay loaded into the loft before supper, but little Jo had brought out dinner to him in the form of cold ham and sour pickles, and they had taken their meal on top of the haystack to share.

"What's that?" Jo asked when Gideon produced a silver object from his pocket and buffed it on his sleeve. She reached out to snatch the trinket from Gideon's palm.

"A compass." He nodded importantly, allowing Jo to take the shiny bobble, though he could have easily held it out of reach.

"Where'd ya get it?"

"My pa."

"Oh ..."

The usual silence fell as it always had whenever the subject of Gideon's pa came up. The weight of it hung thickly in the air. It had been two years now since Pa had left to follow the Red Mountain silver rush. He had never returned.

Jo gingerly rotated the etched silver disk, watching the arrow glide back and forth across the red line. "What's it do?"

"It shows you the way, silly. See here? These letters stand for a direction: north, south, east, and west. The arrow always points north so you can find your way home." He paused. "Maybe if Pa had kept it ..." Gideon let the sentence trail off, leaving a hollow pain in its wake.

Jo handed the compass back to him with the gentle care of someone entrusted with a valuable artifact. She rested her cheek on the back of her hands, pillowed on the billowing haystack.

A hawk glided high above the prairie grass in the sloping valley below them. Gideon turned his head, discretely dabbing the drip at the end of his nose on his grubby shirt sleeve. He squeezed his eyes shut tight to stop the welling tears, knowing he may never see his pa again.

The predatory bird made a sharp dive and snatched its prey from the grass. It soared away from them, growing smaller and smaller until only a pinprick of black showed in the vast blue sky and then winked out of sight.

"I wish I were a hawk." Jo sighed in a dreamy voice that floated on the breeze.

"A hawk? What on earth you be wishin' that for?" Gideon lowered a questioning eyebrow in her direction.

"So I could fly away and go wherever I want." She rolled over onto her back and spread her arms wide, looking like she might soar right into the sky above them.

"And where is it you think you want to go?" He couldn't keep back the chuckle at her free-spirited ways. She didn't know much beyond the ranch and the one-room schoolhouse where they attended church and school.

"I want to fly to the top of a mountain far away and live in the top of a tall pine tree." Jo wiggled her bare toes back and forth, smiling up at Gideon. The freckles on her nose seemed to darken and stand out more and more by the minute as she bared her face to the summer sun. If Jo's sister, Elaine, caught her out without a bonnet, she'd be running straight for the house to tattle. Jo's older sister always insisted on asserting herself as a proper young lady who had no time for their kind of tomfoolery.

"Do you want to fly away with me?" she asked.

"Well, I ain't stickin' around here." He plucked a strand of hay and worked the end of it between his teeth. The fresh herbal tang contrasted with the bitterness of the dried grass.

"You ain't?" Jo asked wide-eyed.

"Nah. I'm going to find him." He looked down at the compass, pointed to the west.

"Your pa?" Jo rolled to her side, her head propped on one fist, and looked at the compass in his hand.

"M-hmm. When I get older, I'm going to Colorado to find him."

"Can I come?" she asked, popping up to a sitting position at full attention.

"I guess so. You sure you want to? I hear it's a mighty wild country out there," he said gravely.

"I ain't afraid." She lifted her chin.

A smile tugged at the corner of Gideon's lips, and he put the compass back into the pocket of his overalls. "No, I don't reckon you are."

He shook his head and gave her a sidelong glance. "But maybe ya oughta be."

Jo rolled her eyes and puffed out a sigh that lifted the coppery hair off her forehead.

"You better take me with you, Gideon Cross, or I'm gonna go off on my own adventure without you."

"Well, if I don't get this hay in the loft before supper, we won't be able to have no more picnics, much less go on any kind of adventurin'." He stood and brushed the shiny bits of dried grass from his overalls and took Jo's hand, helping her gain her balance. "Now you get on back to the house before Elaine the Pain goes tattlin' on us to your pa again."

Jo gathered the cloth napkin that had contained their lunch and slid off the back of the wagon. She ran across the dusty farmyard in her bare feet, scattering chickens and leaving a flurry of feathers in her wake.

GIDEON BROUGHT DOWN the heavy maul with a crack that echoed through the crisp mountain air, sending the two halves of a pine log flying out to either side of the stump he used for wood splitting. He picked up the pieces and added them to the growing wood stack under the extended eve on the side of the cabin.

He had several cords of wood already split and stacked but needed several more if he wanted to keep warm through the winter. The prickle of cool air nipped at his cheeks. Winter wasn't too far off. The sensation of cold tickling its way through the short stubble of beard reminded him of his foolish mistake of gettin' all gussied up for some filly, only to be sent out to pasture.

Not once, but twice.

It wasn't as though the loss of his potential bride, Leah, had been a real loss in any way. He'd practically been clicking his heels as he left Pastor Walton's home after receiving the news she'd found someone else to latch on to. They both would've been as miserable as two tomcats in a gunny sack.

The loss of Jo again, after two years of grieving, was what left him feeling like he'd swallowed a boulder.

He rolled his shoulders against the constriction of the too-tight, buckskin shirt and sheared off the line of thought as he sheared another log in two with a single, furious stroke.

Getting ready for winter was what Gideon should be concerned with now, not the trail of mistakes he seemed to leave behind like breadcrumbs. At this high elevation, the weather was unpredictable at best and downright dangerous at its worst. It wasn't uncommon to have a beautiful day with blue skies and sunshine shift into a blowing snowstorm within minutes.

There had already been light flurries of snow whipping and twirling through the bright yellow leaves around the cabin this past week. This time of year, the snow shouldn't amount to much, at least until November came around, but Gideon was behind on getting the wood he needed to store up for the winter.

As soon as he finished getting these last few cords split and stacked, it was imperative he leave for Pueblo soon.

There was barely enough time to get one more trip in before the winter weather would make the journey, if not impossible, at least unwise.

Gideon hadn't been to Pueblo in far too long, and the guilt needled him like a cucklebur in his shirt. It was a three-day journey to Pueblo on horseback. By the time he made the journey and settled things there, he would be gone for a week. When he returned, he should have just enough time to get things buttoned down before the snow should start sticking around in earnest.

While this would only be Gideon's second full winter on the mountain, he'd learned well enough how much earlier winter would set in and how much colder it would be here in the Rockies than it ever had been back home.

How strange it was, the dramatic change in his life over the past few years. Though he hadn't traveled far, at least not as far as it would have been to go off to California or the Yukon Territory, the climate and terrain of this behemoth of a mountain were something vastly different than Gideon had ever seen. Temperatures in the summer here were almost as cool as a Kansas winter but without the bitter wind.

As it always did, the memory of life in Kansas brought a fresh wave of pain and guilt. Was Gideon even deserving of a happy life when so many had been harmfully affected by his mistake?

The mouths of fools are their undoing. His mother had often quoted the verse in Proverbs while reprimanding Gideon as an overly talkative boy. Her warning had been nearly prophetic.

One fateful evening, Gideon had regaled his parents with the tale of the new railroad that caused a resurgence of silver from Colorado with all the polish of a master narrator. Pa's eyes had widened, and Gideon had been proud to be the bearer of such exciting news. But the following day, he had felt the soul-crushing remorse of his actions. Pa was gone.

Gideon's unbridled tongue had been the undoing of so many lives. Since then, he'd made a conscious effort to keep to himself, avoiding saying too much and firmly rejecting empty twaddle and gossip.

Perhaps his own self-restraint wasn't enough, though. Maybe the reason God had seen fit to close the door of marriage for him was chastisement in payment for the lives he had ruined. Would he be destined to live a lonely life in the Colorado Rocky Mountains, with only his horse to talk to? Was his solitude the consequence of his reckless mouth?

Whatever a man sows, that shall he also reap. Gideon had sown idle gossip, and now the silence of the mountain would be his harvest.

Chapter 17

Evening came, and though Jo begged the sun to linger, the sky began to darken, and so had her spirits. She had done her best to prepare. She washed the bedding, then used the wash kettle to heat another pot of clean water. She filled the basin and ewer to wash away the grime and fatigue of the past few days.

Jo opened a small bag she had brought with her from the brothel. She withdrew a collection of small tins and lined them up on the dressing table. First, she applied a layer of paste over her entire face, finishing with a generous dusting of rice powder, thick enough to camouflage her scar. Hazel may not have thought the make-up was enough, but this wasn't the parlor house. She continued applying the rest of the mask that had been her defense this past year. Next was a wax layer on her eyelashes and charcoal powder to cover her eyelids and coat the wax on her lashes. The last item from her magic bag of tricks was a paper tube of bright red wax lipstick.

"What in the name of St. Nicholas are you covered up in all that for?" Myra appeared at her side, and Jo's heart leaped into her throat.

"In what?" Jo blinked slowly. The dread of this night weighed heavily and slowed her wits. Myra pinched the pale blue fabric of the dress Abigail had given her and cocked her head. "Ya ain't gonna need this thing on. It'll just get ruined."

Jo scanned Myra's own disheveled appearance. The woman was clad only in a dingy, sagging chemise with a strap that kept falling over her shoulder.

"It's all I have," Jo answered stubbornly, not wanting to admit to herself the dress was unnecessary.

"That's just it, love." Myra shook her head. "They'll ruin it with their grubby hands and rip the buttons clean off."

Jo choked back the sour taste that clogged her throat. It was nonsensical to be so disturbed by what she faced. She was already ruined. But after living in the clean and bright world of someone like Abigail, being thrust back into the darkness of this reality was more than she thought she could bear.

"Best get that pretty dress off and get to work," Myra spoke over her shoulder as she strolled to the back door. "Ain't no use in pretending you're some fine lady here."

Jo sank to the bed and began to unbutton the dress with shaky hands. Myra was right. There was no use pretending Jo was above any of this.

As darkness fell, Jo lit the oil lamp on the bureau and locked tired eyes with her reflection. She studied the woman in the mirror with a sensation of pity and contempt. Weak arms hung at her sides, her chest was sunken in, and her head hung low like a marionette without a puppet master.

Where had the feisty girl gone who had a fire in her eyes and had loved to laugh? That girl was gone now, lost in the badlands of her consequences. If she gave in to the grief over her lost identity, it would drain away what little life she had left, so she drew her shoulders back in defiance and pushed down the heartbreak and regret deep within her.

The reserve of energy she needed to tap into was a meager supply. She hadn't eaten anything for two days. The queasy, aching sensation of hunger that had been her companion the past two days faded along with her appetite for self-preservation.

She turned to face the door that would open to the street and the dozens of men who would come and turn this new nightmare into reality. A cacophony of laughter, shouting, and the thumping of boots on the wooden boardwalk outside her door filled the air.

The world closed around her, and the edges of her vision quivered. Her heart pounded so hard it might just explode from her chest at any moment. She braced herself with one hand on the brass bedpost and willed herself to take in a shaky breath. *Get it together, Jo.*

Her mouth was dry, making it difficult to swallow. She remembered the flask she had given the last of her coin for and turned back quickly to retrieve it from the small table by the potbelly stove. As though it contained the last drops of hope available on earth, she pressed the bottle to her lips, seeking its promise of detachment.

Her mistakes, crimes, her year at the brothel, and what her life would be like now, all closed in around her. All of it echoed in her mind like a song that would never end. Layered over the lament of her mistakes, an eerie descant haunted her. *You will never be more than this. You made your choice. There is no way out.*

Finally, through the din, a distant memory disrupted the discordant composition.

A name. Someone she had once known. Pearl DeVere.

The madam who had taken her in and given her a start at the parlor house. The woman who had taken too much opium one night, never to wake again.

Jo thought of Pearl and oblivion. She tipped the flask and drank deeply.

JO PONDERED THE WHITEWASHED ceiling above her. It appeared blurry at first, slowly coming into sharp clarity and seeming much too close. She blinked languidly, realizing she must be floating, and any moment she would be able to touch the smooth, warm wood.

Warm. It was pleasantly warm here, like being wrapped in a fuzzy, woolen cape. The sensation shrouded itself around her mind, cloaking her and clouding her vision again.

She was aware of a distant rumble of sounds but could not be bothered any longer to distinguish what the sounds were. She spread her fingers out beside her slowly, seeking some purchase to connect her to whatever buoyed her.

The cloud she seemed to be resting on was comfortable, soft, inviting her to sink deeper within its depths. Slowly, she was becoming submerged in the quiet, velvet fog. It engulfed her, and her pounding heart began to ease and slow.

She was growing sleepy, so sleepy. The breath that had been so difficult under the weight of anxiety before came so leisurely it was insignificant. A needless task she was reluctant to go on with. Letting go of the habitual need to draw more air into her lungs, she allowed the tranquil mist to swallow her in its warmth and soothe her into deep somnolence.

Something stirred within her. Some nudging of a vital notion warred to penetrate the thick fog surrounding her, disturbing her contentment and bringing pain to her chest. She wanted the uncomfortable feeling to leave her alone. Burning pressure traced the pathways of her lungs. Her cells were screaming for air, desperate to be freed from the bondage of suffocation. Violently, one single demand battered at her cocoon, badgering her. She fought to sink deeper into the darkness and find the comfort of sleep, but the unrelenting voice continued to call to her through the mist.

Breathe! The solitary demand broke through her defenses and the thick fog of drug-induced slumber. Her body responded with a mighty gasp, and she abruptly awakened.

With rasping, gasping breaths, Jo sought to find her way through the fog, but the blanket remained snugly wrapped around her mind. It smothered her ability to understand what was happening. The soft cloud was drowning her, the desire to sleep beckoning to her.

Jo forced herself into a seated position. In the dim tunnel of vision she gained, she found herself on the sagging mattress of her crib-house apartment. The quilts beneath her were rough and scratchy in comparison to the softness that wrapped around her a moment before.

The rumble of sounds in the distance grew louder and more abrupt. Though her heart was pounding violently in her chest, Jo became aware there was another pounding outside herself that she couldn't identify. Thumping and shouting accosted her senses. She blinked, trying to make out her surroundings. Her murky field of vision was partly due to the slowly sputtering oil lamp, running out of fuel.

She struggled to her feet, and the world tilted around her. She clung to the bedpost beside her, willing her mind to tear itself free from the stupor of opium. The pounding and shouting came into clarity as she became aware of someone banging on her door.

"Open up! We know you're in there." Through the blur of laudanum and tattered, lacy curtains, Jo could make out the commotion of a mob of drunken miners clamoring at her door.

"Ain't no waiting lisst here, Schweetheart," one man slurred. "Open up!" They were laughing and shoving one another out of the way.

Adrenaline shot through Jo's veins like lightning, and her breath came quick and shallow, each one seeming to draw less air than the one before it. She opened and closed her fists repeatedly, trying to relieve the tingling sensation from her fingers.

As Jo's vision began to clear, she searched the room for any solution to the trap she found herself in. She couldn't go through with it.

Scanning the room, she caught her reflection in the mirror once more. This time, charcoal was smeared around her eyes, leaving black trails in stark, white rice powder.

Had she been crying? She couldn't remember. Her hair was disheveled. Several pins had come loose, and it stood out in all directions. In the flickering shadows of the sputtering oil lamp, the image before her sent a chill down her spine. The marionette had transformed into a ghastly specter. Pale and gaunt with flames for hair. Jo covered her mouth with a trembling hand to stifle a scream.

"God, help me, please!" She fell to the floor and whispered a desperate prayer.

Drawing in a steadying breath and blocking out the raucous carousing outside her door, a presence of peace stilled her frantic mind, and she crawled across the floor. She clumsily fumbled for the carpetbag that contained her last few worldly possessions. She fled the room, knocking over tins and bottles in her haste and sending charcoal and rice powder flying.

She stumbled out the back door and ran as though the hounds of hell pursued her. Crossing the vacant lot behind the building, she ran through the darkness, tripping over rocks and dried clumps of mud, sagebrush snagging at her stockings. She didn't know where she was going, only that she must run far away from this place. She was forced to an abrupt stop when she barreled straight into a short, wooden fence, doubling her over and sending her flying over the top. She landed face down in what must have been the last mud left anywhere around this time of year.

She lay in foul-smelling mud, too weak to pick herself up. The adrenaline had worn off, leaving heavy limbs and a pounding headache in its wake. Slowly, she lifted herself to her elbows. An overpowering stench surrounded her, and she retched, though there was nothing to relieve her body of but the dregs of laudanum and whiskey. She rolled to her side and sat up, leaning back on the fence made of boards.

Her eyes adjusted to the moonlight, and she found a low-lying roof jutting out from a barn wall. Sounds of groaning and heavy sighs came from the low lean-to. She stood and stumbled closer, peering into the shelter.

Pigs.

Jo had landed face first in a hog pen. She couldn't hold back the illogical snort of laughter that burst from her. Oh, the irony. Hazel's parting words may have meant the mean-spirited comment metaphorically, but here Jo stood after all.

She wavered on her feet, fatigue and weariness overtaking her. She leaned a hand onto the sleeping pigs' shelter and smiled at the sight of them. Piled up like cordwood—"cheek by jowl" she had heard it called. They looked so content, having the warmth and companionship of one another.

Beside her, a low wooden trough had been filled with crusty, moldy bread, most likely begged off of the local baker. The sight of the bread caused the formerly absent saliva in Jo's mouth to begin working again, and a pitiful, painful rumble in her belly reminded her she hadn't eaten in almost three days. She dropped to her knees and picked up a crusty, dark roll. Lifting the bread to her mouth, the sharp scent of mold hit her senses. Her stomach convulsed, painfully heaving, and her arms shook as she tried to brace herself. There was nothing left inside her to surrender.

Leaning back, she rested her head against the outside wall of the pigs' shelter behind her. The inky black sky twinkled with pinpricks of white light. A chill nipped the skin on her bare arms, and she rubbed them. It was late fall now, and the nights were growing colder. Even the pigs snuggled warmly together. She had nothing and no one.

What a fool she was. Here she was, jealous over the companionship of pigs and ravenous over the slops in their feed trough. How could she have come to this? How had she fallen so low?

She did have someone. How had she not recognized that she had friendship and the offer of help, only a few blocks away with Abigail and John? When she had a family back home who, no doubt, still loved her and grieved the loss of her. Fear and guilt had blinded her, and she'd believed she didn't have any other choice.

But she did have a choice, and in that moment, Jo chose life.

Chapter 18

The smell of bacon and coffee thick in the air woke Jo. Her head was heavy with exhaustion and the after-effects of whiskey and laudanum, and it refused to rise from the feathery depths of the pillow. She lay motionless, slowly coming around to consciousness and taking a slow inventory of her current state of being.

The cool, smooth softness of the sheets gave a delectable contrast to the warmth of her body. The tiny feathers that filled the mattress prickled at her sensitive skin with a pleasant reminder that she was, indeed, alive.

Though fatigue weighed heavily upon her, the familiar sound of humming from a distance brought a sleepy smile to her lips, and she stretched luxuriously in her cocoon of contentedness. She blinked languidly and sent all of her available strength into her arms, propping her up. The tantalizing smell of food caused her stomach to cry out for sustenance. She fumbled her way out of the quilts and up on her feet. The scent of the lavender soap Abigail used lingered in the fresh, white nightgown she wore. She dressed quickly in the simple, rust-colored skirt and white blouse she found laid over the bed's iron footboard and peeked from the room to make sure Abigail was alone before venturing out.

"Well, well," came Abigail's soothing tone. "The prodigal returns." Her glowing smile brought out a dimple in her left cheek and softened her teasing tone.

Though Jo wasn't quite feeling up to the level of witty banter yet, the lightness in Jo's own heart allowed her to see the joy emanating from Abigail like the warmth of a wood stove.

"How exactly did I get here?" Jo remembered her moment of clarity in the hog pen but had no memory of how she had ended up clean and warm in the familiar feather bed.

"Not sure how you made it to our door, but when John stepped out on the porch this morning for his early rounds ... there you were. Sleeping by the door, covered in mud and wearing ... well ..." Abigail gave a slight shrug as she turned the bacon in the pan.

"Oh, Abigail, I'm sorry." Jo's light heart clouded over with shame.

"Don't you worry yourself about it one bit. It'll sure give the town gossips something to chatter about, but I suppose they'll move on the moment the next Harper's Bazaar shows up in the mercantile to fill their cauldrons with scandal." Abigail gave Jo an almost imperceptible wink as she turned around with a platter full of bacon, toast, and eggs. "I should be asking you the same thing. How did you get here, or more precisely, what brought you here?" She placed the platter on the table and poured a cup of steaming, black coffee for each of them before sitting down.

Jo sighed and blinked back the rising tide of tears.

"Oh Abigail, I—I just couldn't go back. I couldn't go back to that life." Her shoulders quaked with the effort to repress the sobs rising within her. "I don't know what I'll do, but I won't do that."

All the tension in her relaxed, and the dam broke. Abigail stood from her seat and wrapped her arms tightly around Jo's back as a mother would lean down to embrace her child. Jo wrapped her arms around Abigail's waist and soaked her apron in tears of remorse, regret, and relief.

"Be still," Abigail whispered into the top of Jo's head. "Be still."

THE NEXT AFTERNOON, Jo sat with her feet curled under her on the floral patterned wingback chair in Abigail's sitting room. She relished the comfort of the sensible skirt and blouse Abigail had given her. It wasn't tight and pinching like a corset and didn't make her feel on display. She cradled a cup of Earl Grey tea in her hands and took a deep breath, savoring the wafting essence of bergamot that would fortify her for the conversation to come.

It was time her friends heard the rest of her story about how she came to be crumpled on their doorstep, streaked with mud. She traced the daffodil pattern on the delicate cup with a thumb as she tried to conjure the words lodged in her throat. She attempted to make out the story in her mind, but it was like a blurry landscape, poorly painted, in shades of gray.

Jo looked up from her cup of tea and caught a glance between husband and wife, suggesting they were having one of those unspoken marital conversations the way Ma and Pa used to. Jo dropped her eyes again. The sight of this happy couple stirred a longing within her Jo didn't know how to process.

John reached over and laid a hand over Abigail's, where it rested on her thigh, and squeezed it. The look seemed to be one of comfort and encouragement. He gave his wife a slight nod and a half-smile.

"Did Mr. Cross find you the morning you left for the parlor house?" Abigail began the conversation. Jo straightened in her seat and set her cup down on the table next to her.

She had tried to forget her encounter with Gideon the moment she turned away from him and toward her return to life at the parlor house. She had become an expert at cutting sensitive or emotional matters away from her. Simple as cutting the bruise from a peach. Now, with the memory so abruptly brought back to her, Jo hadn't time to smooth over the topic with bland indifference or even to come up with a reasonable change in subject. Her stomach tightened, and her breath came up short. She gave a slight shrug and pursed her lips before speaking.

"He did ..."

What had happened that morning? There had been a heated conversation, and he—had Gideon proposed to her? He hadn't *wanted* to marry her. She knew that. It was clear he had only been acting on a sense of duty to rescue her from such a disgraceful path.

The delicate cup and saucer vibrated and began working their way nearer to the edge of the table. She placed a hand on her knee, willing the involuntary bouncing motion to stop.

"He seemed quite anxious to reach you before you went back." Abigail's blue eyes were intent as she studied Jo for answers. "He seems quite protective of you."

All of Abigail's statements sounded more like questions, but Jo didn't want to talk about Gideon. She would spill all her other secrets, but that hurt was too deep. She stared down at her empty hands as Abigail spoke, envisioning the life she had always wanted but was now lost.

"Is he a good man, Jo?" Abigail's hinting finally boiled down to the real question.

A good man? He had taken care of his ma and little brother James when his pa had left, had always done an excellent job working for Pa, always putting in a full day's work, and had even been diligent in his schooling when most boys of his age would have given it up. He had looked out for Jo and protected her when they were out on their adventures. He had been a good boy, a good friend, but what did she know about him as a man?

He had abandoned her when he left for Colorado, refusing to take her with him. He had gone months without corresponding after he'd found his pa's journal about the silver. She wasn't sure she did know him anymore. If she were honest, she did know he was a good man, though. It had never been in his character to be anything else.

"Good?" Jo sighed, "far better than I deserve." Jo's voice cracked with this consent.

"We didn't know what might have become of you after you left us. We had wondered whether you would have gone with him. Judging by your reappearance on our doorstep,

I suppose you parted ways from him and returned to the brothel?"

"I did." It seemed safer to offer only the briefest of answers so Abigail wouldn't get any ideas about Jo and Gideon.

Seeming to accept defeat on the topic of Gideon, Abigail waited for Jo to continue the story. She told them of her eviction from the parlor house and her plan to earn money for a train ticket. Feeling safer and more comfortable the longer she spoke, she continued to tell them all about her inability to go through with going back to prostitution. When Jo admitted to her attempt to end it all with the laudanum and whiskey, John shook his head in disbelief.

"You are a fortunate—no, a blessed—young woman." He nodded as if he were confirming something to himself. "For you to have drunk as much of that awful concoction as you did and still be sitting here speaking with us is nothing short of miraculous. By what you describe, you were on the verge of coma and death." He turned to Abigail with a smile.

"What an answer to prayer!" Abigail blinked back unshed tears. "We were praying for you last night with Pastor Walton," Abigail told her, beaming. "We didn't know where you had ended up after you left here, whether you chose to go with Mr. Cross or back to the parlor house. But last night, I had such a burden for you, I asked John to drive us to the pastor's home for an unannounced call. We all came together in prayer for you and asked God to spare you from whatever harm might be in your path." She sat back against the pink velvet cushion of the couch, at ease, with a radiant smile.

"Well, I honestly don't know that God had anything to do with it," Jo said with a wry quirk of the mouth. "But if he did, I sure wish he hadn't seen fit to dump me off in a hog pen."

"The Bible speaks of that, you know?" Abigail looked at Jo pointedly. "In the Psalms, King David wrote, *He brought me up out of a horrible pit, out of the miry clay and set my feet upon a rock.* That's precisely what he did for you, Jo." Abigail raised both fair eyebrows, sipping her tea with an air of satisfaction.

"I do thank you both for your kind concern and prayers. Honestly, I do. But I think I'm a bit far out of reach, even for God Almighty. I know this. I'm sure I won't go back to prostitution. I can't." A shiver skittered across Jo's shoulders as she remembered the voices shouting and the pounding on her apartment door. "But I've fallen too far to find redemption."

The room lay quiet for a moment as Jo clammed up, and Abigail looked out the window with a soft, pensive expression.

"Do you like my tea set, Jo?" Abigail sat straight again and asked pointedly.

"Yes ... it's quite lovely," Jo answered with a furrowed brow and a cocked head at this rapid change of subject.

"You know, it was a wedding gift from my Johnny." Abigail took a moment to lock eyes with her husband and give him a fond pat on the knee. "Daffodils, you see?"

Jo looked down at the delicate cup in her hand with scalloped edges and a soft pattern of pink and yellow daffodils. Jo nodded in agreement though she didn't truly understand Abigail's point.

"Daffodils are a symbol of new beginnings, rebirth," Abigail continued. "You know my story. Why is it you can't believe our good Father would do the same for you?"

Jo stared at the cup and pondered the possibility. It all sounded good in theory, but all she had done, and where she had been this past few years, she couldn't imagine a way across. It was too much. The chasm was too wide to make that kind of leap.

Chapter 19

Gideon rode back into Cripple Creek with the satisfaction of knowing all was well in Pueblo, and he wouldn't need to return until after winter. It was never an easy trip. The formidable four-story building with its towering gables and long rows of neatly made beds always left an uneasy lump in his belly. The stark immediacy of being faced with the consequences of his failures was much worse. His only small token of comfort was that he knew all was as well as it could be, and the silver he provided would ensure the quality of care would continue.

Now that he had ensured things in Pueblo were as well as they could be, he had one more thing to make right. One more life he had to try and salvage from the wreckage of his past mistakes. He had to find Jo.

She'd made it clear that she wanted nothing to do with him, but he couldn't shake the need to see her again. The thought of her in such a miserable place plagued his days and terrorized his nights. She didn't belong in this life she seemed to think she was trapped in.

But how could he convince her to come with him? What could he offer her when she wanted nothing to do with him? There had to be something here that would speak the words that always lodged in his throat. Something that would remind her of who he was and what they once had. He didn't have the words.

He found himself browsing the shelves of the Rocky Mountain Mercantile. Searching. He passed slowly by the cabinets filled with china place settings and silverware. She'd never had use of such frivolous things. When he found himself in a maze of colorful fabrics, he ran a thumb over a bolt of green fabric. It was fuzzy like a summer peach.

Green had been Jo's favorite color once. Was it still? He didn't know. Didn't know her at all anymore. The fresh sting of grief pricked his eyes. To have found her, even changed as she was, and then lose her again was a cruel blow.

"That'n is a fine fabric for a winter dress." A woman's gentle, shaky voice penetrated Gideon's thoughts. "Nice and heavy for warmth."

"Hmph," was all Gideon could manage in reply. The gruff sound cleared the lump in his throat.

"Looking for a wife?" the shopkeeper's wife inquired. Gideon's head snapped up. The approaching woman was a grandmotherly type, with strands of silver swept up into a lace cap on the top of her head.

"No." Gideon jerked his hand back from the fabric as if it were on fire. "Don't need a wife." He could feel the deep furrow carve its way across his brow. The older woman's gentle peel of laughter rang clearly through Gideon's gloomy mood, and he softened, realizing what the woman must have meant by her question. "No ma'am," Gideon gave a reluctant half-smile. "No wife."

"But your thoughts are on someone ..." She gave a knowing smile and tapped her lips with an index finger. "Someone you care for?"

Gideon cleared his throat and looked around frantically for an escape.

"There, there," she said and took one of his hands in her own, patting it gently. "We'll find what you are looking for ... and I'll never tell a soul what a nice man you are," she added with a whisper and a wink.

A short time later, Gideon tucked the small brown paper package into his saddlebag. Maybe the candy would trigger some memory of their youth for Jo and snap her out of this madness.

As children, Gideon had the charge of Jo, Elaine, and Jimmy to walk to and from school each day. Gideon would often stop in at the general store on their way home. It was the perfect opportunity for Gideon to listen in on all the gossip and goings-on around town.

Elaine would huff and fume over the detour, tapping her toe and biting her nails, but Jo was always eager to make the stop. She was a favorite of the shop owner, Mr. Casey. Mr. Casey would prop her up on a stool at the counter and sneak her the bits and pieces of the salt water taffy, made by Mrs. Casey, that weren't large enough to be wrapped and sold.

As Gideon rested his forearms across Sarge's saddle, he scanned the busy street to the left and right, seeking some revelatory answer that would tell him what to do.

"Well, what then? Am I supposed to go into that God-forsaken place and hand her a piece of candy?" Gideon asked

Sarge, who turned a chocolate-colored ear in his direction and swished his black tail impatiently.

The idea seemed absurd now that he faced going through with it. "She doesn't want to see me. You know it, and I know it." Gideon let out his breath with more of a groan than a sigh and scrubbed a large hand over his face.

Sarge craned his neck around and began nibbling at the fringe of Gideon's buckskin shirt. "*Ach*." Gideon pushed his companion's soft nose away. "A lot of help you are." He resolutely stepped into the stirrup and tensed his thigh muscles, giving Sarge the go-ahead and turning toward Meyer Street and The Old Homestead Parlour House.

By the time he reached the front door of the brothel, Gideon's stomach was threatening to turn itself inside out. Was she here? Had she been here all this time? He pounded on the door with the side of his fist, and a lean, dark-haired man answered the door.

"May I help you?" the man asked in a thick accent, giving Gideon a look that said the man had no ambition, much less intention, of helping him at all.

"I need to speak to Jo," Gideon grumbled, not wishing to be heard, or seen, anywhere near this place.

"There is no ... *Jo* here, sir."

"What do you mean—" Gideon stopped short, remembering Jo hadn't gone by her real name here. He racked his brain for the memory of what the liveryman had called her.

"I'm sorry, sir, but we have no one here by that—"

"Kate," Gideon nearly shouted, then lowered his voice to a conspiratorial whisper. "I need to see Kate."

The man's eyes widened with recognition. "Oh. That one." His nostrils flared as if he smelled something unpleasant. "She is not here." The sallow man's French accent became stronger as his irritation increased, and he grabbed the edge of the door to swing it closed. Gideon stopped the door with his boot and gripped the edge of the door fiercely.

"Where is she?" Gideon spoke through a jaw clenched so tightly his bones ached.

"She is no longer employed by this establishment. Now, may you please leave at once?"

The man elevated his nose a fraction of an inch higher. It was clear, had Gideon not been two inches taller than him, the man would have been looking down his nose in condescension. Gideon took a slow, steadying breath and stepped back, fighting the urge to bash the uppity man's head in the door. He stepped back, and the slam of the door reverberated through him.

Gideon's abrupt dismissal from the doorway of the parlor house left him more disconcerted than he'd been before. It was bad enough knowing Jo had chosen that life over a life with him, but now if the French fop had been telling the truth, she was missing all over again.

Where could she have gone? Did it even matter? Gideon lifted a hand to his cheek, now bristling with a short, bushy beard, and remembered the sting of her hand and her words. *Get out of town and get out of my life. I don't need rescuing.*

He was a fool to even care anymore. All evidence suggested the Jo that had loved him before was nothing but a memory. This Jo wanted nothing to do with him.

Still, Gideon needed to find her. The ride to Pueblo and back had given him ample time to think. If he'd never run his ever-moving mouth about the silver rush on Red Mountain all those years ago, his father wouldn't have left. He, Ma, and Jimmy wouldn't have been left alone to fend for themselves. He never would've left Kansas in search of his father, and Jo never would've had cause to run away and fall into disrepute. Although he may not know *how* she'd ended up in a brothel, he did know it all started with him and his big mouth.

Jo had been right when she rejected him on the street a few weeks ago. It wasn't only because he loved her that he'd wanted to marry her and take her from this place. It was his fault she was here. He had to make it right somehow.

Gideon mounted the saddle once more. Where could she have gone? He considered Pastor Walton. Gideon had first seen Jo in the front pew of the church, speaking to the pastor. Though her face was hidden with a veil at the time, he now knew it was her. But when he had spoken, or fought, with her last, she hadn't seemed the least bit interested in turning her life around. She had seemed determined to go on with it.

The thought nauseated him, and he spat the taste of acid from his mouth. If Jo hadn't been ready to turn her life around, she wouldn't have gone to the pastor. But she had seemed cozy with that doctor and his wife. Perhaps, if anyone in this town knew anything, it would be them.

Gideon gripped the reins tightly. Jaw-jacking had never done him any good, and he'd no desire to start now.

He sat rigidly on Sarge's back, his muscles tense with defiance against the task before him. He took a long, deep breath, feeling his nostrils flare, and avoided any twitch of the leg that would cue Sarge into action. Sensing Gideon's tension, Sarge began to paw at the dirt and tug at the reins, shaking his black mane, anxious to get on the move.

"Alright, boy," Gideon surrendered. "Let's go find her."

With a click of his tongue and a tightening of Gideon's legs, Sarge trotted into motion, carrying Gideon off to face his fear.

Chapter 20

Jo - Age 15

Gideon - Age 18

Jo swayed back and forth in front of her mother's tall mirror. The dress did look lovely, though it pinched something fierce. And the shoes, good gravy, these new colonial high-heeled shoes were going to be the death of her.

"You look simply regal, Jo." Elaine untied the bow at the back of Jo's dress and straightened it.

"I can't breathe." Jo put a hand flat on her stomach, exaggerating her distress.

"Oh, hush and come sit. It's almost time to leave." Elaine motioned Jo over to the stool. "I'll help you with your hair."

Jo turned her back to the mirror and dropped onto the stool like a sack of grain.

"You know, if you'd been wearing your corset like a proper young lady this past two years, like a young lady should have done, you would be used to it by now." Elaine lowered a delicate eyebrow at Jo.

Of course, Elaine would think so. She hadn't even waited until thirteen to start wearing her corset. She'd begged their mother to wear one at the age of ten, insisting that she wanted the proper posture of a lady.

Jo, on the other hand, had avoided the contraption like it was treated with poison. She'd been lucky enough not to develop any sort of womanly figure until the past summer and had only recently been forced to join ranks with her sister. A snicker fizzled through Jo's nose in a very unladylike snort at the thought of Elaine and her friends lined up like soldiers in their corsets.

"What's so funny?" Elaine narrowed her hawk-like, tawny eyes as she forced the tortoise-shell comb into Jo's hair.

"Nothin'." Jo waved her hand in a dismissive gesture and sat up straighter, sighing. "You live for this stuff, don't you?"

Elaine had always been somewhat of a mystery to Jo. Why would anyone choose to be so stuffy?

"I feel honored to have been created as one of the fairer sex. Why shouldn't I be a good steward of the role God has placed me in by embracing it and all the finery it comes with?" Elaine waved a delicate hand in the vicinity of the pearl earbobs that their mother had allowed Elaine to borrow, then placed a hand on Jo's shoulder. "You are lovely, sister. Someday, you might even have the patience to let me style your hair like mine."

Elaine's elaborate style had taken her over an hour to achieve. Jo doubted she'd ever be patient enough to go through that kind of effort. Jo grimaced at the thought of all that fuss.

"Don't look at me like that, Jo." Elaine laughed as she put her hands on her hips. "You look like it'd be torture to make yourself look your best."

Jo shuddered dramatically. "It would."

They both giggled, something Jo had rarely done with Elaine in recent years. Elaine gave her a rare, genuine smile and turned Jo back toward the mirror to show off her finished work. The sides of Jo's hair were swept up, the rest hanging down in loose waves.

Jo peeked at her sister, who was fixing a loose strand of her hair in the mirror. Maybe Jo had been too hard on Elaine? She couldn't be all that bad.

A jingling harness outside told her the wagon was out front.

"Our chariot awaits." Elaine giggled and squeezed Jo's hands.

Elaine was in an unusually good mood tonight. A barn dance was not a treat they were able to enjoy often.

While Elaine hurried outside, Jo held back, giving the mirror one more glance. She sure looked different. Unlike her rather plain church dresses, this dress cinched tight at the waist, and the sleeves had large puffs, the size of her head. The airy, pink fabric swept out dramatically in the back. She almost didn't look like herself at all. Maybe that was a good thing. Gideon was never going to see her differently as long as she was in her usual mud-streaked britches and messy braids. Maybe tonight, he would see her as more of a woman than just a fishing buddy.

When Jo came out onto the porch, Gideon stood holding the team while Elaine stepped up into the wagon. He stared at Jo, mouth agape.

A small bubble of excitement swirled in her belly at the attention. She held the sweeping skirt dramatically to one side and sashayed down the tall porch steps. She made it almost to the last step when the shoes finally got the best of her. Her ankle gave way, and she stumbled down the remaining steps. Gideon caught her by an elbow, the undercurrent of his barely contained laughter vibrating through him.

"So much for being graceful." Jo chuckled and climbed into the wagon, feverish with embarrassment.

"Jo, you look different." Jimmy, seated by Gideon, who drove the wagon, looked back with a confused expression.

Gideon elbowed his younger brother.

"What happened to her?" Jimmy shook his head, laughing.

Would she ever be able to prove she was more than a tangled mess? Gideon had seemed shocked, but in a good way, before her stunt on the porch steps. Maybe Elaine had worked some magic on her after all. Now, if she could just manage to act like a proper lady and not embarrass herself again, there might still be hope.

The sun had already begun to set upon their arrival at the dance. Glowing lantern light spilled out into the barnyard from the large front doors. The appealing whine of a fiddle flowed from the confines of the barn, making Jo's heart light with anticipation.

A fiddler stood on top of a barrel. His legs kicked out as he danced a jig while he played. It was a wonder he didn't fall off.

"Jo, you just look so pretty tonight. All the boys will be flocking to you." Elaine squeezed Jo's hand and patted Jo's hair into order after the wagon ride.

"She'll never last all gussied up like that." Gideon shook his head. "She's the same old Jo she's always been."

Gideon's remark caused a twinge in Jo's belly. He didn't see her any differently at all. He didn't even seem to like her when she was all dressed up. If she couldn't get his attention like this, how could she ever hope to?

"Gideon Cross, you just hush your mouth." Elaine turned her nose up at Gideon and pushed Jo forward. "She looks lovely. She should've been dressing like this all the time instead of traipsing around in the mud with you." Elaine continued speaking over her shoulder.

"Doesn't suit her." Gideon tugged at his nose and sniffed. "She ain't some Arabian filly, you know." His voice lowered to a murmur. "More like a good solid mule."

Jo's heart sank. Why had she let her heart long for more? Gideon would never see her as anything.

"Come on." Elaine grabbed Jo's hand and practically dragged her the rest of the way into the barn.

Jo's eyes pricked, and she wanted to hide. Sulking over a cup of lemonade, Jo shot daggers at Gideon, who seemed to be likewise stewing on a barrel top in the opposite corner of the barn.

Good solid mule, indeed. He was the mule. Stubborn, sullen, and thickheaded, that's what he was. Jo scratched at her neck as the flush of her temper boiled to the surface. Heat crept up into her face.

Jacob Sinclair slipped in beside Jo and leaned ever so slightly, pressing his arm against hers and snapping her out of her mournful moping. The warmth of him radiated through the sheer pink fabric of her sleeve. Her breath came short, and her heart fluttered in her chest.

He was a year older than Gideon, long and lean with a boyish charm. It was clear he was a favorite at the party. Girls clustered nearby, hovering as close to him as they could. The room always seemed a little more crowded wherever he was standing.

"Why, Jo Bradford, you've grown into your skin nicely since I saw you last," Jacob whispered into Jo's hair. "Will you do me the honor of a dance?"

The prickle of anger that had been burning under the surface since Gideon's insult found a new purpose. Her whole face tingled. She pressed her lips tightly together to hide the wide grin that would've discredited her mask of ladylike decorum.

"I'd be delighted."

He took her hand and bowed slightly in a mock gesture of a formal ball. He winked at her as he swept her onto the dance floor into a waltz. He held her back firmly, drawing her close, but not so close as to alert any unwanted attention from her father, who was animatedly sharing stories by the refreshment table.

At each point and turn, Jo found her mark, locking a challenging stare on Gideon. His knee bounced rapidly as he watched them, and he seemed to be radiating enough steam to power a horseless carriage. She had no real interest in the dashing Jacob Sinclair, but maybe if someone else saw her as more than just a mule, Gideon might take notice.

As the soft music continued, Jo seemed to be finding herself fractionally closer to Jacob's chest. Inch by inch, his arms supported her a little tighter. He smiled down at her and leaned in closer, his lips brushing the top of her ear as he spoke. "You are so beautiful."

The dripping honey of his words set her teeth on edge. She leaned back a bit and forced a smile. Maybe this wasn't the kind of attention she wanted after all.

The song ended, placing Jo and Jacob right in front of Gideon's corner. Jo stepped back, a little wobbly again on her high-heeled shoes.

"Thank you, Jacob. You're a wonderful dancer." She added a dramatic inflection to her tone, making sure Gideon could hear every word.

A huff of air escaped from Gideon behind her, like a train coming to a stop. The exasperated sound made his opinion of Jacob's dancing skills quite clear. Jo smirked, proud of her ability to finally get Gideon's attention.

Jacob's hand remained on her back as they talked, rhythmically running his fingers up and down. The subtle motion wasn't enough to warrant any attention from her parents across the room, but it made an uneasy itch creep up her spine. She wanted to flick his hand away like an annoying spider.

Hopping down from his barrel, the fiddle player turned over the entertainment to a German farmer who began squeezing out a lively polka on his small, concertina accordion.

Gideon slipped between Jo and Jacob, taking her hand on his way through, and dragged her onto the dance floor.

"Gideon! What are you doing?" Jo gasped.

"Think you can keep up?" Gideon placed a hand on her waist and spun her around and around until she was off-balance. When she faced him again, the flash of his mischievous smile disarmed her. Regardless of what he'd said before, his rascally antics were much better than the oozing charm of Jacob Sinclair.

The lilted motion of the polka was jarring after the smooth waltz with Jacob. The stiff high-heeled shoes were not only pinching now, but her feet ached. She couldn't keep her balance.

"Ready to kick those things off yet?" Gideon asked, cocking an eyebrow at her.

Jo narrowed her eyes at him, but he was right. She wasn't going to last fussed up like this after all. Gripping Gideon's arm for balance, she slipped off the shoes, and Gideon spun her around to the outer edge of the circle, where she chucked them into the corner of the barn.

Without them, the motion of being bounced and jostled was no longer uncomfortable. Jo couldn't help but start to giggle as they tried to keep in step with the fast-paced music. He spun them in circles, all the while maintaining the one-and-two, one-and-two rocking step. They turned round, round, and round again until Jo couldn't keep the step anymore and fell into Gideon's arms, dizzy and laughing.

"Let's get out of here." Gideon jerked his head toward the barn door.

Breathless, they stepped out into the chilly, autumn night. A harvest moon hung low in the dark sky, casting its warm glow over the barnyard. She was still irritated, but he was her best friend. It was so hard to stay mad at him.

"So, I'm a mule, huh?" Jo looked up at him in a side-long glance.

"That's not what I meant." Gideon shrugged against the fabric of his shirt.

"What then?" Jo lifted the length of her thick, wavy hair off her neck to allow the breeze to cool her off.

"It just doesn't suit you, that's all." He scuffed the toe of his boot in the dirt and started walking toward the corral fence.

"What doesn't suit me, Gideon?" Jo followed, matching his slow step.

"All the frills and fancy stuff." Gideon leaned his arms over the top rail of the fence and sighed. "That's Elaine, not you." The warmth in his eyes clenched at her heart. "You're a free spirit, like a wild rose, not a cut flower in a jar."

His words threatened to unravel her tightly wound frustration. Could this be the moment he'd finally speak up on how he felt?

"And what was all that moody pouting in there?" Jo pointed a thumb over her shoulder toward the barn.

"I don't pout."

"You pouted." Jo turned around and leaned her back against the fence.

Gideon hesitated and huffed. "What are you doing hanging around that imbecile?" He scratched the back of his neck, clearly uncomfortable with the topic.

"Jacob? He's not an imbecile. As a matter of fact, he's very nice." *Liar.* Jacob was an imbecile, but Jo wasn't going to allow Gideon to know she agreed with him.

"He's vile." Gideon pushed away from the fence and turned to face her. "So, is that what you want? Some rake with a lot of money?" His voice was growing in volume.

Jo stepped up to him, toe to toe, impatient with all this dilly-dallying. "You know what I want? I want you, you big numbskull." She pushed his chest forcefully. "Can't you see that?"

He stumbled back, wide eyes blinking slowly. Jo stormed off back to the barn, leaving Gideon to stare dumbfounded in the wind.

Chapter 21

The hollow clunking of Jo's boot heel on the wooden platform of the train depot had Jo's heart soaring with hope. She was going home, and although the shame she would be burdening her family with weighed heavily on her heart, the simple fact she was leaving this place kept her spirits high.

She cradled the worn carpetbag to her chest and sidled through the narrow doorway onto the train car. Spying a seat in the front row, she quickly staked her claim on the space, grateful she wouldn't be sitting across from other passengers. She dreaded the discomfort of sitting across from some highborn lady and suffering the scorn of Jo's shameful appearance would attract.

Jo stored away the carpetbag containing the modest beginnings of her new life in the rack overhead. Abigail had insisted on outfitting Jo with some clothes before she left on her journey. She had pressed to be allowed to wear bloomers, the loose pants that were coming into fashion for walking and bicycling, but Abigail wouldn't allow it. With Jo's copper-colored, cropped hair, adding a pair of pants would only increase the number of scandalized looks Jo would have to endure.

Instead, she packed the skirt and blouse Abigail gave her the first morning back, a calico print dress, an apron, and the necessary delicates she would need. Last was the three-piece Chavaret traveling suit, which she now wore, with a shorter, ankle-length skirt for walking and a double-breasted jacket with ridiculous puffed sleeves.

She tolerated the green velvet hat for the sake of its sheer black, spotted veil to cover her face. But the moment she was back on the ranch, she would toss the feathery thing for good. Well, not really. That would be incredibly ungrateful for the generosity the Thorntons had shown her. But she just couldn't abide the fussy trimmings of feathers and frills any longer.

She would give the hat to Elaine. Her sister would love it. What Jo longed for now was a quiet life, her trouser pants and broad-brimmed hat, a good horse, and a cabin of her own. Maybe Pa would take pity on her and allow her to work with the horses. Perhaps even build a sod house near the horse pasture where she could hide away from the world.

She removed her jacket and laid it across the seat next to hers. With any luck, the boarding passengers would assume the seat was taken. People filed onto the car, bumping and shoving one another, setting things in order. A girl, about the age of sixteen, boarded with her parents. She was the picture of innocence with her sandy, blond hair and straw bonnet.

Had Jo ever been so young, fresh-faced, and pure? She certainly didn't look like that anymore. She stared down at the hands in her lap, clasped so tightly her knuckles must be white under the calf-skin gloves. When the final, "All aboard," was called, Jo let out a sigh of relief. The seat next to her remained empty.

With a sudden jerk, baggage and passengers alike shifted, and the car rocked side to side as the train pulled out of the depot. Jo stared out the window as the tracks skirted around the edge of Cripple Creek and headed south, rounding Gold Hill and making a short climb to the summit at Altman. The expansive mining district below, covered in gleaming yellow leaves, was on stunning display for just a few moments before the train began its steep descent from what seemed like the top of the world.

The swaying train car soothed her, and she became lost in the breathtaking scenery. For a short while, Jo wasn't concerned about what lay ahead for her or what she left behind. She drew a deep breath, propping her cheek on one hand, and watched the world slip by.

The train continued to wind through the rolling, golden hills dotted with mining claims. Bare, treeless mountain tops were lightly dusted with snow in the distance, jutting up from a patchwork blanket of brilliant yellow aspens and deep green spruce, adorned with an embroidery of orange and red threaded throughout.

As the track's descent carried Jo away from her fallen life, the terrain slowly changed from golden mountain splendor to one of sagebrush, juniper trees, and jagged rocky outcroppings. A part of her grieved at leaving the beauty of the colorful mountains behind. She had lived the last year confined to the stuffy brothel, surrounded by mountain grandeur but forgetting their magnetism.

While she lived rough with the outlaws, the quiet serenity of the mountains had been Jo's only consolation in her turmoil of uncertainty. Whenever Kane was absent, Jo would steal away, making excuses of needing to wash pots and pans in the creek or gather pinon nuts to roast with their coffee. She would find an aspen stand to hide in and marvel in the dancing sunlight as it peeked through shifting leaves overhead or find a patch of hillside and soak in the warm sun and the breathtaking sights. Those moments would be her only reprieve from Kane's continually shifting moods that would determine her fate for the evening.

When she'd first been taken hostage, Kane had been concerned for her safety and had protected her. He'd kept her from the fate of being passed around the gang like a bottle of whiskey. It had meant giving herself over to him, but what else could she have done?

In time, she'd begun to find solace in his company and had come to believe he truly loved her. He spoke of reform and starting a new life, one free from the gang and a life of thievery. He'd said she made him want to be a better man, and they could start over together. They just needed to work a few more jobs. The other men were greedy, and it would take time for Kane to save aside enough money to make a good start for them. But as the months passed, Kane grew more and more frustrated with Jo and the pressure he said she put on him to change. His moods were volatile and violent one day, apologetic and kind the next. The constant shifting kept her in a continual state of wary tiptoeing, gingerly avoiding the risk of angering him.

Kane stole the mountain's serenity from her, and time spent within the walls of the brothel had smudged out the remainder of their beauty. Perhaps leaving the mountains, and the memories they harbored, far behind was best. The reminder of the constant dread she had lived under still made her breath come short, and her heart began to race. She leaned her head back and pinched the bridge of her nose, tightly squeezing her eyes shut and willing herself to shake off the cloud of bad memories.

How might it have been different if she'd never fallen into the hands of Kane Blake? What if she'd been living here in Colorado with Gideon instead? *No.* She couldn't allow herself to even consider it. The sharp contrast of what life could have been and what it had become was too painful to consider.

She heaved a deep sigh and opened her eyes again, gazing back out of the train window. With a gasp of surprise, she looked out over the open air. Her heart leapt into her throat and stopped beating as it lodged there. She leaned forward ever so slightly, looking down into the bottomless canyon. It must have been at least a hundred-foot drop down to the creek below. The steel trestle had taken her by surprise. It left her with the notion that her own life had been launched out into the open air with no way to see what was holding her up.

Once back on solid ground, the tracks' descent grew even steeper as the notorious Phantom Canyon grew more and more narrow. The tight curves and rapidly descending motion gave a dizzying impression of falling through the vegetation-peppered, vertical canyon walls. Folks called these rocky, winding curves The Narrows. One particular crack through the steep rocky cliffs held especially true to the name. The crevice was so narrow and crooked you couldn't see one end from the other side. Only a sliver of light alluded to the way out. The train squeezed through the crack. The canyon walls were so close she could've reached out and grazed the cool, dusty surface of the rock cliff.

As the train entered a tunnel carved out of the impending mountain, Jo leaned her head back, fatigue weighing heavily on her limbs and eyelids. The past few weeks had been so fraught with changes and emotions, her reserves of energy had diminished.

The gentle motion and the darkness of the tunnel lulled her like a child being rocked to sleep. She was on the edge of drifting into peaceful dreams when a sudden BOOM thundered outside and reverberated through her chest. She was thrown forward and sent sliding across the polished floor. She slammed her head against the metal radiator at the front of the car, and everything went dark.

JO'S EYES FLUTTERED open, and the starry, black canvas began to clear into the forms and shapes of the things around her. She took in her surroundings and struggled to sort out what had happened. She lay on the floor of a passenger train car with luggage tumbled and tossed around her. The small space was dark and filled with noisy chaos. Shouts, cries, and demands to know what happened carried over the wailing of a small child. The train seemed at a standstill.

People were opening the windows and trying to see out. Smoke and rock dust permeated the air, along with the acrid scent of gunpowder filling the train car.

"Shut those windows, you fools!" a rotund man in a business suit shouted as he made his way to the back of the car. He covered his face with a handkerchief and quickly slipped out the door, presumably to see what was going on.

Jo lifted a shaky hand to the throbbing knot on her head. At the sharp stinging sensation of her touch, she pulled her hand away, covered in blood.

Muffled shouts and the loud crack of two shots echoed in the tunnel. Jo's heart raced, and her breath came short. The shuffling sound of boots crunching on gravel approached the car. Jo intentionally steadied her breathing, willing herself to settle back into the present.

The door opened at the back of the car, and Jo expected the businessman to return with news.

It wasn't him, but it was a man Jo knew all too well.

The tall, lanky form materialized in the doorway, ducking as he entered the train car. Though he wore a bandanna tied around his face, Jo recognized Slim Daniels immediately. He always wore the same grimy, sodden hat that drooped around his too-large ears. He held a shotgun at the ready, barking orders at the passengers nearest to him to empty their purses and pockets.

Jo's hands began shaking again. Sweat stung the cut on her forehead, mixing with the blood trickling down the side of her face. The floor tilted as a wave of dizziness came over her, but she drew a slow breath and placed her hands flat on the dusty floor. Now was not the time to be overtaken by fear.

Ducking her head, she crawled quietly back to her seat, hoping not to attract any attention to herself. She retrieved the hat from the seat next to her and quickly put it on, tying the veil. When she had tied it in a large bow at her jawline to help obscure her face, she crept up into her seat and turned sideways, trying to observe his actions but avoiding any eye contact with the outlaw.

What were the odds the Blake Gang would rob this train? Kane had always avoided the trains, focusing only on the stage line to prevent contact with the Pinkertons who policed the railways and protected the mining payloads. He must be getting greedy or desperate to have resorted to something like this. Or perhaps—perhaps the gang had scattered, and Slim was working for another outfit. She sent up a quick prayer that this was the case and that Kane Blake was far away from here.

Slim worked his way up the aisle, threatening and bullying people into giving over anything of value. When a man refused to give up his pocket watch, Slim slammed the butt of the shotgun into the man's face and jerked the watch free, tearing the fabric of the man's vest.

The door burst open in the front of the car, and Jo swung in her seat at the sudden sound. *Kane.* Her blood ran cold, and she covered her mouth with icy, trembling fingers to stifle her whimper of dread.

He hadn't seen her. His attention had been on Slim in the aisle.

The blond tips of his wavy hair curled out from under a slouch cowboy hat, and laugh lines crinkled at the corners of his eyes above the black bandanna. He lived for this.

"What would be takin' ya so long there, Stretch?" The men had developed the habit of using false names when they were on the job to maintain anonymity. "You wouldn't be wasting our precious time, trifling with the young lassies, now would ya?"

"Ain't none here to be trifled with, O'Malley," Slim responded with a tone of disappointment.

"No?" Kane scanned the passengers, appraising the women. His gaze lingered over the young mother who clutched the wailing toddler to her bosom. The twitch of a smile tugged at the corner of the bandanna, and Jo's stomach turned. "Well, now, I'd say you risk offending these lovely lassies here." He walked toward the mother with a swagger in his step. He passed right by Jo, and she let out a silent sigh of relief. He hadn't seen her.

As he walked toward the woman and child, his attention suddenly shifted as he neared the young girl with sandy blond hair. Every muscle in Jo's body locked with tension. She clenched the back of the seat with white-knuckled determination not to make her presence known. *Be still, be quiet. He mustn't see you.* She breathed slowly and intentionally, despite the blood rushing in her ears and the heartbeat pounding against the boundary of her chest.

Kane stopped in his tracks and bent low to whisper something into the girl's ear, trailing a lazy finger along the top edge of her bodice.

Jo snapped. She leaped into the aisle, an arm's length from Kane, pressing a knife firmly under his jaw.

"Get away from the girl," Jo hissed through clenched teeth. She hadn't remembered drawing the ornate dirk from her garter but was grateful she had. She would be a victim no longer, and this innocent girl wouldn't become one either.

Chapter 22

Gideon shuffled his moccasins on the Thorntons' porch and cleared his throat. "If ... if you can just tell me if you know where I could find Jo—Miss Bradford, that is, I'll be on my way."

The couple exchanged a long look, communicating something in the way married folk did, and Abigail spoke up.

"Please come in, Mr. Cross, and join us for supper." She opened the door wide to allow entry. Twin snakes of dread and discomfort in Gideon's belly writhed and intertwined in uneasy anticipation of a conversation requiring both vulnerability and the sharing of information he would typically keep closely guarded.

"Please, I insist." Abigail bent her head toward the kitchen, where the warm, rich aroma of roasted meat beckoned to him. He removed his broad hat and nodded his appreciation as he stepped inside. The table was laid for two, and Abigail quickly went to a cupboard to retrieve another place setting.

Gideon sat in the offered chair and breathed a grateful sigh. Unlike the doll furniture he had encountered at the pastor's home, this one was made of sturdy wood and didn't threaten to splinter under his bulk.

Gideon scoffed. For a man who strictly tried to avoid conversing, he sure had found himself doing a lot of it lately. A shopkeeper's wife, a French doorman, Pastor Walton, Leah, Jo, and now, these people; Gideon might as well've been a squirrel hopping from tree to tree, chattering away. How he had ever, as a young man, thought useless gab entertaining was beyond him.

The supper of roast beef, carrots, and potatoes swimming in a dark, rich gravy, settled his stomach and gave him something to focus on other than the curious faces seated across from him.

"Mr. Cross—" Abigail began.

"Please, just Gideon."

"Gideon, Jo is on a train to Kansas to reunite with her family. She left just this morning." Abigail seemed timid, unsure of Gideon's reaction.

He couldn't blame her. The last time they'd told him Jo was gone, he'd acted like a buffalo jabbed with an arrow. Rather than upset, though, he was relieved. The comfort that Jo had chosen to go home was only tinged with disappointment that she'd already left and he hadn't had the chance to see her again.

"How?" Gideon asked. "How did you convince her to go?"

Again, the couple exchanged a look.

"She realized she couldn't continue with that life and came to us for help," John stated. "She stayed with us for a few weeks while we gathered together enough money to set her on her way."

The weight that had burdened Gideon for the past few weeks lightened. He dropped his elbows to the table and pressed his hands over his eyes to stop the welling moisture, but it was no use. His shoulders shook as the tears washed all the tension out of him. It was over. She was safe.

After a few moments, he wiped the wetness away with a handkerchief. He didn't even care that these strangers witnessed his blubbering.

"Forgive me, folks. I'm just so glad she's out of that life." He tucked the damp cloth into the pouch he wore at his waist.

Abigail sniffed and stood to clear the plates, returning with a coffee pot.

"How is it you know her so well?" John asked.

Gideon had planned to leave emotion and any information about his past out of it. But when asked about his connection to Jo, Gideon found himself opening up.

He shared about their childhood friendship and the responsibility and the love he still felt for her. The words came from him in a rush. Once a few spare facts were loosened, all the others gave way until it was all tumbling out of him like a rock slide. He spoke freely for the first time in many years.

At a sudden rapping on the door, John rushed to answer it, Abigail close behind him. Someone must be ill. Gideon should go and allow the Thorntons to tend to their latest patient.

He stood from the table and gathered the plates and forks, bringing it all to soak in the washtub in the kitchen corner. The sound of rushing voices, questions, and an exclamation by Abigail told Gideon something wasn't right.

He joined the Thorntons in the front parlor.

"Blown up, I tell ya! The whole south end of the tunnel collapsed." A wiry man with a deputy sheriff badge was standing in the doorway, clutching a sodden hat.

"Let me gather my kit and some extra supplies," came John's steady baritone.

"Gonna need that for right certain. Lots of people hurt. I hear two are dead."

Gideon's blood ran cold. The train, Jo's train. It had to be. "I'm coming with you," Gideon informed them as he barged into the room. "You got a saddle horse?"

Gideon remembered the cart pony the Thornton's used to drive around town. That would not do.

"I do," John affirmed, and Gideon brushed past the trio at the door and ran around back to get the horses ready.

ALL WAS PERFECTLY STILL in the train car, and for the space of one heartbeat, Kane looked puzzled. He peered past the black, spotted veil. Then his eyes widened with recognition. Jo took two steps forward, pushing him back with the tip of the knife, forcing his chin upward. She was now positioned between Kane and the young girl, one hand gently resting on the girl's shoulder in a protective gesture.

"You will not touch her." Jo would defend this girl with all the force she should have used to protect her own innocence two years ago. Kane stood motionless, but Jo could read the wild flash of elation in his eyes above the bandanna mask. He must be thrilled to find the girl who he had manipulated and controlled, who had been at his beck and call and done his bidding. The girl who, he thought, knew the location of a sizable cache of silver.

The furrowed brow he had shown when she first pulled the knife had now smoothed into calm confidence. His calm was her unease, and the knife she held to his throat began to quiver. She grounded herself firmer in her protective stance and willed her hand to stop shaking. As long as she held the knife, she had nothing to fear.

They stood an arm's length apart in a deadlock stare. Jo knew what she must do for the sake of her safety and the safety of any impressionable young girl who might ever cross his path. All she had to do was thrust the knife, and it would all be over, her innocence avenged. Yet, she stood like a statue, tears glazing over her vision. His eyes darted behind her, and a rope cinched tight around her neck. She flew backward with the force, dropping the knife. The scratchy rope bit into her skin, nearly choking her. She kicked out, and the slippery soles of her boots slid on the dusty wooden floor, causing her to fall back against someone who pinned her arms behind her and bound her hands. Kane emptied the canvas bag of wallets and jewelry and tossed it over her head. Darkness closed in, and Jo screamed for help.

"Stop. Don't hurt her—" A man's voice shouted and was cut short by the sickening sound of a rifle butt against flesh.

She was dragged backward and down, her heels banging and bouncing on metal and then sliding and scuffling through gravel. She thrashed and fought, kicked and screamed. A sharp, heavy pain cracked across the top of her head. It didn't knock her unconscious, but it forced an abrupt end to her struggling. She was lifted by her heels and shoulders and landed face down on something soft and round. She groaned and sucked in a painful breath as her tender ribs were crushed.

Breathing carefully again, she drew an illogical sense of relief at the faint scent of sweat and dirt. A horse. They had thrown her across the back of a horse.

"Hold his head!" She heard Kane's voice and was roughly shifted and rolled back and forth until her chest and thighs were bound tightly to the horse by the saddle strings meant for a bedroll. She struggled against her bonds but was tied too tightly to move.

"Keep still," a familiar, gritty voice commanded as the harsh sting of a quirt whip was slashed across her back, each thin leather strap leaving behind a line of fire in its place. After several minutes of distant shouts and arguments, one shot rang out, and a volley of thudding and crunching boot steps rushed closer.

"Let's be off!" Kane's voice rose above the commotion in the distance.

A heavy weight brushed over her, bumping into the painful bruise on her head. The horse shifted and sidestepped under her as someone mounted the saddle and spurred the horse into action.

Jo was bounced and bumped on the back of the horse for what seemed like hours. Her head ached, her wrists and ankles burned where the rough rope rubbed and dug into her skin, and bruises already formed where the knotted leather of the saddle strings pressed against her hips and ribs.

The horse's pace eventually slowed, but they had run hard and long. The lathery scent of horse sweat permeated the canvas bag tied over her head. This was the worst horse ride she'd ever been on. The heavy canvas bag around her head was stifling, the stale air heavy on her lungs, each breath becoming more difficult. The horse's pace slowed to a walk, and the choppy, shifting motion became cathartic, allowing fatigue to overtake her.

She must have slept because when she slowly started to become aware of her circumstance again, evening was approaching. The prickle of cold, night air penetrated the thin cotton sleeves of the white blouse she wore, and she shivered. Where would she be when they finally stopped? Had they ridden far enough to be near Cañon City, or even Pueblo, by now? It didn't matter. They would be nowhere near a town. They would take refuge in the vast wilderness where no one would find them.

Chapter 23

Gideon and John Thornton joined a party of other men bound for the train tunnel. They rode through the night, following the tracks as the path of least resistance. Though they all would have preferred to have ridden at full speed, racing to the rescue of their loved ones, the darkness of night and the treacherous landscape hindered their haste.

As they made their way through the cliffs and canyons, where only two riders could ride abreast, John shared a story with Gideon. He spoke of a young girl forced into prostitution and how the Lord saw fit to bring great beauty out of a terrible situation.

"Society would have you think there is nothing but shame for a woman with a ruined reputation." John shook his head in disapproval of the mere idea. "They act as though some women are to be treasured and valued, while others are nothing more than a convenient outlet for a man's lust." He spat with distaste.

The mild-mannered man with waistcoat and pocket watch had transformed for the journey. He'd replaced his satin-puff necktie with a wild rag, twisted and tied about his neck for warmth, and covered his neatly combed hair with a felt, sagebrush hat. Outside of his professional costume, John wasn't the dandy Gideon had first taken him for.

"It's a travesty," John continued. "Miss Bradford found herself in that brothel in a moment of starvation and desperation. Now she's made the choice to leave that life behind, and it's not right for her to be treated any differently than any person who has made a mistake." John turned Gideon's direction, leaning a forearm on the saddle horn and giving Gideon a long, pointed stare.

Gideon had no objections on the subject, but after his initial opening up earlier in the evening, he had once again lost the ease of baring his soul.

"I don't hold it against her, John." He returned John's pointed look but bit back the rest of the response burning inside him. *I don't hold it against her. I feel responsible.*

"All these years with Abigail, and I have not once regretted my choice." A half-smile turned up the corner of John's mouth. "Mind you, that doesn't mean it has been easy," John continued.

Gideon patiently waited while John seemed to choose his words with caution.

"Let me be clear. It has always been easy to love that sweet woman. But it was not always easy for her to accept love."

As they navigated the steep descent of the winding canyons and outcroppings, the path became too narrow to accommodate two riders. They now rode single-file, and the stillness of the night was interrupted only by the soft thudding of hoofbeats alongside the train tracks. Gideon wrestled with the story John had shared and the possibility of choosing the same path with Jo.

Jo had made it clear she hadn't any desire to be with him. Heck, she didn't even want to be in the same town as him. After all they'd been through—all they'd meant to each other—how could she turn away from him now?

Ever since she rejected him that day on the street, he'd only wanted to make sure she was safe. He hadn't held out any hope she would reconsider his offer of marriage.

He did still love her. No question. She'd had his heart for more years than he could remember.

John had said she ended up in the brothel in a state of desperation. Could she ever trust him enough again to not think of him like the men who had just sought her out for their own pleasure? On the other hand, would Gideon ever be able to shake off the worry that their intimacy would remind her, or him for that matter, of what she'd been through? Would the ghosts of the past always haunt their relationship?

He would have to trust God to help him through the hard parts. The question now was, would she be able to accept his love?

WHEN THE HORSE FINALLY came to a stop, someone loosened the saddle strings and rolled Jo off the horse's rump and onto the ground. The impact knocked the wind out of her. The spooked horse responded to the commotion with a solid kick that caught her hard in the thigh.

Someone jerked the canvas bag from her head, and she gasped for air. The hat and veil she wore came off with the bag. Silence filled the clearing. She rolled over and steadied herself on her knees. She looked around to find four shocked faces, mouths gaping, seemingly turned to stone. Three of the four men were familiar. The fourth man must be a new addition to the gang. Kane was nowhere in sight.

Looking around the clearing, she could find no reason for the stunned reaction from the men. It must be the scar on her face and her short hair ruffled from the hat and the rough ride. In her moment of courage on the train, she had been wearing the hat and veil. It must have muted her changed appearance.

"What are you all standin' around f—" Kane stopped short as he rode into the clearing on a high-headed black mare. He looked down at Jo. "Sweet mother of Mary." He crossed himself with the reins still in hand, causing the horse to back wildly and throw her head, snorting. Clearly, he was as startled by her appearance as the other men. Jo hoped the shock value would buy her some time.

Kane dismounted and approached her for a closer look, crouching in front of her. He reached a hand up to her chin and turned her head, appraising the scar. She jerked her head as wildly as the horse had.

"What happened to you then, love?"

No matter how Jo's appearance had changed, there was a familiarity between them, and it made Jo's stomach turn. With eyes downcast, she tried to scramble away from him, but with her feet bound, she only managed to topple over. She couldn't bring words up through the bile in her throat.

How was she right back here all over again after all she'd done to hide?

Kane shouted orders to the men over his shoulder about getting camp set up. Though the sun had set, the evening air held the brightness of a full moon waxing. The men scattered, each to his duties, and Kane helped Jo up to her feet. He dragged her over to a pine tree and tied her bound hands above her head, making sure the rope was secure above a sturdy limb.

"I can't have the fellas thinkin' I've gone soft now, can I? You'll have to bide here like the captive you are until we sort things out." He smoothed the hair back from her face and lifted her chin. "You and I have some unfinished business now, don't we lass?" The look in Kane's blue eyes was tender. "What on earth possessed you to disappear on me like that?" His tone was sincere and smooth. "We have much to talk about, darlin'."

Jo gritted her teeth and looked away. She would not allow herself to be manipulated by him anymore.

"Oh, you'll loosen that tongue of yours"—he crushed her bottom lip between a thumb and finger and drew it downward—" or I'll cut it out of your pretty head." He cocked his head slightly and focused on the scar again. "Looks to me like you'll be knowin' all about being cut. Now, won't you?" He released her lip, trailed a thumb over the scar on her face, and followed it down her neck to the high lace collar of the blouse she wore.

His gaze lingered over the disappearing scar, and he clicked his tongue. He grabbed the collar of the blouse and jerked it savagely. The sound of tearing lace and popping buttons preceded a rush of cold, evening air on the exposed skin on her collar bones. He found the rest of the scar. A shiver of revulsion crossed his handsome face and left Jo with a mingled sense of relief and shame that he found her changed appearance so repulsive.

He left her tied to the tree and gathered the men in a hunched discussion. The men's eyes followed as he cast a look toward her over his shoulder. He would tell them to leave her alone, for tonight at least. But that order would only stand as long as it took for him to get the location of the silver from her. A location she didn't know. Would that lack of knowledge protect her or only infuriate Kane?

Later that night, the men reclined around a campfire, eating a cold supper from a saddlebag. There were wall tents set up, which meant they would be on the move again in the morning.

Kane tossed the bag containing their supper to the man next to him and pointed in Jo's direction. The young man they called Kit scrambled for the strap of the canteen next to him and brought it, along with a strip of jerky and a corn dodger, to Jo. She had no appetite and wanted to refuse, but it would be best not to run on an empty stomach if she were to try and escape. She managed to paint a weak smile across her lips and thanked him for the food.

She had always liked Kit. He'd never struck her as a heartless criminal like the others.

"What ... happened to you, Jo?" Kit asked. His penetrating green eyes examined the scar after feeding her several bites of the food and nearly drowning her in his attempt to give her water from the canteen.

"Seems I'm a magnet for bad men." Jo gave a rueful snort and shook her head at the futility of it all.

Her hands were tied to the limb above her head. Her fingers were numb and beginning to swell and darken. Straightening each finger, she sucked air in through her teeth from the pain of trying to move them. Kit cast an uncertain look over his shoulder to the men at the fire. Clyde was retelling his part of the train robbery with sound effects and the larger than life hand-motions that came with the big man's bulk.

While the men were distracted, Kit quickly worked to loosen the knot and lowered the rope below the branch where Jo could relax her shoulders and change the angle of her hands. Her fingers tingled and throbbed as the blood was allowed to flow again.

Jo mouthed a silent *thank you*. A dimple tucked into his cheek as he gave a wavering smile. She had always known there was something different about Kit. There was a kindness in him that the others lacked. He had been younger than the rest and seemed to have been swept up with the gang the way she had been. Could she rely on his help to escape?

He pressed his lips together, snuffing out the brief smile with a tight grimace. A muscle in his jaw bulged as he clenched his teeth together and huffed out a breath through his nose. He scooped up the canteen and stomped back to the fire. Maybe Jo wasn't going to be able to rely on his help after all.

Chapter 24

Jo - Age 16

Gideon - Age 19

Jo spread out a quilt in the oak grove beside the creek and kicked off her shoes. The tall, springy grass gave the picnic spot a luxurious pillowed effect. She leaned back, relishing the movement of air over her bare toes.

"Will you ever learn to keep your shoes on?" Gideon smirked.

"I most certainly will not." Jo squinted up at him, shielding her eyes from the dazzling summer sun. "I suppose I don't mind these dresses anymore." She sat up and smoothed out the blue calico skirt. "But those pinching, leather contraptions can float on down the creek for all I care."

She picked up a shoe and pitched it toward the water. Gideon caught it deftly and tossed it back to her. *Cocky bugger.*

"You're gonna want that come winter." He shook his head and chuckled.

Gideon plopped down on the quilt, stretching out next to her. He rummaged in the saddlebag that contained their lunch. Retrieving an apple, he leaned back on one elbow and polished it on his shirt. She tried to ignore the way the closeness of him made her bare toes curl.

"Josephina Maude Bradford, you're hopeless." Gideon took a bite and wiped the juices on his sleeve. "Somebody's gotta look out fer ya."

Jo snatched the apple from Gideon and took a large bite. "If I were some refined lady," she spoke around the chunk of apple in her mouth, "like my sister—" She coughed and sputtered, nearly choking on the bite. Snorting with laughter, she tried again. "If I were some refined lady, you wouldn't want to have anything to do with me." She passed the apple back to Gideon, chewing carefully.

"That ain't true." A sheepish smile tugged at the corner of his mouth. "Don't matter to me if you're gussied up or working cows. You sure do make the scenery better." A dark red flush flooded his neck and face. He looked down, focusing all his attention on the knots of yarn on the hand-tied quilt.

Was that a compliment? Had she heard him right? He'd been acting so odd ever since the dance earlier this summer.

"I thought I was a mule," Jo challenged.

"Not what I meant." Gideon cleared his throat. "You don't need all the frilly stuff, that's all." He rubbed the back of his neck and let out a long sigh.

Long moments passed in silence. Neither of them seemed to know how to find their ease in the conversation again. Tension crackled in the silence hanging between them.

"What'd top-hat Tom want after church today, anyway?" Gideon finally asked, shrugging a shoulder.

"Tom? Oh, nothin' much. He and his father were just talking to Pa about a possible partnership of sorts." She leaned back on one elbow and tipped her face up to the summer sun. She was grateful Elaine and Ma weren't around to force her into a bonnet.

"A partnership?" Gideon sat up straight.

"You know, their wheat, our cows. Makes sense, I guess." Jo shrugged.

"If your pa and his are striking a deal, I see no cause for Tom to be hangin' around makin' eyes at you. Seems to me Tom's been noticin' more than the cows around here lately." Gideon braced his forearms on his knees and scowled at the apple in his hands.

"What in Sam Hill are you talkin' about?" Jo shrugged. "I don't see any reason he shouldn't talk to me. He's mighty friendly, and he treats me like an important part of the conversation." She smothered a satisfied smile with her hand. Maybe her stepping a little bit closer to Tom when she noticed Gideon watching had gotten his attention after all.

"Tom Barlow, Jacob Sinclair, they're all nosin' around where they ought not to be. You oughta send 'em packin'." Gideon threw his apple core into the stream.

That kindled a fire deep in Jo's chest. She resisted the urge to hit him over the head with the saddlebag.

"Maybe it's not so bad having a little attention for once."

"What's that supposed to mean?" A deep furrow etched itself between his brows.

"Forget it."

Jo stood up and walked to the bank, picking up a smooth, gray rock and slinging it across the lazy water of the wide creek. Rather than skipping, the rock cut into the water from the force of her throw and disappeared. The growing inner fire was building, and her blood was at the brink of boiling over.

Gideon's sleeve brushed Jo's as he walked up beside her. She had a good mind to push him into the creek. What gave him the right even to have an opinion on who might be giving her attention?

"Come on, out with it." Gideon picked up a rock and sent it flying. Ripples grew from each footprint of the skipping stone before it disappeared near the other bank. Jo huffed and shoved him to the side with an elbow.

"Maybe it's not so bad having some attention for once. Maybe Elaine has the right of it, and I oughta let one of those boys court me after all."

"So they *are* after you, are they?" Gideon hurled another rock, and it landed with a loud splash.

"If you hadn't noticed, I ain't the tomboy in overalls anymore. There's plenty out there who'd be willin' to treat me like a lady." Jo crossed her arms tightly across her chest.

Gideon grasped her arms securely and pulled her to him, kissing her hard with a fire to match her blazing temper. It was short and rough—and breathtaking. Her lips tingled, and she pressed her palms against his chest to catch her balance.

"You think I haven't noticed you?" Gideon shook her gently. "You think I don't watch you every minute of the day? Those fools may have started to pay attention now that you're all gussied up and wearin' dresses. But I've always been right here." Gideon slid his hands up her shoulders and into her hair, combing through the long strands. "You think I don't see the way the sunlight glows in your hair or the bits of gold in the green of your eyes?"

Jo's breaths quickened, and she leaned into the hand that gently cupped the side of her face. He looked down at her with a warmth and intensity that pulled her to him like a tether.

He bent his head and nudged the tip of her nose with his own, whispering against her lips. "I've always known you were special, Jo. Always."

His lips engulfed hers again with gentle pressure, this time soft and firm. In all her dreams of kissing him, she'd never imagined it could be like this. She clutched his shirt, responding to the burgeoning flame that flared between them. All her anger and frustration melted into the inferno, spilling over the edge of the creek bank to be carried away with the current.

THE MORNING AFTER THE train robbery, Jo found herself on the back of Kane's horse. Rather than binding her feet and throwing her over the horse's rump again, he insisted Jo ride double behind him.

"No sense in ya being treated rough, love." He smiled sweetly and grazed a finger along her jawline. "But we can't have ya runnin' off now either, can we?" He tightened the rope binding her hands before mounting the saddle and reaching down to pull her up behind him. She would have no way to dismount and escape with Kane riding in the lead and four other pairs of watchful eyes behind them.

As the horses wandered the dusty trail, the warmth of Kane's back radiated against Jo's face as she sat behind him. In her fatigue and hopelessness, a part of her longed to give in to submissive compliance like she always had. The disturbing feeling churned in contrast against the desire to reach her bound hands over his head and choke the life from him for all of the hurt he caused.

Yet another, more rational side of her was in a panic. No matter how calm Kane acted toward her now, it was only a matter of time before his anger would take over, and she wanted nothing more than to bail off the back of the horse and take her chances sliding down the rocky mountainside in an escape.

The effect of conflicting emotions was that of a tornado, like one she had seen on the Kansas prairie as a girl. It reached its dark finger into her heart, and the violently spinning force was tearing her to pieces like the boards of a barn being ripped apart in a twister.

Jo's meager breakfast of hardtack and acorn coffee was churning in her stomach as the emotional torrent battered her. She had to find a way to gain some kind of distance from Kane, or she was going to be sick.

She grasped the saddle strings from one side of the saddle and then the other, gripping the leather straps tight to anchor herself. She settled herself back on her hips and leaned as far away from him as possible. The small distance she achieved allowed a breeze of fresh air to sweep between them, washing over her and clearing her mind from the storm within.

The inner turmoil was an unwelcome but familiar companion from her time with the outlaw gang. For an entire year, Jo had been torn apart. Torn between the man who made her feel like she was the most precious thing in the world and the man who screamed curses and insults in her face. The man who showered her with trinkets and jewelry from his exploits was the same man who would wrap his hands around her neck in a fit of rage and squeeze until she passed out.

She needed to put her mind to work and get it off of the past before panic set in again. Would anyone be coming to look for her? It was doubtful. The sheriff would have too much responsibility on his hands getting the people safely back to Cripple Creek to bother sending a search party after someone like her.

Would he lead a posse to get the money back from the train robbery? No. The stolen payload from the mine would be under the Pinkerton's jurisdiction, and something told her they had either been killed or paid off. Why else would they not have stopped the robbery? That was the reason they were on the train in the first place.

John and Abigail were the only people on earth who knew she was on the train and who cared about her. But John would need to be there for the injured passengers. She was truly and utterly alone without any hope of a rescue plan.

A rescue plan. That sparked something in her spirit she couldn't quite grab hold of. Something about those simple words gave her a small glimmer of hope. But hadn't she determined there was *no* rescue plan? There was no one coming for her, and she had to accept that.

Chapter 25

The rescue party reached the train passengers just before dawn, and the gray, flat light had yet to give way to the morning sun. A great heap of jagged rocks blocked one end of the tunnel. Whoever these bandits were, they were cunning. The explosion had trapped the train and passengers inside, and the open end would have been easily guarded.

"Halloo," the sheriff shouted as they neared the site. The stranded passengers came pouring out of the train tunnel and out of the few exposed train cars. Gideon anxiously scanned the crowd for Jo's tell-tale coppery blond hair but found nothing. He dismounted from Sarge and began searching the crowd on foot.

John had immediately begun to sort passengers into groups of those who needed medical attention and those who didn't. Gideon grasped him by the shoulder, interrupting his evaluation of an older man who was gingerly holding an arm against his chest.

"What was she wearing, John?" Gideon squeezed John's shoulder.

"What was—Oh, forgive me, Gideon, but she's not hard to pick out of a crowd." John's attention was clearly on his calling now, and Gideon relaxed his grip, knowing he couldn't fault the man for knowing his priorities. He took a deep breath and spoke slowly.

"I can't find her, John. What was she wearing when she got on the train?" Gideon's deliberate speech broke through John's concentration. John blinked behind his round glasses, and his eyebrows drew together.

"Abigail bought her new clothes ... one of those puff sleeve jackets ... and a hat with a veil." John met Gideon's eyes and nodded confidently again. "Yes, I remember the fuss over the hat. You know Jo doesn't like all that frilly business, but Abigail insisted."

Gideon began canvasing the passengers, describing a woman in a hat and veil. Most folks hadn't remembered seeing anyone like that, but he came to a family huddled together against the hillside, and a girl's eyes widened when Gideon gave the description once more.

"Mama, I think he means that crazy woman." The girl stood up from her perch on a large, flat rock. "The one with the knife."

Gideon's shock gave way to exasperation. Why was it the blasted woman couldn't just keep out of trouble for more than a few days at a time?

"A knife?" Gideon wasn't sure he wanted to hear more but wanted the girl to get on with the story so he could get to the bottom of all this.

"That bandit, he was ... well ...."

"He was making inappropriate advances on my daughter." A man who must be the girl's father stood now and took over the story, his face turning scarlet.

"This woman in a veil came out of her seat and put a knife right to the rogue's throat." The man's color was fading to a mottled pink now, but the mother fanned herself and clutched at the girl's hand as if afraid to lose her.

"And?" Gideon was impatient with the story and began scanning the crowd again, looking for a hat matching John's description.

"And ... well, they took her." The man cleared his throat, and Gideon jerked his head back, stepping forward, bearing down on the man. Gideon grabbed the man by his lapel and growled his retort.

"Took her?"

"He seemed to know her, the man who was ... well ..." He glanced at his daughter and then back to Gideon. "They took her from the train. That's the last we saw of her." The man shrugged, looking abashed.

Gideon's heart pounded, and heat surged through him, his muscles quivering. He stomped back to the train where the sheriff stood on the back of the caboose, giving orders and making arrangements. He told the sheriff the pertinent details of the situation, grateful they had a lawman and enough men to form a posse to go after the outlaws.

When the sheriff informed Gideon there would be no posse and that the priority was to get these people back to Cripple Creek safely, Gideon saw red. He resisted the urge to yank the sheriff off the back of the train car and throttle him.

"What do you mean there's nothing you can do? You're the sheriff, aren't you?"

"I have a duty to get these good people back to safety, and I can't abandon them to go off on a wild goose chase." The sheriff puffed his chest importantly and looked down on Gideon from his perch. "The outlaws are long gone and have been for more than fourteen hours. The trail is cold."

Gideon drew his fists into tight balls at his sides to keep from grabbing the man. He stomped over to John to tell him the situation.

John wouldn't be able to help him track her down. Too many of the passengers were injured, and he was the only doctor available. He would have to stay.

When Gideon told him what had happened to Jo, the blood drained from John's face.

"It must be them. The band of outlaws Jo told us about." John shook his head and sighed as he finished bandaging a large cut above a small boy's eye.

"Band of outlaws? Are they the ones who cut her up?" Gideon was vibrating with the need to hit something.

John patted the boy on the knee and sent him back to his mother. He turned around to Gideon and spoke in a hushed tone. "No, that happened at the parlor house, a senseless attack. Didn't you two talk before you left town?"

Heat rose in Gideon's face. They had attempted to speak on the mountain, but they'd both been so riled up they hadn't got to that part of the conversation. He shook his head. It all seemed like too much talk. What was needed was action.

"Her history with the outlaws is how she came to be at the parlor house in the first place." John removed his glasses and wiped a hand over his face. "She'd somehow fallen into the hands of some outlaws and spent a full year in their company. I don't know anything more, only that she escaped. The brothel offered her something. Safety? Sanctuary? Not to mention food." John shrugged.

Gideon's heart abandoned his chest and fell into his stomach. Kidnapped? A captive for over a year and then forced into prostitution as a matter of survival. The emptiness in his chest filled with lead. Had they come back for her?

Gideon paced the dirt until he had found the spot where several horses had been milling about. He located the path the gang took and checked all his gear. There could be no mishaps or mistakes if he was going to track these men alone. John gave Gideon an extra pistol and prayed briefly over him before Gideon mounted the saddle and headed off in the direction of the hoof prints leading southwest.

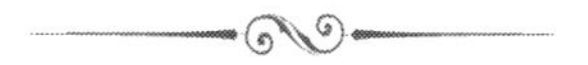

JO PACED INSIDE THE tent, her arms wrapped about her waist like a shield. She was unbound for the first time in two days, and the freedom had her limbs tingling with the need to move. The cramped space didn't offer much exercise, but nervous energy skittered over her and demanded action.

She wished she could take the opportunity of being untied to bolt beyond the tent flap and into the trees. But Kane had a man stationed outside the tent, blocking her escape.

The fear of the unknown terrified her, but the retribution she faced for fleeing into the night a year ago was even more grim.

Kane had been convinced she was lying about the silver, and no matter what she said to him, he wouldn't believe her. She chewed the inside of her bottom lip so intently in her apprehension of his return that she tasted the copper tang of blood. She willed herself to unclench and take a breath.

She would escape or die trying. If she didn't give Kane what he wanted, her life would be over anyway. If he didn't kill her trying to get the information out of her, he would make sure she paid for it either with her body or her blood, and after last night, it was clear Kane wasn't her only threat.

Her attempt to escape the night before had not ended well. As she had slid the rope along the pine bow her hands were strapped over, it caught on a brittle twig that snapped with a tattletale crack, capturing the immediate attention of the man on guard.

In her panic, she'd ignored the traitorous noise and bolted through the sagebrush and cedars. The man on guard had been Jasper, the one outlaw in the bunch she didn't know. He'd caught her by a fistful of her hair and pushed her to the ground face-first in the decaying pine needles and juniper berries.

"Don't worry, sweetheart," he had spat in a slimy whisper next to her ear. "That scar on your face don't bother me none." He wrenched her skirt up to her thigh.

Jo was never going to allow a man to use her like that again. His hot breath had warmed the back of her bare neck, and she threw her head back. The grating crunch of bones breaking had vibrated through her as the back of her head hit something solid. He'd cried out with rage and pain, which brought all the other men up from slumber in a flurry of bedrolls and pistols.

"What's going on out there?" Kane had shouted into the darkness.

"Caught this witch trying to run away," the man had barked back with a stuffy mumble. "Broke my nose, the filthy whore." He'd yanked her upright and shoved her back toward her tree. "This isn't over."

A shiver of trepidation and a wave of gooseflesh crept up Jo's arms and down her spine at the memory of his hissed threat. She rubbed her arms fiercely, trying to dispel the icy finger that walked over her.

The canvas tent flap swept open, and Kane stepped inside. He smiled sheepishly, like a man who wanted to reconcile after a little spat. The warmth of his smile would've drawn her in once, but no more.

"Shame for you to go and cut that pretty hair of yours off." He reached out and toyed with a short lock that fell over her forehead.

Jo stiffened as his eyes grazed the side of her face, following the scar from top to bottom.

His mouth quirked to the side in a pondering twist of the lips. "You should've stayed with me, love. Looks like life hasn't been kind while you've been away." He tugged the strand of hair down hard as he spoke, lowering her head until it bent in submission.

Pain narrowed her vision, and her knees hitched. He released the strand and strode the few feet to the other side of the tent, casually removing his coat.

"Now, it's time you and I have ourselves a wee chat." He unbuttoned the cuffs of his sleeves, rolling the fabric up to his elbows.

She clenched clammy fists into the fabric of her skirt. "Kane, I'm sorry," she whispered.

"Sorry?" he asked, rubbing his chin thoughtfully. "What are you sorry fer then? Sorry fer leaving me?" His eyes tightened, and a furrow crept its way across his brow. "Maybe you're sorry for keeping letters of an old flame after all I'd done for ya?" His voice wavered with intense emotion, and his demeanor softened. The hurt she had caused him was etched clearly across his face.

"It wasn't like that—"

"Are ya sorry for keepin' the rest of that journal to yourself? For hiding it from me?" Kane continued speaking, Jo's ineffectual explanation going entirely unnoticed. "Everything I did, I did for us. All I wanted was to give you the life you wanted."

He reached out and gently cupped her chin with both hands. His eyes softened, and he searched her face, pleading for an answer to her betrayal.

"All we needed was a wee bit more cash, and we could've moved on—just the two of us. But you—" Kane released a short, rueful laugh. "You abandoned me." He dropped his hands, his face downcast, and for a moment, she was ashamed for not having loved him more, for hurting him by leaving the way she did.

"Who is this Gideon the letter was from anyway? Did you go back to him?" Kane stepped close. A familiar shift in his mood was coming 'round, and Jo's heart raced. "Did you think you could do better than me? Just because he had some silver stashed away? You always were a greedy wee thing, weren't you?" He crossed his arms across his chest.

"No, I didn't—I wasn't." Jo shook her head and took a step back.

"He the one who cut you? It would serve you right if he did." He shook his head in disgust. "Did you think you'd get by without me?" He stood with feet spread shoulder-width apart and rolled his shoulders back.

Jo's heart hammered in her chest as if it would burst clean through the torn lace of her blouse at any moment. The pressure in him was building. He couldn't hold back much longer.

Then, it came. The dam burst, and he screamed into her face. "Where's the bloody map?"

"Please." She was shaking her head and trembling all over. "There is no map."

"No map. Alright then, where is the bloody silver?" Each word was punctuated with a sharp jab to her chest with his stiff fingers. He turned away and scrubbed his hands roughly over his face.

"I don't know." A desperate sob escaped her.

"You're lying." The back of his hand connected with her cheekbone, hard as a blacksmith striking iron. She stumbled back, reeling from the pain. She wanted to cower, to grovel, to hide like she always had. Like she had been educated to do.

He grabbed hold of her blouse and brought her back in front of him, nose to nose. Her cheek ached, and anger boiled in her belly. Something savage came over her. She placed her hands on his chest and shoved him across the tent as hard as she could. He stumbled with the shock of it and stared at her. His bewildered eyes were wild and unhinged. She braced her feet and balled her fists at her side.

"There is no map, you fool," she told him between clenched teeth. "And even if I did have it, I wouldn't give it to you." She spat the retort, heedless that she would pay for her defiance.

His weight shifted, and she grabbed the closest thing at hand, a canteen. She swung it, heavy with water, as he lunged at her. It connected with the side of his head and knocked him to the ground. She bolted for the flap. He grabbed her skirt as she passed and yanked her down hard. The force of impact on her barely healing ribs forced the breath from her, and fiery pain shot through her side. He straddled her and pinned her to the ground. His hands, burning with the heat of his fury, closed tight around her throat. Panic surged through her as she fought for air. Stars floated in her vision before the world faded to black.

Chapter 26

Gideon rode up a narrow draw between sheer, rust-colored rock walls, allowing Sarge to pick the best path through the scrub oak and cedars to the top of the ridge. A surge of exhilaration quickened his pulse as the sweet smell of burning cedar permeated the dominant aroma of sagebrush. He tipped his hat back and searched the sky for the cloud of smoke that would lead him to Jo.

There it was. The tell-tale smudge of gray was hazing the orange and pink sunset from the other side of the ridge.

Gideon dismounted quietly and kicked off his boots, sliding into the soft pair of moccasins he retrieved from his saddlebag. He slipped his rifle from its scabbard, checking his hip for the pistol John had given him.

He crouched and crept along for the remainder of the trail, stopping short of cresting the steep hill. A vivid image of bolting elk flashed through his memory from the hunt he had blundered earlier in the fall. With a quick prayer for sharp senses, Gideon lowered himself flat and removed his broad hat. He belly-crawled to the top of the rocky outcropping and scanned the area.

No movement or sound gave him any indication the bandits would be up here. Most likely, they were hiding out against the base of the steep rocks on the other side. Twilight crept in to take the place of the flat light of dusk.

As he took the extra time to wait for full dark, he poured his heart into a more substantial prayer than the *God, help, please* he'd been repeating for the past two days.

When Gideon opened his eyes again, darkness had fallen. The silvery glow of the full harvest moon illuminated the Colorado mountain desert with enough light that he would be able to see below. He crawled along the narrow ridge-top, mindful not to expose his large form at the skyline. When he reached a good vantage point, he crept to the edge and peered over. *There.*

The gang had set up camp against the cliff edge under a rocky overhang. Four men sat around the dwindling fire, and one crouched in a notch of the cliff-side in an elevated position—*night watch.*

A single wall tent was set up to one side. The canvas wall of the tent shook. There was some sort of skirmish inside. Was Jo in the tent? Was someone with her? His stomach turned, and a protective rage grew in his belly.

Shuffling down to a rocky shelf, obscured by scrub oak, Gideon watched the tent for any further sign of movement. All was quiet and still. He couldn't act too rashly. The horses were hobbled in a small clearing fifty yards from the main camp. Gideon counted. One, two, three ... five. There were five horses, not four. The fifth man must be in the tent with Jo. Five men to Gideon's one. He would need to use the terrain and layout of the camp to his best advantage.

The canvas moved again, and a man emerged from the tent, dragging Jo's lifeless form behind him. Gideon's stomach twisted, and bile burned his throat. Why had he waited? Why hadn't he found a way to get to her sooner?

Suddenly, Jo kicked out, her boots scrambling in the dirt. She twisted and fought as the man dragged her. A new, desperate intensity hummed in Gideon's veins. The man anchored her to a tree with a rope stretched across her neck.

Every instinct in Gideon screamed to move, but he had to wait until the outlaws bedded down. It was torture to crouch there, waiting, but it would be a necessity if Gideon was going to get Jo out of there with both of them still breathing.

He didn't know how he would go about pulling off this rescue mission on his own. Jo was still alive, and that was all that mattered for the span of the next few hours.

He waited, and he prayed—all the while, keeping Jo in his line of sight. One by one, the three men around the fire spread out bedrolls and settled themselves down to sleep.

A shifting of oak brush caught his attention. The man on night watch left his post, slowly working his way down the rocky slope. He paused before passing behind the wall tent. What was he doing? Waiting for something? Listening? A prickle of unease crawled up Gideon's spine as the man skirted out into the trees before shifting his path and heading straight for Jo.

Likely, nothing good would come from this, but on the smallest chance there was an honest soul in the bunch, willing to set her free, he held back and watched to see what the man would do. Gideon lowered himself onto his belly. Bracing himself on his elbows, he brought up the rifle, opened the peep-site, and pressed the stock against his cheek. He let out a slow breath. Desperation to free Jo from this mess curdled in his stomach, spoiling with the time spent waiting.

The nightwatchman stood over Jo in a manner that made Gideon's blood run cold, and he slipped a finger into the trigger guard. The man loosened the rope binding Jo to the large tree, and a sigh of relief washed over Gideon. Then the man knelt in front of Jo and grabbed her by the legs, jerking her to the ground. She clawed at the rope across her neck that had stretched tight. She landed a kick square in the man's chest, scuffling and digging her heels into the dirt. The man stood up and reached for a knife at his belt. Gideon didn't wait. Releasing a slow, steady breath halfway out of his lungs, he squeezed the trigger.

The man dropped like a stone. Jo scrambled to get to her feet, struggling against the rope binding her to the tree by the neck. The men in camp jumped up, shouting and looking wildly around the clearing.

Gideon had stirred up a hornet's nest now.

JO COUGHED AND WHEEZED as Slim dragged her back to camp. The pressure of the rope binding her to the tree had nearly crushed her airway when she'd tried to fight off the attack. A scuffle of voices rose around her as she was shoved down onto a stump by the fire.

"Where'd that bloomin' shot come from?" Clyde shouted.

"It could've come from anywhere. We could be surrounded," Slim added in a panicked tone. "It's a posse!"

"Pull yourselves together, ya fools," Kane demanded. "Clyde and Slim, split up and search the area. Handle it. No witnesses. I'll not tolerate any interference from the law. This haul from the train is too fine a prize, and we've even bigger fish to fry now that we have Jo back with us again."

The two men gathered their pistols and split up, creeping into the quiet darkness, and Jo feared for whoever was out there trying to help her.

Lord, help. Please help, Jo implored silently. She didn't know why she had suddenly taken up praying again, but maybe God hadn't forgotten her, and there was a rescue plan after all. Jasper, who had tried to assault her, was lying dead in the trees. Surrounded by the rocky red cliffs, the shot had echoed across the canyon, giving no clear explanation of its origin.

She sat huddled by the fire, wondering who would come for her. Where had that shot come from?

While Kit stood guard over Jo, Kane barricaded himself in his tent like the coward he was. Jo leaned on Kit's sympathy for her and tried to convince him to let her go.

"If you let me go, I'll tell the posse you helped me. They'll go easier on you, I'm sure of it."

"Kane will kill me if I set you free."

"I won't let that happen. Untie me, and I will help you. I know you don't belong here, Kit. You know it, too."

Kit looked around the camp, warring with his conscience.

"Please," Jo whispered desperately. "Please, help me."

He looked down at her and back at the tent, slipping a knife from his belt. There was a moment of silent stillness as he came around behind her. Had her words produced a decision to help her or to shut her up? Jo's heart pounded so hard she was sure it must be audible. There was a quick tension of the rope binding her wrists and a sudden release of pressure.

Jo let out a sigh of inexplicable relief. Kit had decided to set her free and cut the ropes rather than her throat. She blinked rapidly and mouthed a quiet *thank you* as she rubbed the soreness from her wrists.

"Run. Run away from here. Don't let him catch you!" she whispered fiercely.

The fire had died down in the commotion. The embers glowed orange but no longer offered any light. Kane's face appeared in the darkness over Kit's shoulder, sending a thrill of panic up Jo's spine.

"And just what is it ye think yer doin' there, boyo?" Kane's voice was cold as steel.

Kit let out a defeated breath, the shadow of a dimple tucking in his cheek as he accepted the inevitable. Kane raised the pistol behind Kit. Jo dove forward and grabbed the knife Kit had used to cut her ropes. The motion slammed Kit's weight into Kane, and the loud crack from Kane's gun echoed off the surrounding cliffs as they tumbled in a heap to the ground.

GIDEON HID BEHIND A patch of oak brush, watching to make sure Jo was safe while also trying to listen for the men who had disappeared into the trees. Rocks tumbled down the hillside below him. He slowly turned in the direction of the noise and repositioned his rifle, resting his elbows on his knees for a steady shot. The faint, metallic, double click of a hammer being drawn back behind his right ear froze him in place.

With a split-second prayer, Gideon shifted and knocked away the gun pointed at his head. It tumbled down the hillside, and a furious wrestling match ensued. The man he tangled with didn't have the reach Gideon had, but he was heavyset and was capable of more force than Gideon would have expected.

The glint of moonlight on a metal blade caught his eye, and Gideon grabbed the man's hand, clenching his wrist with all his might. The man pressed the knife down toward Gideon's chest. Gideon relaxed the tension in his arms long enough to gather enough force to give one enormous shove, knocking the man off of him. The outlaw tumbled to the side and went limp, having landed on his own knife.

Gideon struggled quickly away, untangling his legs from the dead man's, and reaching down, he retrieved the man's other pistol from his gun belt, to be sure.

The shock of what had happened staggered Gideon. When he looked back down the hill where he had first heard the noise, a tall, skinny man stood gaping at the scene. He met Gideon's eye, and his hand flashed to his gun belt. Gideon already held the dead man's pistol in his hand. He fired before the second man had a chance even to clear his gun from the holster. The tall silhouette dropped to wobbly knees and fell sharply to one side. The flat, hollow sound of his head hitting the cliff's rock shelf caused Gideon's stomach to lurch.

Another shot rang out below, and Gideon leaned over the edge of the embankment to see what had happened. All was silent and still below. Three bodies lay heaped together by the fire. Motionless.

He scrambled down the hillside, sliding in the soft sand and grasping at sagebrush to steady himself on his way down.

"Jo?" Gideon hollered in a state of shock. One shot. There had been only one shot. Had he missed something? What could've happened? "Jo!" he desperately repeated.

A sudden rustling came from the pile of bodies as Gideon reached the bottom of the slope. A wild crop of strawberry tendrils rose to the surface, and Gideon's heart soared. He ran for Jo and scooped her up, raising her from the apparent carnage. He cradled her in his lap on the ground, crushing her to himself, burying his face in her hair.

"Are you alright? Are you hurt?" His voice trembled as he looked her over. He gently grazed his shaking fingers over her face, seeking to assure himself she was alive.

"I'm okay, Gide—Gideon? What are you doing here?" Jo whispered hoarsely, her airway constricted by his shoulder as he crushed her to himself.

"Thank you, God. Thank you, Jesus," he whispered over and over. One of the men beside them stirred. Gideon dumped Jo off in the dirt, raising a pistol.

"Gideon, no!" Jo laid a hand over his, bringing it down in a gentle motion. "He cut me loose. He's not going to hurt anyone." Gideon stared down at the young man. "Two are dead up on the hill. Are there any more?"

"No, sir." The tall, young man removed his hat and looked Gideon squarely in the eye.

"You gonna be a problem for us?" Gideon asked, not lowering his gun yet.

"No, sir."

Gideon hesitated but dropped his hand and hung his head, pressing it against the side of Jo's as he clutched her. The adrenaline from the evening leached from his veins. He nudged the form of the man on the ground, ensuring there weren't going to be any more surprises.

"What happened here?" Gideon looked back to the young man who sat, dazed. "Did you kill this one?" Gideon cocked an eye at the prone form on the ground.

He said nothing but gestured back to Jo.

"Kit cut me loose." Jo began to stir and shifted in Gideon's arms uncomfortably. He reluctantly relinquished his grip on her, and she stood rubbing her forehead with one hand, an arm wrapped protectively around her waist. "Kane saw it—he would've shot him." She pressed a hand flat over the bare expanse of skin on her chest, breathing heavily. "I couldn't let that happen." She looked pleadingly into Gideon's eyes as though seeking his understanding.

"Of course you couldn't." Gideon stood and reached a hand out toward her, wanting to offer comfort. She stepped back a pace and nodded her head in a jerky fashion.

"I want to go home." Jo's voice cracked. The sound squeezed at Gideon's own heart. He would do whatever it took to mend this damaged girl, even if it meant taking her back to Kansas and losing her all over again.

Chapter 27

"Gideon, you have to let him go." Jo held her hands outstretched, completing the electric current between the two men. "Kit never wanted this. He never hurt me. He protected me."

"He's an outlaw, Jo," Gideon growled. "He needs to pay for his crimes."

"Gideon, you can't—you don't know how it was. You don't know the kind of fear, the power Kane—" She choked on the name. Had she indeed killed him? Killed the man with whom she'd spent a year of her life? It had been the right thing to do, hadn't it? He would've killed Kit, who'd just set her free.

Jo shook her head to clear the confusion and continued. "The power he had over people and the things we found ourselves trapped into doing, he had a way of making it all seem normal."

"We? What do you mean, we? And doing what? What are you talking about, Jo?" Gideon asked.

Jo shared a long look with Kit. She was going to have to tell Gideon the whole story.

"If you turn him in for being part of the Blake Gang, you'll have to turn me in as well." She dropped her hands, her shoulders slumping.

A deep line cut a trench in Gideon's forehead. "Jo, you were kidnapped. You were a hostage. That wasn't your fault." He stood firmly with a rope in hand, shaking his head like a stubborn mule. "You had no choice in being dragged along with them."

"It was my choice, Gideon. I may have been a hostage at first, but I—I was one of them." She looked back at Kit, the sentence hanging heavy in the air between them. Gideon's eyes narrowed, and he rubbed his chin.

"Not ... this time." She waved a hand and sighed. "Two years ago, when I left Kansas, the gang held up the stage I was on. I was taken hostage, but I didn't remain a hostage for long. Not really." Her voice wavered and cracked. She pulled her hand back, covering her mouth as the shock of the evening's violence washed over her.

"You don't have to do this." Kit stepped forward and placed a hand under her elbow to steady her. "I'll stand for my crimes." Kit met Gideon's eyes and straightened to his full height, squaring himself.

He was nearly as tall as Gideon but had a whipcord leanness and a narrow face. He wasn't such a young kid after all. It must have only been comparing him to the rough outlaws that made it seem that way. There was something about him that wasn't hard and cold like the others.

"Gideon needs to know what it was like." Jo regained her composure. "The way Kane conned and used people. Including you and me."

Kit stood rigid, defiant against the insinuation he had been folly to Kane's manipulation, but it wasn't in his true character to have been a party to what they had done any more than it had been in hers. She'd seen that. Both of them had been young and impressionable, and both had been swept up in Kane's game.

"Kane convinced me the only way to protect me from the other outlaw's advances was ... well ... was if I was with him."

"With him?"

"Yes, with him." Jo turned her back, unable to face Gideon any longer.

"What are you saying?" Gideon's voice was almost a whisper behind her.

"In the beginning, I was just trying to survive. I was terrified of what would happen to me if I didn't give myself over to him." She rubbed her arms to dispel the chill that crept over her. "I thought it was better to have control of my choice." She shrugged a shoulder. "Better to have one in that way than to have four of 'em at me." She brushed a treacherous tear from her cheek and turned back to face Gideon.

He bore down on Kit with a murderous glare.

"Not him." Jo stepped forward and stopped Gideon's advance with a hand on his chest. "Kit didn't come along until a few months later." She paused long enough to seek out rationality in Gideon's eyes.

He puffed a harsh breath through his nose like a horse that was about to blow.

After his breathing took a slower, calmer pace, she continued. "Kane was charming and conniving. He talked about exploring the territory and seeking fortune. He made it all sound so exciting." Jo hung her head, rubbing a tired hand over the back of her neck. "By the time I realized his version of fortune-hunting was robbing the stage line, I had been a party to a crime."

"Why didn't you run or fight back, for mercy's sake?" There was no tone of judgment in Gideon's voice, only frustration.

"I was naive." Jo looked deep into Gideon's eyes. "I believed that he wanted to protect me, and I could see no way out." She walked a few paces and turned back again, clutching the torn shreds of her blouse in a vain attempt to cover her shame. "I was as much a part of the gang as Kit. They used me as a decoy and Kit as a lookout."

Gideon's silence was as cold as the grave. This was it. She had lost the trust of the only man willing to look at her differently than all the rest. The only one who saw her as being worth rescuing. Worth risking his life for.

Now he knew the truth, and she had severed any remaining thread of respect he may have had for her. Kit had risked his life to set her free, and she would do the same for him. Besides, it was better to get the truth out there and get it over with so Gideon would stop looking at her like a victim. He needed to know the truth of what she had done and what she was so he could move on with his life and forget her.

RIDING UP THE MOUNTAIN, Gideon noticed the marked lack of leaves on the trees along the trail. A whisper of snow was swirling in the air around them so slowly it never appeared to touch the ground. It was nothing as substantial as a flurry. Pinpoints of white, silent and weightless, hovered in the air. The sky was clear and sunny, with large, puffy clouds hovering high above. Only in the Colorado Rocky Mountains would there be snow falling while the sun shone in blue skies.

The outlaw's camp had been a day's ride northeast of Cripple Creek. Gideon and Jo had been on their way back to town to return the mine's payload when they ran into the sheriff and a posse, returning to assist Gideon in apprehending the outlaws.

Gideon had been grateful to meet the sheriff along the way. Maybe he wasn't such a bad guy after all. He'd only been doing the best thing he could with the resources he had and needed to ensure the safety of all the people on the train before going after the outlaws.

Gideon had been relieved that Kit, or rather Matthias, they had learned, was well on his way out of the territory before they had come across the posse. He had assured Gideon he would start a new life, taking back his proper name and turning his back on outlaw life for good.

Gideon was still unsure if letting him go had been the right thing to do. But if turning Matthias in meant Jo being arrested as well, there was no way he could have allowed that.

The sheriff had explained the damage to the train tracks was so devastating it would be months before the train would be operational again. The responsibility to get Jo back to the family ranch in Kansas before winter was on Gideon's shoulders.

There wasn't much time. Winter was close at hand. They would need to leave as soon as possible. With this unexpected trip back to Kansas, there was a chance this would be the last time he would be able to return to his cabin before spring. Once winter set in, the narrow pass leading to his home would become insurmountable.

He didn't want to think about the possibility of being forced to spend the winter months in Cripple Creek, but if it meant Jo would be safe, home again with her family, it would all be worth it.

The realization that he, himself, would be returning home to Kansas struck him like a knife to the belly.

Ma. What would he say when he saw her? What could he say? He cut off the thought. That was one worry too many for him to face right now.

As the trail climbed farther into the mountains, the knowledge that Jo would, at last, see the home he had built for them but not stay, twisted the knife in his gut.

What would she think of his mountain haven? Would she find his cabin in the woods as comforting as he once had hoped? And what about his unique neighbors? For that matter, what would Florence think of Jo? Florence had an unusual perception when it came to people. It was how Gideon had come to know her and her grandson so well, so quickly. Even with his hermit ways, she pushed past all his barriers and got right down to his heart. Would she be able to do the same thing with Jo?

Gideon himself didn't even know what to think about Jo anymore. She wasn't quite the same girl he had left behind in Kansas. She had the ferocity of a wildcat one moment and the tender skittishness of a kitten caught in a fox hole the next. It clenched his heart to see her so lost. She had always been so strong. It was probably the only reason she had ever been able to bear his buffalo-like tendencies. She'd always been strong enough to put up with him.

He didn't know what to make of her life as an outlaw and the relationship she had with the gang's leader. That was a bit of information that had him reeling.

She had done all of what she did in fear for her life, that was certain. But she was taking too much blame upon herself. She wasn't an outlaw or a prostitute. She was a girl who had been doing what she could to survive.

Jo's weight rested against Gideon's chest, moving with him as they made their way up the trail. She must be sleeping again. He was glad she had finally come to relax. The first part of their journey had been rigid and awkward at best.

They may have been comfortable with each other in their youth, but now things were different. She hadn't resisted when he'd clutched her at the outlaw camp, but that had been a momentary shock for them both. Neither had questioned the embrace, having found peace and relief in the closeness of their familiarity. The relief of finding her alive had been enough to make him forget his own name, much less anything else.

Gideon bent his head down and breathed in the fresh scent of her. She had washed in the creek this morning, and her hair smelled of mountain spring water and honeysuckle. He wanted to follow the fragrance down her neck and behind her ear. Having her close to him again was intoxicating.

He pulled himself away so as not to disturb her sleep. What was wrong with him? He had no business acting like a coonhound on the trail.

A few nights ago, he'd been sure he wanted a life with her, regardless of her time at the brothel. He had wanted to bring her home to his cabin in the woods. There, maybe he could have helped her heal and waited for her to be willing to accept love again.

He huffed out a sigh of frustration. So much had changed now. Even if he did want to be with her, Jo had made it quite clear she had no interest in him. She had rejected his offer only a few weeks ago and now had asked him to escort her back to Kansas.

Gideon sighed. Kansas would be the right thing for her. She had loving parents and a home, and maybe the distance would give her what she needed to heal.

Chapter 28

The rhythmic motion of the horse and the creaking of saddle leather greeted Jo as she awoke. The scent of the buckskins Gideon wore wrapped around her like a blanket. She couldn't remember the last time she had felt as safe as she did now, nestled back against his broad chest.

When they first set out for Gideon's cabin, she fought to keep distance between them, sitting straight-backed, her arms resting on the pommel of the saddle. The proximity of a man being so close, even if it was Gideon, had been disturbing. But exhaustion from the last week weighed on her until she couldn't hold her rigid posture any longer. Fatigue overcame her, and she eventually relaxed, leaning back against him and falling into a deep sleep.

It was unnerving and yet perversely comforting to have Gideon so close again after all these years. All of the anger and uncertainty she'd harbored against him since he left Kansas hung in the balance against the absolute peace when he was near. Their chance at love had passed, but at least she was protected as long as she was with Gideon.

She had to fight this false sense of security that would evaporate like a mountain mist once they separated again. But some small part of her also wanted to relish each moment and soak it up like the flowers soaked up the rays of sunshine in spring.

Wood smoke replaced the scent of leather, and Jo stirred, now on high alert. She gripped Gideon's arm as it controlled the horse's reins. The smoke was billowing from the chimney of a low-roofed trapper's cabin across a clearing ahead.

"Where are we?" Jo tried to blink the sleep out of her eyes.

"We need to stop here." Gideon's voice rumbled in her ear, causing a tickle to run down her neck. "These are my neighbors. Well, as close as it comes to that in these parts. They've been watching my place for me while I was in Pueblo. I need to find out if they're well and if they can continue to watch things while I take you back to Kansas."

Pueblo? What on earth had Gideon been in Pueblo for? The question disturbed her more than it should have. They had once known everything about each other, but things were different now.

How had he ended up so far from Red Mountain, where his pa had been mining? What in Pueblo was so important he'd leave his homestead when winter preparation was so necessary? The security she absorbed in her sleep started to trickle away. She was an intruder, an outsider.

She squirmed, uncomfortable at the thought of meeting anyone new right now. The tenderness of bruises from her last words with Kane meant her face must still be painted with shades of blue and green. The last thing she wanted was to be a spectacle for pity or gossip. She hadn't much choice, though. For now, she was at the mercy of Gideon until he could get her back home to Kansas. She appreciated his looking out for her but longed for the day she could rediscover her own life and desires.

The moment Sarge stepped out of the trees and into the clearing, a great, black beast came barreling from behind the barn straight at them. Jo's heart leapt into her throat, and she wound her fingers around the course black mane with one hand and gripped the saddle horn tightly with the other, bracing herself for a wild ride. To her surprise, the horse didn't crow hop, buck, or even shy away. He only groaned and blew out a great puff of air as if tired of this usual greeting. As soon as the animal was within attack range, it sat abruptly with a tongue lolling out one side of its smiling mouth.

"There's a good girl," Gideon spoke affectionately and threw something down to her. She happily chomped it out of the air and pelted straight back for the cabin as quickly as she had come out to greet them.

Jo let out the breath she'd been holding. "What was that thing?"

"That's just my girl, Bonnie," Gideon told Jo with a chuckle.

As they approached the cabin, a young man walked out and leaned forward, resting his arms on the hitching post. He had long, glossy, dark hair, braided back, and wore a buckskin get-up similar to what Gideon wore. The young man greeted them with a big wave and took hold of Sarge's bridle as she and Gideon dismounted. Climbing on and off of a horse wasn't quite as painful as it had been when she and Gideon first rode out of Cripple Creek to reconnect a month ago.

"So, you brought back a wife to the mountain after all?" The young man looked Jo over with a half-smile and one eyebrow raised.

"Nope." Gideon's short response didn't seem to affect the young man one bit.

He grinned amiably and nodded toward Jo in a slight, respectful bow. "Clay Anderson, ma'am." Clay loosely wrapped the reins around the hitching post and welcomed them into the cabin.

It took a moment for her eyes to adjust to the dim, one-room cabin. The aroma of drying plants and curing hides filled the small space.

"Look who it is, Grandmother." The tall, young man addressed an older woman in a rocking chair by the fire. Her hair was white, and her skin was the color of chocolate. She smiled up at Jo, missing several teeth, and struggled with her hands on the arms of the rocker. Jo quickly knelt beside her, laying her hand on the woman's to let her know there was no need to stand up.

"Jo, I would like you to meet Florence." Gideon bent down and kissed Florence on the cheek, the tenderness and respect of the gesture touching Jo's heart. "How are you feeling?"

"I'll do, Gideon, I'll do." She patted his hand and held it fast, clasped between her own hands with skin as thin and delicate as brown paper. "And who is this you have brought? A present for me, perhaps?" She smiled a broad, toothless smile.

"Florence, this is Miss Josephina Bradford," Gideon introduced her formally. Florence looked back at Jo and smiled. Florence didn't speak for a long moment. The site of Jo's cropped hair, a scar down one side of her face, and the new bruising down the other side must have made her a frightful mess. Yet, for some reason, the woman's evaluation of Jo didn't make her uncomfortable at all.

"Who are you, child?" Florence's gaze penetrated straight through all of Jo's layers of self-preservation and denial and spoke directly to her heart.

"I don't know anymore," Jo answered automatically and was shocked by the truth of it.

Florence shook her head. "You are a child of God," Florence responded confidently. "*That* is who you are."

Jo swallowed hard and pulled her hand back from Florence's fragile arm, giving a slight shake of the head and looking down.

"You haven't lost Him." Florence lifted Jo's chin and looked deeply into her eyes. "He's here." The gentle touch she placed over Jo's chest sent a vibration straight to her heart.

Jo shivered. Was it the cold or the woman's touch that sent chills down to her toes?

"Why don't you come over here and dry off?" Gideon dragged a chair over in front of the fire for Jo.

By the time they had reached Florence's cabin, the sky had taken on a darker hue and held a damp chill from the hovering snow that melted as soon as it touched the ground. The cotton and lace of Jo's torn blouse had been soaked through by the lingering moisture in the air.

Florence motioned to Clay, who helped her to her feet. She shuffled over to a chest in the corner, and Clay lifted the heavy lid. She pointed out different items, speaking to

Clay in what must be the Ute language, though Jo had never heard it spoken before. Clay withdrew the things and brought Jo the bundle, which consisted of a colorful calico blouse and a set of buckskin leggings, jacket, and moccasins.

Jo sat in the ladder back chair and lifted her sodden skirt hem to unlace her stiff boots. Gideon's eyes darted to her ankle and quickly away. He stood up, tugging at the hem of his tunic and starting for the door.

"Clay, we'd better see to the horses." Gideon cleared his throat and stalked outside, nearly slamming the door behind him in his haste.

Jo was perplexed by his sudden sense of discomfort. It had been so long since someone had shown any deference for her modesty. She was almost as shocked by his reaction as he was at the sight of her leg. She smiled to herself at his discomposure. It was refreshing for once to be treated as a respectable woman and not merely an object meant to serve a man's animal lust.

She dressed in the supple leather buckskin and calico behind a flannel curtain tacked up in one corner of the room. The warm, dry clothes smelled of earth and herbs, and she breathed a sigh of contentment. Wearing pants would have been the cause of shock in most places. But here on the mountain, it was a simple necessity. They would keep her dry in this damp weather, and she took confidence from the practicality of them.

She fluffed her wet hair by the fire, running her fingers through the choppy waves, allowing the radiant heat to dry it. With her short hair and buckskin leggings, she might simply look like a young man traveling with Gideon on their trip to Kansas. That would be safer for them on the road anyway.

Florence began pulling down jars and bags from a set of shelves in the kitchen and set to work, crushing the fragrant leaves in a wooden bowl. She applied healing herbs and salves to Jo's face and pasted a thick poultice she called boneset over the faded bruising on Jo's side from the cracked ribs and covered it in a smooth linen cloth.

Florence never asked Jo questions about her injuries or what she was doing on the mountain with Gideon. She only offered kindness and healing. She taught Jo about the different herbs and plants used for medicine, making Jo recite each of their names and applications. Jo didn't see any reason she would ever need the information, yet, like everything Florence did, it filled another empty corner in Jo's soul.

At supper, Jo savored a bite of warm cornmeal mush. Something about the hearty simplicity of the meal was a balm to her shaky nerves after the trauma, not only in the past few weeks but also the last few years. The dimly lit cabin with its rustic, hand-carved furniture gave Jo a new picture of a life she had never known before. None of the gaudy trappings that painted a false veneer of glamour over the sordid decay of the parlor house. None of the expectations or pressure that life on her father's cattle ranch put on her. It was life in its most pure form, and it was beautiful in its modesty.

"We'll head to my cabin at first light so I can set things right before our trip. It's a good distance, but we'll be back by dark and stay here one more night before we set out for Kansas." Gideon pushed the cornmeal around in its wooden bowl. He'd already tried to convince Jo to stay behind with

Florence and Clay, but Jo insisted that she would go along. She wanted to see his home and the life he had built in this wilderness.

"I s'pose it'd be alright for you to come if we make it in one day. Wouldn't look right—" Gideon scratched the back of his neck. "—us stayin' there alone." He cleared his throat and turned away as a dark red hue crept up his neck. "You can sleep here with Florence in the cabin, and Clay and I can find a bed in the barn."

Jo scoffed at the idea of propriety having any place in her life, but as usual, Gideon seemed stubbornly oblivious to the reality of Jo's disgrace.

Chapter 29

Jo was overwhelmed by the stillness and tranquility of the clearing where Gideon's rustic log cabin was. The horse's hoofbeats padding through the blanket of yellow leaves was the only sound to break through the silence of the forest. The few leaves left clinging to the white branches glowed yellow and orange as the morning light illuminated them.

On both sides of the trail, the imposing mountains rose high and magnificent. A quiet creek wandered through the small valley. The trees began to thin, and the space between mountains opened up into a narrow clearing. Remnants of pink rose hips and a few dull red raspberries that hadn't been picked still clung to bushes that were turning brown with the passage of fall into early winter. A curious rock wall connected the cabin to the hillside, creating the illusion that the home had grown right out of the mountain. A little farther up the narrow valley stood a modest barn and corral. Jo released a sigh that relaxed her down to her toes. She could stay here forever.

Once inside the cabin, Jo was surprised by the touches of detail and comfort Gideon had included when he built his home. It was far from the small, sparse space Jo had expected. The ceiling stood at a comfortable height for Gideon's large frame, and little touches like a washbasin, countertop, and cupboard were something more than Jo assumed an average mountain man's cabin would boast. The bed in the corner was much larger than most. It, too, seemed to be made to accommodate Gideon's size.

She ran her fingers along the table that would seat an entire family. Taking in all of the details of this home, it was clear he'd planned to share it with someone and not to live here alone.

How long had Gideon's plans to marry Leah been in the works? All of this had to have been built with a wife, and perhaps a family, in mind. Had Jo's sudden reappearance gotten in the way of that plan? Had she been the cause of two lives being torn apart? It would be just like her to ruin things, not only for her own life but also for two other people.

Jo marveled at the beauty of the reds and blues in the multicolored rocks framing the hearth. This place was something right out of a dream. Well, her dream, at least. She doubted Leah would have appreciated the beautiful simplicity.

If she were honest, she was glad things hadn't worked out for Gideon with the dark-haired beauty he'd brought to the Thornton's that day. While fresh-faced and beautiful, the girl had the sour disposition of an unripe crabapple. And yet, if that was what Gideon had wanted, Jo was sorry to have mucked it all up.

Gideon's coat was covered in a thick layer of large, white snowflakes when he returned from settling Sarge and Jack outside.

"What—Where did that come from?" Jo asked in surprise. When they had arrived, there had barely been anything but wet, white specs in the air. She peeked out the cabin door behind him.

Heavy snowflakes the size of silver dollars fell rapidly to the ground, stacking up in heaps over logs and rocks, swallowing the landscape in a sea of white. Gideon leaned over her shoulder, looking up to the sky above.

"From up there, I reckon." He nodded a furrowed brow and sagely rubbed his chin, covered in a thick growth of beard. A wry grin betrayed the serious tone of his voice. She gave his shoulder a hard smack, showering herself in snow as it dislodged from the thick fur on his coat.

"Whoo!" Jo whooped and gasped. Snow covered her face and trickled down the neck of her blouse. Gideon's eyes sparkled, and his white teeth gleamed through his dark beard. He grabbed her, holding her close, and tipped his hat, shaking it wildly and creating a flurry of snow flying in all directions.

"You scoundrel!" She shrieked and tried to wriggle out of his grasp. Spinning around, she ceased her struggles when they were face to face. The ability to breathe abandoned her as she looked up at him. His hands rested lightly on her arms, and she could easily have pulled free, but the warmth in his eyes held her captive.

Her heart stopped for the space of a beat, and she let out a slow breath. She flushed and stepped back, bumping into the door and turning away.

For a moment, she'd been sixteen again, carefree and alive. But she couldn't afford to forget herself like that. She wasn't that girl anymore and never could be. Shame's shadow crept back into place around her heart, and the moment passed.

EARLY THE NEXT MORNING, Gideon lay on a pallet by the fire, with one arm stretched beneath his head. The sighing and wailing of wind outside had kept him awake for hours. The oiled hides covering the windows rattled and snapped at the edges. The chill in the cabin told him what he would find outside. Still, he was not all-fired anxious to see the effect of the night's storm.

When the rapidly falling snow had turned into icy sleet, he figured they'd best give it a day or two to melt off before trying to get back to Florence's cabin. There were parts of the trail that would be far too treacherous if it was iced over.

He didn't like how it looked, he and Jo sleeping under the same roof, but there was nothing to be done about it. These mountains sometimes took those choices away, and Gideon couldn't argue it.

It was still early in the year, with days warm enough to ensure the snow wouldn't have any reason to stick around. The blizzard that blew in last night, however, had changed everything.

Rising, he added wood to the fire and swung the kettle of water over the flames before crossing over to the front door. The gale forced its entry when he cracked the door, blasting past him with a flurry of snow and creating a snowdrift at his feet. He pushed against the wind to force the door closed again and threw down the internal latch. Well, this was not part of the plan.

When he turned again to face the room, red-gold spikes, like an Indian paintbrush, peeked up out of the Buffalo robe on the bed. Jo stared down at the drift of snow at Gideon's feet. Disappointment etched across her freckled face.

"Is it that bad?"

"Pretty bad." Gideon scratched his cheek, trying to smother the grin warring to take over his face. She wrinkled her brows in confusion. A soft chuckle escaped him before he could clamp his lips down tight.

"What is so funny?" She asked skeptically.

He ran a hand over his wavy locks, and Jo rolled her eyes upward as if she could manage to see her own. She cringed, bringing a hand up to her hair, which was floating out in all directions.

"Purty as the morning sun." He gave her a broad grin, knowing she was ashamed of her short hair. She smoothed it down and wrapped the robe snugly around herself, coming to stand beside him by the door. She braced her hands against the door and rested her cheek against the wood, listening to the wind.

"No use bringing more of it in here with us," Gideon told her. "Why don't we eat something and wait for this to blow over."

Jo shuffled over to the fire, comfortably wrapped in the buffalo hide, and warmed her feet. He crouched down and stretched out some fatback on the cast-iron spider in the open hearth.

"How long do you suppose it will be before we can set out?" Jo stretched out her bare feet toward the hearth and wiggled them. Gideon couldn't help but smile; she looked so cozy and content here.

Distracted by the familiar sight of her long toes, he almost missed what she had asked.

"Set out?" Surely Gideon had heard her wrong. She had to realize there was no going to Kansas now. At least not for quite some time. Hesitating to answer and standing instead, he went to the counter to mix up cornmeal, salt, and water for Johnny Cakes. Back in Cripple Creek, he had splurged on some maple syrup, and in light of the tumultuous times Jo had been through, he hoped to offer what comfort he could.

"We'd best not be going anywhere just yet. I'll check it out when the storm is over, but I reckon the pass is covered right now." Gideon tried to look regretful. She would be disappointed, but some small part of him hoped maybe this would give them both some time.

Time for her to change her mind and feel settled here. Time for him to reason out whether that was what he even wanted. Last night, she had laughed and teased as she used to when they were young, and it had been easy for them. Could it be like that again?

Jo drew her bare feet up under her and wrapped the hide tightly around her. "Quite some time, huh?" She bit the inside corner of her lower lip, and Gideon's heart clenched to see the unease she was feeling at the prospect of staying. Minutes passed before she spoke again. Only the pop and sizzle of grease in the pan broke the hush that fell over the room.

"Gideon—I can't—we can't ..." She looked up at him, pleading. "I have to get home." She clutched at the opening of the hide around her neck and bound it tightly in her fist, nearly choking herself with it. Her hand shook, her eyes frantic as if she was looking for an escape.

"Ain't nothing to be done about it now." Gideon watched as she burrowed deeper into her wrappings, a panicked look in her eyes. He sighed in defeat. Was she so afraid of being alone with him? Afraid of what he might be expecting if they were left alone together for too long? Irritation coursed through him. Hadn't he killed three men to save her from that kind of abuse?

"Land sakes, Jo. What do you take me for?" He ran his hands through the waves of his thick hair. "What difference would it make if we were here or if we were out on the trail? You've never been afraid of me before, and you got no cause to start now."

The smell of burning fat-back in the skillet recalled him to his chore. He turned his back and began stabbing savagely at the meat, pulling it out of the pan. Would she ever be able to trust him or accept love again?

Chapter 30

The past week had boasted more ups and downs than breaking in a bronc. It was as if Jo didn't know who she was or how to feel at all anymore. When she wasn't sleeping, she fussed around the house, picking things up and putting them down at random. Most days, she was cold as the weather outside, avoiding simple eye contact and having little to say.

He needed to find something to clear the air between them. They had been penned up in this cabin for too long. Jo was restless. With the unusual series of odd winter storms this past week, they hadn't been out of the cabin much.

The weather had turned on them so fast. It had snowed a solid two feet the first night, and the days since then had doused them in a series of cold, wet sleet and freezing rain followed by another wet, heavy snow the night before.

The storm had finally relented now, and although the air remained cold, it was the clearest day they'd had since arriving at the cabin a week ago.

Some fresh air would do them both good, and he happened to have the one thing that might ground her and remind her of who she was.

"Got somethin' to show you." Gideon set aside the antler button he was carving and walked to the front door, jerking his head, indicating that she should follow. She narrowed her eyes and gave a slow smile.

She put down Gideon's copy of *The Adventures of Huckleberry Finn* that she had been absentmindedly thumbing through and rose to follow. They bundled up in bearskin coats, and Jo tied a scarf over her head while Gideon pulled on the fur hat he had made from a wolf pelt last winter.

He motioned to Jo to hold on to the rope stretched out to the barn. The rope acted as a guide when blizzard conditions made the lack of visibility dangerous. Today, it offered support as they walked across the icy clearing.

When they arrived at the corral, Sarge and the big gray gelding stood nose to tail, sheltering each other from the crisp breeze. The new gelding raised his head from behind Sarge and nickered in greeting.

Jo's eyes lit up. She looked at Gideon with surprise and curiosity.

"I expected to see Jack out there with Sarge." She looked around for the big black mule.

"Ah, that greedy gus is probably in the barn hogging the hay I put out this morning." Gideon shook his head and leaned his forearms on the top rail of the fence. The horses came trotting over, nipping and nudging at each other. The cold air had everyone feeling a bit feisty today.

"I know this horse." She smiled, wrinkling her forehead. "Horace had him for sale at the livery in Cripple Creek." Jo looked up at Gideon with curious eyes.

Gideon nodded. "Saw you there, you know."

"What? When?"

"Day before I saw you at the doc's house, I s'pose." Gideon looked down at the ground, ashamed at his recollection of the way he'd acted at the livery that day.

"How do you know it was me? You sure seemed shocked to see me the next day." She gave him a half-smile.

As the horses approached the fence, Gideon reached into his pocket, drew out a handful of brown lumps of sugar, and dropped a few in Jo's hand. She smiled and stretched her hand out, knuckles first, as the horses came over, nosing around for a treat. After letting the gray gelding get a good sniff, she rotated her hand, palm out flat, letting him take lumps of sugar.

"He's yours," Gideon said matter-of-factly, giving Sarge some sugar as well.

"Mine?" Jo stared at him, dumbfounded.

"Suppose you'll be needing a good mount when we go back to Kansas."

"Oh ..." Jo's shoulders slumped slightly, but she smiled and patted the horse on the neck. "Thank you. He'll make a good companion on the trail."

"I mean for you to keep him." Gideon smiled warmly, hoping to reassure her.

She looked up at him, bewildered, her eyes glossy and bright.

"New tack for ya in the barn, too, if you want to go for a ride." He tipped his head in the direction of the barn.

Jo threw herself hard against him, burying her face in the front of his jacket.

"All right then." He chuckled. "Let's get saddled up."

"Wait, if the weather is clear enough to ride now, shouldn't we be packing up to leave for Kansas?" Jo asked as they walked over to the barn to retrieve the necessary tack for riding.

"Soon, I hope, but the pass between here and Florence's cabin is mighty treacherous with the layers of snow and ice we've been getting. I reckon we'd better give it a little more time to melt off before we risk it."

"But what if it doesn't melt off? How am I going to get back to Kansas then?" Jo looked up to the snowy peaks surrounding the cabin, twin lines of concern etched between her brows.

"It's too early in the year for all this to stick around much longer. Why don't we ride out to the west a way where the trail isn't so steep and see how this new gelding rides." Gideon handed Jo a bridle from one of the nails by the door, where he kept the halters, bridles, and harness tack.

The beaming smile radiating across Jo's face warmed Gideon enough to thaw the entire mountain. For once, maybe he'd done something right.

JO'S EMOTIONS HAD BEEN a convoluted jumble for longer than she could remember. Having been trapped in the cabin had only amplified the turmoil. Gideon's homestead was every bit as serene as Florence's had been, but the apathy she had learned to guard herself with at the brothel was beginning to fade. Like a vanishing mist, it was lifting away, leaving Jo's emotions raw and exposed. Shut up in the cabin for so long, she'd been restless and trapped, like a caged bird that was desperate to fly.

But now, for the first time since Jo left home, she was back in the saddle on her own horse. Not thrown over the back with hands bound or riding with a man who held the reins. Gideon let her lead the way, exploring this mountain he called "home." She was free and independent, just a girl and her horse. The mountain air and liberty were incredibly refreshing.

She followed a game trail behind the cabin that led to an overlook with an incredible, full view of the Front Range Mountains. It was spectacular. Pikes Peak rose not far in front of them, blanketed in snow with its rocky crags and peaks jutting through the white. If she'd thought the mountains had been breathtaking from town, she'd no idea what real beauty was.

Here, there was no pollution of man's ambitions or selfish desires, no alterations to this glorious landscape God had created. She could feel His presence here and wished she could stay in this moment forever, basking in the light of His glory. She wished her life could be like this landscape. Unadulterated and unmarred by man.

She widened the panorama of her gaze to include the man sitting tall on his paint horse beside her. Wearing a fur hat in the mountain-man style and a bearskin coat, he blended into the scenery as if he belonged as a permanent feature in it. The whole scene looked like a Bierstadt painting.

Life in these Rocky Mountains was something entirely different than what she had experienced on the run with an outlaw gang or from the stifling brothel in the booming mining town. Could she paint herself into the scene with him, or would she mar the canvas with her tarnished past?

Gideon dismounted, bringing her out of her reverie, and reached out to take hold of her horse's bridle, cautioning her to watch her footing in the icy, slick crust of snow.

"Name him yet?" He scratched behind the gelding's ear as Jo swung down.

"Shadow, I think." She patted the horse's neck and smiled up at Gideon.

He had given her back something she'd never dreamed she could have again. These days, she had been feeling like a broken vase, fragmented and scattered. With this single gesture, he had picked up a large piece of her heart and set it back in place.

She tipped her head back to look up into his eyes, glowing with warmth. "Thank you for this." Stepping closer, she took hold of the reins, her cold fingers grazing over his rough, work-worn hands. Warmth flooded her body at the touch. She closed her hand tight around the reins, wanting to capture the tingle in her fingers and not let go.

Was it possible? Could she have those feelings again? What would it be like to let go and give love a second chance?

As they trekked back to the cabin, she tried to get her head sorted out. She'd never thought she could be in such close proximity to a man again and not feel dirty or uncomfortable. She'd resigned herself to the life of a spinster and accepted it as her reality. Before today, the idea of being with a man ever again had repulsed and frightened her. But the quickness of her breath and the tingling in her fingers where they had brushed Gideon's was showing something entirely different.

Could she pursue these feelings? Was it safe or smart? Since leaving Kansas, she hadn't known any man to show her attention that didn't come with its own selfish, self-serving desire. Yet with Gideon, it seemed as though he genuinely cared for her. Could he be trusted, or would he be like the rest?

Chapter 31

The following morning, Jo cracked the door, filling the cabin with pink morning light. Anxious without Gideon in the house, Jo hadn't slept well at all. He'd been insisting on sleeping in the hayloft. He wanted to make her more comfortable, but the result had been just the opposite. Without his reassuring presence in the cabin, she tossed and turned.

When she did sleep, the nightmares plagued her. Fighting off Mr. Carver, the sickening sensation of Kane's life passing from him as she jerked the knife free from his body, there were plenty of horrors to keep her up at night. Often, fighting the demons of her past wasn't worth it, and she forced herself to stay awake.

She looked out to the barn. Had Gideon been warm enough? Did he lay awake all night as she did? She wished he would hurry up and come back inside. She was growing accustomed to his company, and not having him around bothered her more than she expected.

This morning she had already stoked the fire, boiled the coffee, and was heating last night's stew over the crackling flames. Maybe if she spent some time doing something constructive rather than puttering around the cabin and waiting for Gideon to come inside, she'd be able to put her demons to rest for a while.

She began by setting the bed straight and smoothing out the quilts and furs she'd been sleeping under. The pile of her few belongings lay at the foot of the bed. She really should try to find somewhere to put her things. In a house this small, every inch of space was beginning to feel cluttered.

She knelt on the floor to tuck her things under the bed. As she pushed them under, her hand bumped into something hard, skinning her knuckle. Bringing the injured hand to her lips, she retrieved the candle she'd been reading with this morning and peeked beneath the log frame to see what she had hit. Several rough wooden boxes lined the log wall under the bed.

She ought not to be nosing around, but she needed anything to keep her mind occupied. She worked a box out from under the bed. It was cumbersome, about the size of a small traveling case, and constructed of rough wood with hinges on the back.

She lifted the lid and gaped at the contents. Neatly stacked inside, bricks of silver gleamed back at her from the light of her candle. There must've been thirty pounds or more of the metal. Had Gideon found his Pa's silver after all? Even with the value of silver dropping, this was a small fortune.

She closed the box quickly and pushed it back into place. What had happened to Gideon's Pa? Why hadn't Gideon spoken of any of this? A pang of regret needled her chest. She'd been so selfish and lost in her misery that she'd not made any effort to hear the rest of Gideon's own story. Just what had he been through during their years apart?

She retrieved the corn husk broom from the corner and started to sweep the rough boards. Guilt over nosing through Gideon's things, and even more so, over not having considered what Gideon must have gone through all this time, weighed heavy on her. Charles Cross must have died. Otherwise, he'd have returned to his family. But how had Gideon found his journal and silver?

Gideon was such a closed book. Would she even be able to get him to open up? Her heart ached for him and what he must've gone through. She longed to go to him. After he had saved her life, the least she could do was to try and comfort him, even if it was three years too late.

She replaced the broom in the corner, took down the heavy bearskin coat that Florence had given her, and slipped into its secure warmth before braving the crisp mountain air.

Morning light reflected off of the snow. It was blinding in its brightness and caused her eyes to water. The wind and sleet had died down, and it was cold and clear out. Blue sky overhead contrasted the sheer mountainside and towering pines above the cabin. All was silent and still. It was breathtaking here.

Jo stepped into the thick, hay-scented air of the barn, and her heart warmed like baking bread. She shed her coat and located the ladder leading up to the hayloft. She climbed up quietly, not wanting to disturb Gideon if he still slept.

She paused at the top of the ladder. The sun shone in through the cracks of barn wood and sent streaks of morning light across his bare chest. Lying on his back with one arm resting under his head and the buffalo robe cast aside, she had the full advantage to take in every curve of muscle that graced his arms and chest. Heat washed over her, and her breath came short. The warmth of the barn loft suddenly seemed stifling. Shocked by her response, she quickly tried to climb back down the ladder.

"Do you come as a thief in the night?" His voice came down to her from the loft. She looked up to see that a sleepy smile gleamed through the thick growth of his beard as he peeked down at her. Cracking one eye open, he raised an eyebrow at her.

"Hardly the night, you lay-about. You've slept the day away!" She was rewarded in her jest as Gideon jerked up to a sitting position and looked around himself for the first time, noticing the light shining in. He scrambled to his knees and opened the loft shutter, allowing brisk winter air to rush over them. He sighed and ran a hand over his face.

"It's barely full light out, you imp." He rested his hands on his thighs as he knelt and took in the sight of the glorious morning.

Jo couldn't help but notice how the buckskin stretched tight across his thighs and marveled that the leather fringe didn't unravel at the seams. What had gotten into her? *She* was unraveling at the seams.

She cleared her throat. "I've made coffee and warmed the stew if you want to come back to the cabin." She nodded toward the pillar of smoke coming from the chimney across the clearing. Trying to keep her eyes averted, she picked up the buckskin tunic that lay crumpled in the hay. Meaning to hand it to Gideon as a hint he should cover up, the scent of him wafted up from the leather. It smelled of wood smoke and hay and his masculine essence. She closed her eyes and breathed in the intoxicating combination.

When she opened them again, Gideon was watching her with a curious expression. Heat crept up her neck and face. He took the shirt from her trembling hands, his fingers brushing her own. He held her gaze. Their eyes locked in a heated, silent exchange. He ran the back of his hand down the scarred side of her face and grazed a thumb over the bottom lip she had clenched between her teeth. His eyes focused on her lips with the look of a Viking marauder ready to claim his plunder. The blood hummed in her veins, and something fluttered in her belly. Was he going to kiss her?

Gideon was the first to break the connection, looking away and pulling his hand back as if he might be burned. Rocking back on his heels, he cleared his throat and slipped the shirt over his head.

"Well, let's get something to eat then. I'm starving."

What happened? Had she imagined it? She was left bereft at the loss of the connection they'd shared, and her lighthearted spirit sank as she descended the ladder.

GIDEON WORKED THE BARE elk hide, pulling and stretching it as he massaged the wet brain solution into the softening leather. He was grateful to have a job he could come out to the barn to work on alone. The off-putting smell of the brain tan was something that would discourage company.

It wasn't that he didn't love having Jo up here on the mountain with him, but there had been a new tension in her since their close encounter in the barn.

"Almost went and ruined things all over again," Gideon spoke over his shoulder to Sarge. "Almost gave in." He shook his head. "And Lord knows what kind of mess that would have stirred up."

It had taken every ounce of self-control he had not to reach out and claim her mouth with his own, putting an end to all this dilly-dallying between them. But he had known kissing her would be like drinking saltwater. The more he drank, the thirstier he would become, and he couldn't afford to quench that thirst.

"I know. It was a foolish thing even to consider." Gideon sat back on his heels and ran a sleeve over his forehead. Sarge nickered in apparent agreement.

He sighed, resisting the urge to fling the sopping wet mass of animal hide in his hands against the barn wall.

He'd done the right thing, hadn't he? It had been a mistake when he'd jumped the gun and tried to kiss her back in Cripple Creek. He couldn't forget the look of terror in her eyes when she'd jerked away. After that, he had decided he wouldn't be so foolish again. She was mighty unpredictable these days, and it wouldn't do either one of them a bit of good for him to be acting like a single-minded brute.

When things in the loft had leaned that direction again, he had to put a stop to it, hadn't he? He was trying to protect her, but judging by her shift in mood, maybe she hadn't wanted to be protected. All he seemed to have done was to make things worse.

"What else was I supposed to do?" Gideon looked up at Sarge again and shrugged one shoulder.

Before the incident in the loft, she had begun to act more like herself. She had been spending time with Shadow each day, and it was clear having something familiar to do had been helping. She'd even been cooking some meals. Though neither of them was any good at the task, it was beginning to feel downright homely around the cabin. It had been everything he had wanted when he'd first built this place.

The puzzle was coming together with Jo around, and she was the missing piece that would bind it. But after their moment of near intimacy in the barn, she was retreating into her shell again.

Gideon stood, stretching his back, and sighed. So, what now? If she was his missing piece, how could he possibly take her to Kansas and leave her there? There had to be a way to show her how he felt.

He crouched back down over the bucket of brain tan and began stretching and pulling again, the motion reminding him absurdly of—taffy.

That was it. He'd forgotten about the taffy he'd bought at the mercantile in Cripple Creek. He meant to bring her the gift when he found her, but what with train robberies, outlaws, and blizzards, he had forgotten.

Gideon hung the hide to dry and scrubbed his hands in the icy snow outside. Grabbing his saddlebag from the barn, he strode purposefully back to the house.

The aroma of roasting meat wafted over him when he opened the door. Jo was buttering sourdough bread at the small counter. She was so lovely in the glowing lantern light.

"I have somethin' for you." Gideon gave a half-grin.

"Another horse?" Jo looked up from her sourdough with a raised eyebrow.

"Close your eyes." Gideon reached inside the leather bag.

"What? Why?"

"Do you trust me?" Gideon asked but regretted the question when she hesitated. "Just do it. Please."

She looked at him sideways, evaluating him for a moment. The corner of her mouth turned up to form a crooked smile, and she obligingly closed her eyes.

He pulled out the taffy and removed the layer of brown paper. "Now, open your mouth."

One green eye glared at him through a squinting eye.

"Do you trust me?" he repeated.

She hesitated, but after a few moments, her lips parted. Gideon dropped the treat in her mouth, trying not to notice the brush of her lips on his fingertips. There was a moment of silence as she chewed and then an intake of air as her breath caught. Moisture glittered on her auburn lashes as she blinked up at him.

"Do you remember?" he asked, his stomach in a knot.

"How could I forget?" she whispered.

Gideon released the breath he didn't realize he'd been holding. Maybe this would be enough to speak the words he couldn't find on his own.

Chapter 32

Jo came to the surface of sleep, heavy darkness weighing down upon her, smothering her. She jerked upright in a panic, gasping for breath, only to realize the suffocating darkness was the heavy bearskin she slept under and not the drug-induced stupor of laudanum.

Heart racing and breaths coming short, she ran her hands through her hair, trying to clear the cobwebs from her mind. Her cheeks were wet with tears she hadn't even realized she'd shed, and she wiped away the traitorous wetness that betrayed her weakness.

The cabin was dark and quiet. The nightmare had shaken Jo to her core. The cold night air prickled at her bare arms, but she couldn't bear the stifling weight of the blanket again. Not just yet.

She hadn't slept well in weeks. The ghost of Kane plagued her nightmares. She had taken the life of a man who may have loved her, even if it was in his own, twisted way. Did it make her a murderer that she'd thought about it many times before when he abused and berated her or when he hurt people on the stage line? She couldn't pretend the thought hadn't crossed her mind that it was the only way to stop someone like that. And so the time had come, and she'd done it.

As much as it had torn her soul in two to take the life of someone she knew so well, hadn't she wanted it, even just a little? That was the question he asked her in her dreams. "*You wanted it, didn't you?*" Now she was doomed, not only to be haunted by her own past sins but also that question and the dull, blue eyes staring back at her each time she closed her own.

When she was with Gideon during the day, all of it faded to the background. He anchored her in the present and brought calm to the chaos of her mind. She didn't feel lost or crazy when she was with him, but she couldn't rely on his presence forever. She had to find peace of mind on her terms and not rely on him to keep her grounded.

This past week, she'd begun to feel like herself again. Perhaps even opening up to the possibility of love and the unguarded recklessness of hope. But something had made Gideon turn away from her that morning in the barn. Regardless of old feelings lingering between them, something was holding him back. She couldn't blame him. Not really. There was so much damage in her own heart and soul. So much brokenness between them. Why wouldn't he hesitate?

But then, last night, Gideon gave her the saltwater taffy. And heaven help her, all of the memories she'd tamped deep down rose to the surface. The friendship and the love they once shared came flooding back when she'd tasted the treat.

Like a fool, she'd looked up into his warm brown eyes. At that moment, her heart was open and exposed. The vulnerability was terrifying. She'd meant to guard herself better than this. She had no business even considering love. But it was too late. She'd already made the mistake of allowing hope to find its way into her heart.

Regardless of how he protected her or the gifts he had given her, he had hesitated in the barn, hadn't he? He must be at war with himself, just as she was. She couldn't let old feelings crowd out his better judgment.

She was damaged. Plain and simple. It wasn't fair to Gideon for her to clutter his life with her broken pieces.

The sun had been out the last two days, melting much of the snow and ice. Surely they should be on their way by now. Gideon had still stubbornly maintained it wasn't safe yet for them to travel, but she suspected he was just conflicted. She had to decide for him.

She was a confident rider, and Shadow was surefooted and calm. If she took it slow and careful, she could make it back down the pass. If she borrowed some of the silver Gideon kept beneath his bed, she could pay for a stage line fare. With the Blake Gang meeting its end, the stage line would be a way for her to return to Kansas safely. She could leave Shadow at the livery with Horace, along with a note for Gideon explaining everything. She would have her father send money to replace the silver she took. Making this journey back to town alone wasn't ideal, but it would be better than holding on to false hope.

Her heart ached to have to leave Gideon without a goodbye. He had been her only true friend in this world and was still the only source of comfort she had right now. But she had to go. She had to leave before things got any more complicated.

She bundled herself in the bear-skin coat Florence had given her and gathered up what few things she had. Light glinted up from the glossy, melting snow. The full moon would see her safely down the trail.

Holding her breath, she pushed open the barn door enough to reach in and lift Shadow's bridle from its nail on the wall inside the door. She would have to do without a saddle just for tonight. There would be no way for her to get it out of the barn without Gideon's notice.

She slipped through the pole fence into the corral, clicking her tongue and holding out a handful of the brown sugar lumps she had been using to train Shadow for the past few days. The big gray gelding trotted over and nudged at her hand, greedy for the treat. She slipped the bridle over his ears, guiding the bit between his teeth.

"Time to go, boy," she whispered as she scratched the white star under his forelock. She led him to the back gate, and after securing the long pole back into its carved latch, swung up onto Shadow's back.

The glowing moonlight that had lit the open clearing around the cabin was absent once she moved into the trees. Snow, still blanketing the ground, swallowed the sounds of the night, and an eerie hush filled the forest.

She was right, the snow had begun to melt, and the trail was easily passable on the south-facing slopes. But as the trail wound downhill, the snow remained fairly deep in heavily treed sections. Far deeper than she had anticipated. She gave Shadow his head in the sloping drifts on the narrow trail, trusting him to find the surest footing.

GIDEON SNUGGED UP THE cinch on Sarge's saddle a bit firmer than necessary, eliciting a groan from his companion.

"Sorry, boy. It ain't your fault." He scrubbed a hand over his face. "But you could'a at least sounded the alarm, though, eh?"

He checked the cinch, too tight to tuck a finger under, and loosened it a notch. He sighed and patted the horse's neck. Jo didn't even have a saddle. All she left with was a bridle and the clothes on her back. He thanked the Lord she at least had the sense to wear the buckskins and bearskin coat Florence had given her. The buckskin would keep her dry, and the heavy fur coat would be warm. But she was riding bareback down a mountain pass. If she reached the creek crossing before he did, the snow might obscure it, and the ice would be too thin to support the horse's weight.

Things had begun to get better these past few days. She had been elated by his gift of the horse and had been growing more lighthearted by the day. She'd been more herself lately. So, what could've brought her to do something so foolish?

A sinking feeling in his gut brought all the pieces together. He was the fool. Jo had been tense since their heated moment in the barn. She'd been in no shape for that close call, and he shouldn't have allowed things to progress so far. Even if he had cut the moment short, he should never have let it get so close. And then he'd gone and pushed her even farther with the taffy.

Now she was going to get herself hurt or even killed.

She couldn't be too far ahead. She had to have left in the dark, and travel would have been slow. Shadow had only traveled this trail once. Sarge had made the trip more times this past few years than Gideon could count. He would take the old high-trail and try to get ahead. From the top of the ridge, he would have a better vantage point and, hopefully, locate her from above.

The steep trail was far more dangerous than he had anticipated. The snow was deep and wet. He was lucky he'd made it up the sharp incline of the slope without much trouble. The trail he hoped would lead to the ridgetop descended from the top and down toward the upper bowl.

He rode out of the trees into the smooth, snowy expanse. Mid-way across the bowl, he spotted Jo, and his heart sang with relief. She was still safe and dry. But she was approaching the deceptive creek crossing.

"Jo!" He had to get her attention and stop her now. He nudged Sarge back into action. "Jo!" he hollered louder, terrified she would make a mistake and injure herself or the horse. The echo of his voice bounced back up to him as Jo looked up, shading her eyes with one hand.

"Gideon! Just let me go." Jo's desperate voice rang clear in the early morning air. Something stirred. What was that? It didn't feel right. The snow shifted under his horse. Panic surged through his veins as a rumbling vibration rolled through the mountain beneath him. Snow began to slide above him on the hill.

Gideon twitched his heels, and his horse's muscles bunched and gathered under him, lunging forward.

Too late. Running had been a fool-hearty notion. There was nothing to run on. The world was falling, slipping, sliding, shifting. Sarge stumbled to a knee, throwing Gideon over the gelding's head, causing Gideon to fly headlong into the churning sea of snow. He turned to look at the mountainside above him in time to see the wave of white towering over him.

The hungry wall of snow swallowed him, and the world went black. Tumbling and rolling in the angry waves of snow, he curled his arms protectively around his face. He had no control over anything else.

When the turbulent, rushing motion stopped, Gideon jerked and fought to free himself. Nothing moved. He was frozen. Immobile. Everything was dark. The pressing weight of the snow bound and crushed him. He was unable even to raise his chest to breathe. He frantically tried to draw air into his lungs, but all that would come were tiny sips of air.

It wasn't enough. He couldn't get enough air with these rapid, shallow breaths. Even the twitch of a muscle was beyond him, though he struggled with every ounce of strength. The crushing weight of the snow turned him to stone.

He couldn't breathe, couldn't move. There was no way out.

The panting respirations brought no relief to the burning pressure in his lungs. He was going to die here. The sound of his heart racing thundered in his ears. Dizzy and disoriented, he had never been so powerless.

A violent rage coursed through his veins, his muscles screaming to break free, yet he could do nothing. The sweat of his exertion trickled over his face, stinging his eyes.

Amid the chaos of his mind, a gentle nudge to his spirit stopped his struggling. His mind cleared. If he didn't calm down, he would run out of air in a matter of moments. He willed himself to fight the panic. Focusing on slow breaths, insignificant as they may be, he allowed the meager sips of air to satisfy. He begged God for a miracle and began to seek any small weakness in the tightly packed snow—any vulnerability that would allow movement. A slight twitch in one finger gave him a grain of hope.

He began working one finger back-and-forth, gaining more mobility as the movement shifted the snow. First one finger, and then another and another. He now had a minute range of motion in the hand pressed against his face in this coffin of snow. With the mobility in that hand, he dug the snow from around his nose and mouth. The space he'd created allowed the scant bit of air to flow more freely, though he remained unable to lift his chest to draw a real breath.

Little by little, the snow began to collapse in on itself, and the icy grains of snow trickled down onto his face. He must be lying on his back. As he dug, a small tunnel, no bigger around than a rifle barrel, began to form above him. After the crumbling of snow falling onto his face stopped, a glow of light shone through the small opening far above him—a pin-prick of hope and a light at the end of the narrow tunnel.

Chapter 33

The distant rumbling of thunder was faint, but it vibrated in Jo's chest as it drew closer. A white cloud of fog was rising from the snow on the slope above Gideon. She watched in panic as Sarge spooked and lunged forward, trying to get across the clearing. Horror paralyzed her as the foggy cloud on the mountain began to grow, looming up behind Gideon, a great white wall that enveloped horse and rider.

"Gideon!" The shock wave of what was happening hit her with the same force of the avalanche that hit Gideon. She caught glimpses of a paint horse sliding in and out of the fog but had no visual of Gideon himself.

She could do nothing but pray. She prayed as she had never prayed before, and at that moment, Jo had no doubt she was speaking to the Creator of this mountain. She had no doubt God was bigger than this scene in front of her, but she didn't know if he would listen to the heart-cry of a soiled prostitute, an outlaw.

Her heart pounded with great heavy thumps like the drumbeat of a warrior clan readying themselves for battle. While she wasn't ready for this battle, she would fight to save him with every fiber of her being.

The rumbling, shifting snow stopped. Jo flew off Shadow's back, not wanting to risk him being buried as well, but the snow she ran on was hard-packed as the brick-and-mortar buildings she'd seen constructed in Cripple Creek.

Screaming Gideon's name, she frantically scanned the snow for any sign of him. The hillside was a vast sea of white, and the only sign of disturbance was Sarge, who, miraculously, had not been entirely covered but was heaving and clambering at the ground in front of him.

His entire back half was locked into the hard-packed snow. Jo tried to speak soothingly to him as she scanned the immediate area, looking for any sign of Gideon himself. She didn't dare approach the frantic horse, who threw his head and pawed with his front hooves. If she came too near, he would seriously harm her. The sound of the frightened horse, screaming and bellowing, tore at her heart, but she had no time to waste. There was *no time*.

Jo's moccasin caught on something, and she tripped, falling hard. She spun around. Her heart palpated into double and triple beats. Gideon's wolf-hide fur hat was partially buried in the snow and had tripped her. She grasped at the ear flap and frantically swept away the top layer of fine, granular snow. Below the loose top layer, the snow was hard as sandstone. She continued to dig, and to claw, scraping until her fingertips bled from the tiny cuts caused by the icy crystals. It was no use. She would never find him this way.

She ran back down to the trail, flying as though the fringe on her buckskin leggings were wings. She broke off a branch from a dead tree by the trail and ran back to the place where Gideon's hat had been.

She ran around screaming his name, using the stick to prod here and there into the snow, hoping to find a weakness in the snow's fortitude. Sarge's bellows and screams had lessened to a low groan. He had worn himself out in the struggle and rested his nose in the snow as there was no way to lay his head down. He seemed reconciled to accept defeat.

Had Gideon given up too? If he had survived the violence of the avalanche itself, he would surely run out of time and air within moments. As she ran back and forth, a muffled sound came from behind her. She stopped dead in her tracks and waited. There it was again. She spun around and crawled across the snow, calling for Gideon.

There it was—a small hole, smaller than her wrist and deeper than her arm.

"Gideon!" she screeched.

There. A muffled voice, so low she almost missed it. "I'm here."

"You're alive!" Jo began sobbing as she used the stick to chisel the snow away from the tunnel down to the spot where Gideon lay, nearly motionless. She stroked his face and brushed back the sopping wet, dark waves from his forehead. "I'm sorry," she whispered. "Gideon, I'm so sorry. I never meant—I never thought—" She swiped away the tears streaming down her face.

What had she done?

JO HEATED ANOTHER HOT kettle of water over the fire and threw in a handful of crushed herbs from paper packets Florence had given her. If she remembered correctly, the white willow and wild cherry barks should help alleviate some of Gideon's pain.

She dipped a finger into the basin of saltwater cooling beside her. It was still too hot. She would need to wait until it had cooled before soaking his feet. She removed the hot stone from the edge of the hearth and wrapped it in fabric she'd cut from her old skirt, and brought it with her to the foot of the bed. She slid the warm bundle under the buffalo robe, mindful that it wouldn't make direct contact with his feet.

The avalanche had stripped Gideon of moccasins and coat, and his shirt had been brought up, high on his chest. His feet and much of his torso had been exposed to the wet snow. She'd been able to dig out his face and chest quickly, allowing him to breathe more easily, but it had taken too long to dig out the right foot, and the skin was swollen and red from chilblain.

It must have taken hours to chisel him out of the snow. Even after Jo had dug him out down to his waist, the snow remained impossibly constricting. He still hadn't been able to move his legs until she'd dug them out of the snow inch by inch.

"Leave me be, woman." Gideon's voice had been slow and sluggish. He wasn't himself at all. The cold must've addled his senses. He was unreasonable and challenging as a sullen mule and had fought her attempts to extricate him from the snow. He hadn't been violent, only difficult. But she had feared he would suffer further injury if it took much longer.

"Get Sarge out," he'd growled and motioned back to the exhausted horse. Taking the large digging stick from her and breaking it over his exposed knee, he had given one half of it back to Jo for each of them to dig.

Knowing she wouldn't be able to manage Gideon until she'd seen to his horse, Jo had left to do his belligerent bidding, fighting the urge to knock him over the head with her stick and drag him out unconscious.

Eventually, she'd released both horse and rider and checked that Sarge could walk. It had been a slow, limping pace, but they made it safely back to the cabin with Gideon riding double behind her. Thank heaven he hadn't been injured to the point of immobility. She wasn't sure how she'd have managed.

She walked around the side of the bed where her now unconscious patient lay, dozing restlessly on his stomach. The confusion clouding his mind had lifted, but there was still the problem of the angry red swelling on the toes of his foot and a nasty abrasion on his left side from where something had nearly impaled him.

She would need to soak his feet in the warm saltwater and put an onion and bread poultice on the wound to his side. Barring infection, it was a minor concern in comparison to the chilblain on his right foot. *Don't let it be frostbite. Please, Lord.*

She retrieved the bar of silver from her reticule and replaced it under the bed. What had she been thinking? What a mess she'd made.

She sat down beside Gideon and grazed her fingers along his cheek and across his upper back. No fever. Yet. She was glad he was resting, fitfully as it may be, but some contrary part of her wanted to wake him. She longed to look into his eyes again and feel their warmth. Would they still look on her with affection, or would they be glassy and bright with fever?

She longed for the caring touch of this man who had risked his life to rescue her. Who had been willing to leave his own life behind to see her safely to her parents' home, even knowing he wouldn't be able to return to his own home until spring.

The weight of guilt was heavy on her shoulders. It was all her fault. If Gideon lost a foot or died from the complications of exposure, she would never be able to live with herself. Was there no end to the damage she would do to her own life and others?

He stirred, and her chest tightened. She couldn't face him yet. She rose from the bed and hurried back to the fireside. The water was at the perfect temperature now. Its warmth radiated through her fingers.

"Jo?" The crack in Gideon's voice ran straight through her heart.

"I'm here." She steadied her tone as much as she could and picked up the basin of water, carrying it to the bedside. "Can you sit up?"

Gideon lifted himself to his elbows and groaned. "I feel like a herd of longhorns trampled me." He gave her a half-hearted grin.

"That's about what it was. Though I'm not sure which would've been worse," Jo spoke, keeping her eyes on the floor.

She knelt by the bed and guided his reddened feet to the warm salt water as he sat up. He sucked in a hiss of air between his teeth as he submerged them.

"What in the Sam Hill were you thinking, Jo?" Gideon grimaced and adjusted his position on the bed.

Jo sat back and drew her knees up to her chest, wrapping her arms around them. "I thought—I couldn't stay here with you any longer. It's not fair to you to burden you with the baggage of my bad decisions. You shouldn't have to spend the winter away from your homestead just for my sake." It was a weak excuse. Though it was true, it was far from the entire truth.

"So you'd rather risk both of our lives instead of accepting my help?" A bushy brow lowered, and he scratched his cheek, ruffling the thick growth of his beard.

"Of course not." Jo sighed and pressed her forehead against her knees. "I feared that old feelings between us were clouding your judgment. Before you found me that day in Cripple Creek, you were making plans to marry and move on with your life. Now you're stuck up here with a whore for a houseguest—"

"Don't you dare call yourself that." The pain in his eyes bored a hole straight through her.

"It's the truth, Gideon. I am so sorry that my rash decision put you in harm's way, but I'm more sorry I'm up here at all." She swiped at a tear that tracked down her cheek and stood up.

"You are no burden to me." Gideon reached out and grasped Jo's hand. "I would do anything for you, don't you see that?"

She could see, but she couldn't understand it. She wasn't the same girl he'd once loved. How could he possibly still care about her the same way?

"I need to see to the horses." Jo couldn't talk about it anymore. Not yet. Her reasons for running off now sounded flimsy and foolish.

She took additional hot stones from the edge of the hearth and placed them in a canvas bag along with the excess fabric she had gathered from the remnants of her skirt and blouse.

She brought them out to the barn where she had boxed Sarge into the single stall. He would need weeks of rest and isolation from Shadow and Jack to ensure he didn't push his injuries too soon.

His lack of serious injury had been as miraculous as Gideon's survival. By the time Jo had dug Sarge's back legs out of the snow, he had no fight left in him. Breathing heavily, he had stared past her with a far-off look, focused on something beyond. Exhausted, he had been reluctant to even move out of the hole she dug around him.

She had allowed him to rest while she finished digging Gideon out of the snow. The sweet horse limped back to the cabin behind Shadow, but it was a slow and painful journey. He had been dead tired and extremely sore. Stiff and stove-up in cannon and fetlock, it was clear he had strained muscles and ligaments. She prayed they would heal with time.

Jo spoke calm, sweet nothings to the valiant horse as she wrapped the warm stones, pocketed in swaths of fabric, around his legs. While she waited on the warm compresses to relax the stiff muscles, she brushed him down as well as she could manage with him lying down.

There was a sore on his withers where the saddle had rubbed him raw as he struggled. She would need to bring out a poultice for that as well. Working slowly and speaking calmly, she unwrapped one leg at a time, gently massaging. He groaned restlessly but had no energy to fight her.

She marveled at his strength to endure such a trial. It must've been by God's grace alone that he hadn't broken a leg. If not from the avalanche, the force of him fighting the bondage of hard-packed snow should have done more damage.

The sheer miraculous nature of his survival was astounding, and it resonated deep within Jo's heart. If God would turn such mercy on a mere animal, wouldn't He do even more for Jo?

Chapter 34

Gideon lay on his side in the large bed, watching Jo as she sat by the fire. Being stuck in this bed for the last day and a half was nearly unbearable, but having ample opportunity to watch Jo working around the house wasn't so bad. Just now, she was weaving long strips of leather into a five-strand round braid. She must be making a new set of reins for Shadow.

For a short time, it infuriated him that she'd been so reckless, taking off as she had. But now, after he'd had ample time to think about what she'd said, it pained him that she was so convinced she was a burden. She was determined not to accept love. John Thornton had warned him of that, hadn't he?

Gideon needed to give her more time, but all he wanted to do was stomp all the demons that plagued her to a pulp. If only he could conquer her fears himself, so she didn't have to fight this battle on her own.

Firelight danced on the walls of the cabin and played in the waves of her hair. Something in the softness of her expression drew him to her. He had an irrational desire to lift the hair from the nape of her neck and kiss the pink, strawberry birthmark hiding underneath. Without his intention or even his notice, he found himself hobbling over to the fire, walking on the outside edge of his foot to avoid putting pressure on the blistered toes.

Stopping himself before he could touch her, he reached for the long piece of wood from the shelf above the hearth. He settled himself in the other chair by the fire. The polished grain of the wood was gold and tawny in the firelight and reminded him of the shades of Jo's hair. He blinked hard, trying to dispel the image that had brought him over here in the first place. He ran a thumb over the band of intricate beading wrapped around one end.

"What on earth is that?" Jo laid the leather strands across her lap, leaning forward in interest.

Rather than answering, Gideon put the end of it to his lips and gently blew in the mouthpiece. The soft tone filled the cabin, and Jo's eyes lit up.

"A flute," she whispered. "And you play it?" She gave him a skeptical look.

Gideon nodded. "A gift from Florence."

He polished the wood with his sleeve and played a few measures of a hymn. The flute made any melody sound haunting in the minor key.

The open, innocent delight on Jo's face warmed his heart even more. He tipped the wooden flute in her direction, and she took it, the motion stirring up the scent of cedar from the warm wood.

"She saw I tend not to say much." He scratched the back of his neck. "Said I needed another way to speak." He looked down shyly. "Guess maybe she was right." He paused and bunched his lips to the side, struggling to say more. "Helped me pass many evenings up here on the mountain alone."

A pang of regret shot through him at having used such a vulnerable word. Alone. It hung in the air between them and left him exposed. His chest was as hollow as the flute. Would that one word make him appear weak?

"Why is it you don't say much anymore?" Jo weighed the flute in her hands, and Gideon weighed his next words carefully.

He drew in a long, slow breath. "When I was a boy ..." He sighed. "Well, you know how I was. I'd talk the hind end off of ole Jack out there. I liked to talk, and I did a whole lot of it."

Jo smiled at the memory, but there wasn't anything about it that could make Gideon smile.

"But Pa left and ... well, I was the cause of that, wasn't I?"

"Wait, why would you say that?" Jo shook her head and looked confused.

"If I hadn't been running my mouth, spreadin' gossip, Pa might not have left at all, would he?" Gideon sighed and rubbed his thumb and fingers over his forehead.

"Gideon." Jo reached out to take his hand. "Just because he left after you told him about the silver rush doesn't mean it was your fault."

"It's the truth," Gideon responded abruptly. "He'd had no reason to leave in the first place."

"You couldn't have known that." She stroked the back of his hand, lightly circling with her thumb. "The way I see it, he left and never reached out to your family again." She handed the flute back to him. "I hate to say this, Gideon, but I don't think he was ever planning on coming back."

"He was." He clenched his jaw at the crack in his voice, exposing his weakness. "Got the journal to prove it, don't I?"

He motioned to the bookshelf on the opposite side of the hearth with a jerk of his chin. Jo's eyes widened.

"The journal. I'd forgotten." Jo nodded. "So, what happened?"

He lifted the wooden flute to his lips absently and played out a few notes. He lowered it again and stared hard into the fire.

Gideon rose and placed the flute back on the hearth. He shuffled over to the bookshelf, slid out the battered black book, and thumbed through the pages.

"Says here, he fell in with another miner who offered to share a tent and go in on a claim together. They hit it big but kept their findings secret." He leaned an elbow on the shelf of the stone hearth, looking down at the page. "Afraid they'd be robbed or have their claim jumped, they hid it on the mountain. Guess they spent the next year separating and processing the ore themselves with a small ball mill and quicksilver rather than sending it out on the train. They'd planned to bring their score down in secret eventually and put it in a bank."

Gideon rubbed a hand down over his face. "I—I don't rightly know what happened." He gave a half-hearted shrug. "When I found him, he was a drifter, a pauper in Ouray." He closed the book and crossed his arms, tucking it close to his chest.

"It hadn't been hard to track him down when I showed the tintype I had of him around town. Everyone knew *Crazy Charlie.* He was living in a shack on the edge of town."

Jo sat frozen, her mouth parted in shock.

"He's—er—was … alive?"

"Is."

"Is? What do you mean *is*? Where—where is he?" Her sandy eyebrows rose so high they might take flight. She looked around the dimly lit cabin as if his pa would materialize in the darkness behind him.

"Pueblo." Gideon's voice broke entirely now, and he grimaced. Sighing forcefully, he continued, "Colorado State Insane Asylum."

"Oh, Gideon." Jo set her braiding aside and rose from her seat, running a hand along his arm, her eyes glassy in the firelight.

Silence filled the cabin again. Gideon remembered the sickness and shock when he'd realized Pa was beyond his ability to care for and had been forced to take his father to the asylum.

He'd found Pa sitting by a fire with a vacant expression, and it was apparent he had no idea who Gideon was. Pa had rambled on about the falls and a box in a canyon. None of it made a lick of sense.

When Pa had fallen asleep, Gideon had rummaged through his pack and found the journal. The pages of the journal told the whole story. It had laid out his father's aspirations of striking it rich and buying his own cattle ranch to give his wife and sons a life they deserved.

The increasingly scattered and chaotic journal entries had captured his pa's slow descent into madness. It was rife with fear, suspicion, and paranoia.

The next morning Gideon had been able to convince Pa it was time to take the silver to a bank, and surprisingly, he had taken Gideon right to the secret cache, hidden in a crevice of the rock wall behind the Box Canyon Falls.

It became clear to Gideon, Pa's mind was a jumble of chaos, and there would be no sorting it out. At times he was calm and agreeable, but other times he was belligerent and dangerous.

Gideon had coaxed him to Pueblo, where Pa was committed, and Gideon bribed the staff with silver to ensure his care would be better than it might otherwise have been.

Gideon had settled himself on the mountain, close enough to Pueblo that he could return to visit his father a few times a year. The only thing he had ever, or would ever, use the silver for was to ensure Pa's well-being at the asylum. He never recognized Gideon but often spoke disjointedly about his wife and boys whom he would bring out to Colorado soon.

Jo gently slipped the journal from his hand and opened it reverently, running her fingertips over the ink.

"So you see," he said. "I couldn't tell you. All I could manage was to send you a page of his journal and hope you'd see I was on to something and wait for me." He scoffed but without malice. "It was because of my loose tongue Pa left and ended up losing his mind." Gideon's voice grew raspy. "He's just sitting there, lost and alone, because of me. What else was there to say?"

"Gideon," Jo said his name warily as if she were afraid to ask the question that balanced on the tip of her tongue. "What about your ma? You did tell her, didn't you?"

He knew the blow was coming, but it didn't soften the impact. A sharp pain stabbed in his chest, and his breath came out in a choked sob.

"What could I say?" His eyes stung, and he squeezed them tightly shut, rubbing the heel of his hand between his brows. "How could I write home and tell her that? I reckon she has Jimmy there to take care of her. All I've ever done is wreck things. They're better off without me."

Jo didn't speak but walked to the corner of the room where her belongings were and retrieved the journal page.

"I am so sorry I didn't wait ... I didn't understand." She slipped the loose page back in the book and handed it to Gideon. "But Gideon, none of this was your fault. You are putting too much on yourself." Reaching a hand up, she cupped his cheek. "What happened was tragic. But your pa didn't leave because of you. *I* didn't leave because of you. We all make our own mistakes and follow foolish notions. You are not responsible for all this." She pressed her forehead into Gideon's chest, and her reassuring presence sealed the hole in his heart.

He wrapped his arms around her back and sobbed into her hair like a small boy. The pain was still there, but it was lighter somehow, with Jo in his arms.

THE RICH SCENT OF THE hay filling the barn was an intoxicating reminder of Jo's youth. Her time at the brothel had dulled her senses, smothering them in perfume and tobacco smoke. Up here, her senses sharpened. The crisp mountain air, the dusty smell of sweat embedded in horsehair, and the sweetness of dried hay all brought her out of her stupor and had her thinking clearly again. Jo stabbed a pitchfork of hay from the mound beside her and shook it over the stall gate into the feeder.

Incredibly, Gideon had never fevered. The chilblains responded well to the treatment she had used, and although there was some blistering, there were already signs of improvement.

Even so, the painful red patches made wearing any sort of boot or moccasin impossible. Jo practically had to tie him down to the bedposts to keep him from being out here doing the work himself. He would have found a way if Jo hadn't been around to help, but he also wouldn't have been laid up if she hadn't gone and led him into an avalanche chute, either. Besides, the physical exertion had been healing for her in a way.

There was no sense in him forcing a blistered foot into footwear when she was here and perfectly capable. He'd not been pleased to comply, but some small part of him must have known she was right because he allowed her to take care of him and the animals without putting up too terrible of a fight.

Jo wiped the back of her sleeve across her forehead and leaned against the saddle tree. A heavy piece of canvas slid to the barn floor. She froze. There sat Mr. Cross's saddle. Cracks in the leather showed weather and past abuse. But now, it practically glowed with oil and care. Gideon must oil it near weekly for it to be in the condition as it was. How Mr. Cross had managed to keep it with him in all his wanderings was a mystery in itself.

Her heart tightened. Gideon was piling more guilt on himself than the mound of hay that filled the entire back half of the barn. And all over the simple mistake of a youth who'd had no malicious intent at all.

She was still reeling over the revelation of Charles Cross being alive. It put a new face on all of her assumptions. When Gideon had left Kansas, she was sure it was because she wasn't good enough, wasn't ladylike enough, for him to stick around. Sure, he'd said he liked Jo that way, but they'd been kids then, and most men would want a lady, not a cow-hand for a wife.

But he indeed hadn't any intentions to move on with his life without her. With the amount of silver tucked under his bed, he had the perfect opportunity to start a new life with someone more like her perfect, proper sister, Elaine. Yet, he hadn't spent one coin of the silver on himself. He'd only used what he needed to ensure the best care for someone who would never know the difference. Jo had known many men who would not have done the same.

She propped the pitchfork against the barn wall and re-placed the canvas cover over the saddle. For two and a half years, Jo had guarded herself against looking at Gideon in a positive light. Her fear and insecurity had convinced her she'd been left behind for better things.

Now, she understood that wasn't why he'd been so secre-tive all this time. It pained her that he wouldn't forgive him-self, even though it wasn't his fault.

But wasn't she guilty of the same? She'd stubbornly refused to trust God to forgive her own sins and failures. She hadn't set out to kill Kane in cold blood, just as Gideon hadn't intended to send his pa after the silver rush. And wouldn't Gideon's ma forgive him without a second thought so that she could have a relationship with him again?

Did God see Jo the same way? Even though she'd made choices that led her down crib row, wouldn't He forgive her and welcome her back into His loving arms as well?

Jo slipped into her coat and stepped outside. She tipped her head back and looked up into the night sky. The deep black canvas stretched from ridge-top to ridge-top, sparkling with starlight. She had a limited view of its vast span, nestled into this valley, but if she rode to the top of the ridge, her vision would expand to a panorama of beauty beyond the vast mountain range surrounding them.

"God, I've had a limited view of your grace, haven't I?" She closed her eyes, and tears streamed down the sides of her face. "Forgive me for not trusting you to love me, God—for having such a narrow perspective. I made so many wrong turns I can't see my way out. Take this burden from me, and set me free."

A sense of peace and pure love washed over her, wrapping itself around her, and she understood that not only did she have His forgiveness now, it had always been hers to accept. Even in the famine of her lost faith, He had been right there with her.

Chapter 35

Jo supposed it was time to pack her belongings. Over the last week, Gideon's injuries had improved dramatically, and the blisters on his foot had healed. He had said they would need to ride out and check the trail to be sure, but the weather had been fair enough to make their way back down to Cripple Creek and then on to Kansas. Other areas wouldn't have been as affected by the early storms as they had been up here.

They would need to find a new trail to the top of the ridge to avoid the avalanche chute, but it was time. He'd made it clear he didn't feel it was appropriate any longer for them to be up on the mountain alone if they didn't have the weather or his injuries holding them back.

Jo's stomach was tied in a thousand knots. A part of her was anxious to see her family again and have a second chance at life. But there was an equal part of her, one she tried not to heed, screaming at her to stay. Despite the unfortunate series of events, she couldn't remember a time where she had felt more like herself than these past few weeks.

She went to the corner of the room where she kept her few belongings. There wasn't much for her to pack. She had been wearing her mother's reticule when she was kidnapped, but that was the only possession left to her. She had the buckskin clothing and fur coat Florence had given her, but the blouse and skirt she had been wearing at the time of her capture had been all used for bandages in the past few weeks.

She picked up the Bible and began to skim through the pages. In her stubbornness, she hadn't taken the time to even open it until the past few days. Pastor Walton had marked several passages for her notice.

He marked the story of Rahab, a tale she'd often heard as a child but of which the more profound meaning had escaped her childlike understanding. Rahab had been a prostitute like Jo, and yet God had rescued her and all of her family. Not only that, but she was in the direct lineage of Jesus Christ.

In the New Testament, he'd marked stories of Jesus's direct interaction with women like herself. There was a woman who'd been married multiple times and lived with a man who was not her husband. Jesus offered her redemption and salvation freely. In another case, it was an adulterous woman the Pharisees were going to stone to death. He'd forgiven them all and offered His mercy and His grace to each one of them.

Flipping back through the delicate pages, she came across a passage in the Old Testament she had missed. King David. Jo remembered the story of David's larger-than-life faith when he'd faced a giant and how he'd been called *a man after God's own heart*. Yet, when she read the marked scripture, she found the story of a man who committed adultery and murder, having known better all along.

Here it was—the answer she'd been seeking all along and had been too stubborn to see. If she had just read these passages right away, like Abigail and Pastor Walton had encouraged her to do, maybe she could've avoided all this misery she'd been wallowing in.

She pressed the Bible to her chest, thanked God for his patience and grace, and then opened the bag to put the Bible inside. The compass tumbled out into her lap, and she smiled. Even though it was broken, she'd kept it all this time. It had been a small lifeline she'd clung to. A reminder that someone out there knew the real Jo. Not the outlaw, not Copper Kate, just Jo.

She closed her fingers around the metal disc. Gideon had once told her as long as she had this compass, she would always find her way home. Would Kansas feel like her home anymore? She'd been more at ease here on this mountain homestead than she ever had on the prairie.

Even though she loved and missed her family, Kansas may not be the same. When Gideon had left to find his pa, it had already stopped feeling like the place she was supposed to be.

She rotated the disk back and forth on her palm, and the needle spun in a lazy circle as if encompassing the cabin.

Was that it? Had Gideon been her home all along?

GIDEON CHECKED THE cinch on Jack's pack. Sure enough, there was enough play for the pack saddle to swing loose once they got on the move. He gave the mule a firm smack on the belly.

"Suck it in, ya ole goat," Gideon chided the big mule, who answered him with a loud bray.

This was it. The time had come to leave for Kansas before any more winter storms could compromise the trip. It was the right thing to do for Jo. He'd give just about anything to keep her with him here on the mountain, but staying with him didn't seem to be what was best. She needed a fresh start to heal, and if that meant Kansas, then that was most important.

What would his life look like without her around? His heart ached, and he rubbed the heel of his hand over his chest. If she'd chosen to stay with him, it wouldn't have been an easy road, but he would've gladly traveled that road thousands of times over to keep her with him.

"I think we need to talk." Jo's honey-sweet voice spoke behind him. She stood inside the barn door, leaning against the jam.

"Talk?" Gideon turned his eyes back to the pack saddle in front of him, not wanting to see her looking so radiant in the morning light. "Talk about what?"

"Why did you offer to marry me back in town?"

That brought Gideon up short. He wasn't sure what he'd been expecting, but this certainly wasn't it. He scratched the back of his neck and moved to the other side of Jack, adjusting the halter and looking at the mule as though he would have the answer Gideon needed. Jack offered nothing but a shiver and an impatient stomp.

"Lot of help you are," he muttered to Jack.

"Maybe I don't know." He raised his eyes over the mule's neck, trying to read her reaction.

Her face fell. *Come on, Gideon, you owe her more of an explanation than that.*

"I wanted to get you out of that place. I may not have known what all had happened since we'd seen each other last, but I knew it wasn't where you were supposed to be."

She worried her lip between her teeth before continuing. "The other night, you told me you'd hoped I'd know by the journal pages that you were on to something, and you'd be coming back to get me."

"Mmhmm."

Looking up into his eyes, she said, "Gideon, I believe you." She sighed and shook her head. "I'm so sorry for not trusting you. I—" Her eyes fell back to the ground in front of her. "I don't know what got into me back then."

Gideon came back around to the mule to stand in front of her. The rising sun lit her hair from behind, causing it to glow in the morning light. She looked so tender and fragile, something he didn't see from her often these days.

"That was a lifetime ago." He shrugged. "Besides, it wasn't all on your shoulders, Jo. I shouldn't have waited so long to write. I was so swallowed up in guilt about Pa. I couldn't see my way out of it. It was like being buried in that avalanche." He looked down and scuffed the toe of his moccasin in the scattered hay on the ground. "I couldn't breathe—I couldn't face what I'd done, much less admit to you or Ma."

"I see that now. I look around this place, and I don't see a trapper's cabin. I see a home. A home built for two people, maybe even a family." She searched his face. "So tell me. What is it you truly want?"

"What do you mean?"

Jo straightened and picked up a comb from the shelf. Walking over to Sarge, who was patiently waiting to be saddled, she began methodically combing his mane.

"It's not just that you're careful with what you say anymore, Gideon. Now you don't say anything at all. You don't have to stay buried in that guilt anymore. You don't have to bottle everything inside." Jo tugged the comb through a large knot in Sarge's mane.

Gideon laid the saddle blanket across Sarge's withers and turned back to lift the saddle from the saddle-tree. Jo moved out of the way as Gideon heaved it onto the gelding's back. He braced his hands on the saddle horn and pressed his forehead onto them.

Jo leaned back against the stall gate. "You'd better learn to open up before it's too late."

What in tarnation was the woman getting at?

"Back in Cripple Creek, you asked me to marry you. If you only wanted to get me out of the brothel, then fine. I'm out, and I will always be grateful for what you've done to make sure I'm safe." She sighed. "But is that all it was?"

"What do you want from me, Jo? What do you want me to say?"

She pushed off the fence and planted her feet. "I want you to say *something,* Gideon. Tell me you love me." Her voice broke, and her eyes were bright with unshed tears. "Tell me not to go."

Her words slapped sense into him. All this time, he'd thought if he avoided talking as much as possible, he would somehow keep from causing harm. Now, if he didn't open up, he was going to hurt them both. But old habits die hard, and he wasn't sure how to let go.

"Don't you know it already? You said it yourself. I didn't build this life just for me." He reached out and grazed the sleeve of her buckskin coat.

"All that tells me is you wanted me back then. That was before, wasn't it? Before you knew I was a prostitute and an outlaw." She ran her fingers through the waves of her short hair. The evidence of how much had changed since he'd built the cabin for them both.

The time apart, the frustration of having her back again but not being able to keep her, everything he'd kept pent up inside for so long came erupting in an explosion of emotion. "None of that matters to me. I want you more now than I ever did back then." The raging torrent, battering the breaks of his defenses, broke through and filled every crack and cranny of him with the love he had for this woman. The rush of it was a calming balm to his weary soul.

"I love you, Josephina Bradford. I love you more than this mountain, more than anything I have ever had or could ever want."

The same relief of tension washed over her, softening her countenance and filling her eyes to the brim.

His fingers glided over her shoulders and up the back of her neck.

"What about you?" he asked as his thumbs brushed her jawline and over her bottom lip. "What do you have to say to me?"

She pressed her cheek into the palm of his hand and closed her eyes. His heart hammered as he waited for what she would say. After a long moment, she opened them again, blinking away the tears. She stood on tiptoe and, hesitantly, in an excruciatingly slow motion, pulled his mouth down to hers. It was a tentative, soft caress. He soaked up the sweet softness of her lips, holding back the urge to press her against the stall fence. She needed to know she was safe, that he wasn't a mindless brute. He slowly grazed her lips again with his own, resting his forehead on hers and breathing in the intoxicating moment. She sighed out a shuddering breath that shattered him to pieces.

"I say ..." She smiled. "Will you marry me, then?" she whispered as she pressed her forehead against his. A deep chuckle rumbled in his chest, and a more genuine smile than he had worn in years found its way to his tingling lips.

"Yes ma'am, I do believe I will." His lips found hers once more, and he pulled her close, soaking up all that had been lost between them.

"Well, then." She pushed back after a moment and set her shoulders straight. "In that case, you'd better finish packing up. We're going to town to get ourselves hitched."

Chapter 36

Jo hesitated on the boardwalk outside the Rocky Mountain Mercantile. Her stomach clenched, and her breath came short. She had lived in Cripple Creek for over a year and had not been allowed to walk its streets or frequent its businesses during regular business hours. Would they turn her out? Gideon seemed confident that they wouldn't, and she clung tightly to his hand for support.

He tugged gently on her and opened the door. A small chime announced their entrance, and Jo's breakfast of salt pork and eggs threatened to revolt. She wanted to run and hide.

Mrs. Landry had never been unkind when Jo had reason to come to the store after hours, but the older woman did know who she was and what she had been.

As they entered the store, Jo stepped partially behind Gideon, burying her face in the back of his shoulder.

The petite, older woman looked up from the counter and smiled. "Mr. Cross, how good to see you again. I didn't expect to see you for months."

"Well, I had good reason to come down." He shifted his position, exposing Jo. A warm flush crept up her neck and into her cheeks. "Mrs. Landry, I'd like to introduce you to my wife." Putting pressure on Jo's lower back, Gideon coaxed her to come out of hiding and stand in front of him.

"Wife?" Mrs. Landry came out from behind the counter.

"Well, not just yet, but fixin' to be." Gideon's face glowed like the sun, and Jo couldn't help but soak up a little of the warmth of his confidence.

"Ma'am." Jo bobbed her head and managed a weak smile.

There was a moment of hesitation, and then a look of recognition flashed through Mrs. Landry's eyes. Jo's stomach turned, and she wanted to bolt for the door. Gideon squeezed her hand tightly.

Instead of the stiff response Jo expected, the woman looked pleased. "Well, how delightful. Congratulations to you both."

Jo blinked. Delighted? Congratulations? Could this be possible?

"I don't believe I've had the pleasure of a formal introduction, dear." She held out a hand, and Jo took it, stunned.

Words failed her. Silence lingered in the air. It took a moment, but Gideon eventually came to her rescue. "My apologies. I suppose I've misplaced my manners on the mountain. Mrs. Landry, I'd like to introduce you to Miss Josephina Bradford." He nodded toward Jo.

"Why, Mr. Cross, I didn't know you had so many words in you." She giggled like a young girl, and Jo's roiling stomach settled. "What can I help you with today, then?"

Gideon insisted that Jo pick out two new dresses and some extra fabric, along with any other necessities she might need. She walked to the back wall, running a finger over the bolts of cloth, and beamed.

She'd come to love the buckskin leggings she wore on the mountain. They suited her so well. She was never one for frills, but the ready-made dresses Mrs. Landry had to offer were feminine, yet modest and sensible. The fresh start it represented was exhilarating.

"Why don't you try this on, dear? I think the yellow would look so lovely with your coloring." Mrs. Landry smiled sweetly and handed a folded dress to Jo. "Come to the back room with me, and we'll see if it needs tailoring."

Jo followed her to the back and waited for the older woman to close the door behind her. She clutched the dress to her chest as joy bubbled up inside her. Here she was, shopping for fabric and teapots in regular daylight hours like a respectable woman.

She slipped on the dress and smoothed the fabric of the skirt. It was a simple calico dress with a bit of eyelet trim at the collar and sleeves. Not too fancy, but it made her feel like a lady. She tucked a wave of hair behind her ear. It hadn't grown much yet, but at least it was now laying down mostly on its own. Given time, it would grow back to its full length, and she wouldn't feel so self-conscious about it. There was no help for the scar, though. It was a part of her now. Just like her past, it couldn't be erased, but it didn't need to define her.

As she exited the back room to show the dress off, the tinkling door chime and a rustle of taffeta fabric announced the entrance of another customer. The pink puffed sleeves were so wide the woman practically had to turn sideways as she crossed the threshold. The bright blue feathers and bows of her hat contrasted strikingly with dark hair and a fair face that stopped Jo dead in her tracks.

"Why, if it isn't Mr. Cross." Leah swept into the store with all the grandeur of an entrance to a formal ball. Gideon, leaning casually with an elbow on the counter, jerked upright as if someone had stuck a needle in his hind end.

He stood, rigid and wide-eyed, looking at the young woman warily as if she were some dangerous creature. "Leah ..."

"Mrs. Thompson, now, thank you very much."

Gideon relaxed visibly and let out the breath he must have been holding. Jo didn't know much about Leah, but the impression she'd had was of a petulant child. A child, she wasn't, but it was evident by Gideon's reaction she was possibly not the most pleasant person to be around.

Gideon nodded. "Congratulations, Mrs. Thompson."

A breeze drawn in by an open window swung the storeroom door shut behind Jo with a bang, drawing Leah's attention. She looked from Jo to Gideon and back again. Her eyes flashed wide when recognition set in. The scar must've given her away.

"What is *she* doing here?" Leah pressed a gloved hand to her collar in shock.

A hitch in Jo's chest stopped her heart and stole her breath. She looked desperately from Gideon to Mrs. Landry, pressing herself against the door behind her, palms flat against the wood.

"Whatever do you mean, Mrs. Thompson?" the older woman's voice held a patient tone.

"She's not allowed here during daylight hours." The fever pitch of Leah's tone was shrill. "Don't you know what she is?"

"This, my dear, is Mr. Cross's bride-to-be. Isn't it wonderful?" Mrs. Landry's tone now began to grow firmer and more pointed.

Tears pricked in Jo's eyes.

"His ... " Leah sputtered. "His bride? But she's a prostitute!"

Jo gripped the doorknob behind her, ready to lock herself in the backroom, but her hand had grown slippery with cold sweat on the brass knob. She wouldn't be able to open it now if she tried.

Gideon took two quick steps toward Leah, and for a moment, Jo wondered what he might do. She'd seen him riled up before but had never seen this kind of anger from him. "She is no—"

"I am no such thing," Jo interjected into Gideon's defense of her honor. She wasn't going to allow this woman's petty insults to rob her of the peace she had found.

"Don't try and hide it. The whole town knows what she is." The young woman was shrieking now, baring her teeth in a wicked sneer. "I demand you send her out of here at once."

"Miss Bradford is a dear friend and a customer, and I will not have such base vulgarity spoken in this store." Mrs. Landry darted from behind the counter and stood firm in front of Gideon.

There was a commotion outside. The raised voices coming from the mercantile must have stirred up the hornets' nest of town gossips.

The door chimed again, and John Thornton came in, glancing around the shop, wearing a look of surprise. Abigail peeked in behind him. Scanning the room, she took one look at the outraged Mrs. Thompson and then at Jo. Her lips parted in a silent, "Oh."

Abigail rushed across the store and wrapped an arm around Jo's waist, pulling her close to her side. More people filed in, and although Abigail steadied her, Jo's knees threatened to buckle.

"Stand tall, my dear," Abigail whispered. "Look around you."

Jo wiped her bleary eyes with a trembling hand and blinked rapidly. The faces in the room, by and large, were familiar and kind. The Thorntons, Pastor Walton, Hap, Horace, and Sheriff Walker were all part of the crowd.

Gideon walked back to Jo and took her by the hand.

"What seems to be the problem here?" Sheriff Walker was the first to bring order to the chaos.

"This woman—this harlot—has no business bringing her kind of indecency to such a respectable business." Leah lifted her nose a fraction of an inch higher, and her chest swelled, causing her puffed sleeves to appear to inflate. "I shouldn't have to be exposed to such filth during my daily shopping."

"Wait just a minute." The sheriff put out a hand toward Leah. "To my knowledge, Miss Bradford is no such thing." He looked at Jo, who stood a little straighter and gave a quick shake of the head.

"Please forgive the indelicacy of the question, Miss Bradford, but are you, in fact, employed by any brothel, or do you have any *current* connection to the establishments on Meyer Street?"

"No." Jo gained strength from the supportive, loving faces in the room with her. "No, sir, I am not."

The sheriff turned back to Leah, who blazed with fury.

"Miss Bradford and Mr. Cross not only recovered the stolen mine payload but returned it in its full amount when they could've taken it and run."

"Miss Bradford has also been a frequent guest in our home and has been nothing but courteous and helpful to us," Abigail chimed in now, smiling reassuringly at Jo.

"But—" Leah sputtered. All the venom that fueled her before appeared to dissipate as she searched in vain for an ally.

A woman stepped forward. She was familiar, but Jo couldn't place her.

"She saved my little Robert." The woman's voice cracked. "Pulled him right out from under the fire wagon." The little boy peeked out from behind his mother's skirt with a wary smile.

"Well, then. Is there anyone here who has any objection to Miss Bradford frequenting the reputable businesses of Cripple Creek?"

The unanimous "No," followed by multiple encouragements, was a soothing balm to Jo's hurting heart. There may be people who would always remember what she'd been, but there were also people who were willing to see beyond her past mistakes and give her the fresh start she so desperately had longed for.

The chime of the doorbell sounded again. Mr. Stanley Thompson, banker, and husband of Mrs. Leah Thompson, outraged socialite, walked into the store, blinking at the crowd, confused. He scanned the room and landed on Jo. He gaped at her.

"Kate—I mean—uh," the short, pudgy man stammered and cleared his throat.

"Kate?" Leah whispered. All the fire of her fury had gone out of her. "Who ... is ... Kate?"

Stanley looked wildly around for anything to distract from his grievous misstep. He stood, opening and closing his mouth like a fish out of water.

A pang of regret for the Thompsons gripped Jo's heart. She wanted no more of this ugliness to continue for herself or anyone else. She had been given grace. Didn't everyone deserve that chance?

"Kate?" Jo asked. "There is no one here by that name."

Chapter 37

Gideon laid another pine bow in front of the pulpit in the little church on the edge of town. The scent of the fresh greenery filled the space and set his anxious heart at ease. He hadn't been able to sleep at all that night and had been collecting pine boughs since the early hours of the morning.

He'd been wound tighter than a two-dollar watch in anticipation of what was about to happen. The dramatic change of his circumstances in just a matter of weeks was staggering.

He'd been a man, exiled and alone, yet grasping for anything that would resemble the love and family he had lost. Now he was a man reunited with love and with the hope of reconciliation on the horizon. Nervous energy buzzed inside him like a beehive at the prospect of seeing his family again. It may not have been his fault Pa left, but it was his fault for hiding from the truth and severing the one family tie he had left to save his pride. He'd found forgiveness for himself, and Jo insisted Ma would forgive him as well. She was right, of course, but it didn't make the waiting any more comfortable.

Gideon lit one of the dozens of beeswax candles Mrs. Walton had been generous enough to loan him. He tipped an unlit candle to the first flame and continued passing the light from one cotton wick to another. As each candle flickered to life—all started by a single spark—the dim room grew a little brighter.

He could hardly fathom how God had used the flame of hatred in someone's heart to kindle so much good. Not only had Jo's life been restored, but Gideon's, and hopefully the young outlaw Matthias's as well.

If it wasn't for God's work of grace in Jo, Gideon might never have seen his own need to let go of the past and move forward with real freedom. Who knew how many other lives would change? Perhaps Matthias could be an example of restoration in someone else's life.

Each glowing light was a testament of God's goodness, and all of it had been sparked by something tragic. That foul man had plans for evil, scarring Jo the way he did, but God had plans for good and brought beauty from the ashes and peace from despair.

As Gideon lit the last candle, a small group of witnesses filed into the church. Pastor Walton and his wife, Hap, and John warmly greeted each other, shaking hands and sharing pleasantries. Gideon had no interest in small talk. Not because he feared it any longer, but because he only had an interest in one person today, and until he saw her face, his restless spirit would not settle.

Abigail slipped in the side door, rosy with excitement, and gave Gideon a quick nod as she steered the others into their seats. The blood rushed in his ears, his heart pounding like it was trying to escape his chest.

Finally, after enough time passed, Gideon was near madness with the waiting. A creaking of hinges at the back of the church signaled that his life was about to change.

A stream of brilliant sunlight painted a pathway down the aisle leading straight to him. The light illuminated a vision surpassing anything he could ever have anticipated.

Jo stepped forward into the church with the quiet shuffling of moccasins and the clicking of beads. The white doeskin dress with a colorful sash Florence gave Jo on their trip down the mountain fit like it was made for her. It captured everything he loved about her. She was feminine and lovely. Fierce and strong.

When she came to stand in front of him, everyone and everything else faded into the flickering glow of candlelight and the warm sweetness of beeswax.

This woman was the epitome of all he had ever wanted in his life. She didn't need frilly parasols or flowery contraptions on her head to be beautiful. She didn't need *any* of that to be beautiful.

Her beauty was in the freckles across her nose that multiplied in the summer sun. It was in her free spirit and fiery temper.

Jo smiled up at him, her round, juniper eyes sparkling, and her hands trembling in his. His chest tightened, realizing she would be by his side for the rest of his life. The unfulfilled need to have a wife and family to love and protect had been completed, and not by just any woman. She was the only woman who could ever touch him and heal his heart. She loved him for who he was, with no other expectations. He didn't deserve her, but he was grateful and would spend the rest of his life doing his best to be the man she needed.

Life with this woman was never going to be short on adventure or complications, that was certain. But he was happier now than he had ever been, knowing that he would share a life with her—complications and all.

BACK AT THE CABIN, Jo curled up in a chair by the fire and tucked her feet under herself. The warmth from the crackling flames soaked into her skin. The prickle of cold from their ride home was replaced with the tingling pleasure of heat.

Neither Jo nor Gideon had any wish to spend a minute longer than necessary in town, and they had gone straight back home after the wedding.

Home. That single word warmed her more than the crackling fire.

Gideon came to stand behind her and stroked one finger down the back of her neck, kissing the spot lightly. A shiver ran down to her toes. Although the touch had been innocent enough, it reminded her the night was far from over. There was business yet to be done.

The unwelcome thought made her stomach quiver. She didn't want to think of it like that.

It was not business. This was love. This was marriage.

She stood up restlessly and wrapped her arms around her waist, stepping closer to the fire, warming her back. Why was she acting like this? Gideon would never put her in a position to do anything she didn't want to do. Still, she shifted from one foot to the other, restless.

"You cold?" Gideon eyed her warily, but she shook her head.

He walked over to the large bed and sat down. Jo stiffened and wrapped her arms tighter about herself.

Gideon seemed to think better of his action and got up, pacing back to the table. He pressed his hands flat on the wood and stared down at the table for a long moment.

"Do you want me to go back to the barn?" Gideon looked at her without anger or betrayal, only the resignation of a man who was willing to put his desires aside to make sure she was alright.

"No ..." Jo unwrapped herself, becoming aware of the defensive posture she had taken. She shook out the tension in her arms. "No, I don't want you to sleep in the barn," she said, gripping the inside corner of her lip between her teeth.

He took a slow step toward her, and then another and another like he was approaching a jumpy horse. When he reached out a hand toward her, knuckles out, the gesture made her giggle. Was he going to need to gentle her like an unbroken horse?

He tilted his head at her sudden amusement.

"Are you gonna offer me a lump of sugar next?" she asked with a smirk. The vibration of her internal laughter caused her shoulders to shake. It took a moment for him to catch the meaning of the joke.

He raised an eyebrow at her and clicked his tongue, sending both of them into a riot of laughter. She slipped her fingers into his waiting hand, and he drew her closer to him.

She rested her head on his chest, and they laughed, giggled, and snorted until they were both out of breath.

She sighed with the relief of tension, still smiling. Gideon smoothed a hand over her hair and ran the knuckle of one finger down her jawline. He lifted her chin until their eyes met, locked in a new kind of exchange.

He took hold of her by the arms, the gentleness of his touch holding her captive. His hands were so large they engulfed her wrists, but there was no dominating or hardness to his touch. It was feather-light as he grazed calloused fingertips up and down her arms.

She breathed in his scent, layered with wood smoke and horses. A fire was kindled deep within her, its heat spreading throughout her veins. She pressed her hands against the cool cotton of his shirt, and his heart thudded against her palm.

He didn't move. He was waiting for her. He wouldn't be the first to move, but his breath grew quicker and more shallow under her hand. A thousand butterflies that had lain dormant for years came to life, swirling and fluttering in her chest, building in intensity.

She crept a hand slowly up around his neck, intertwining her fingers into his hair. Desires warred within her, both to pull him closer and to push him away. She smiled and shook her head softly from side to side, drawing in a breath and slowly releasing it. He mimicked her motion, shaking his head, a question in his eyes.

Slowly, he pulled back, and she gripped his hair tightly, drawing his mouth down to hers, their lips grazing in a feather-light touch. Her breath came up short, and she pulled him closer, capturing his shuddering breath with her mouth.

Standing on tip-toes, she deepened the kiss. His hand spread gently around the small of her back, pulling her closer to him. The thousand butterflies swirling inside released all at once, dissipating all her fear and apprehension and setting her free.

Epilogue

Clear skies stretched out from one side of the flat prairie to the other in an enormous dome of blue.

Riding through the rich, green, waving grass with a chorus of bawling calves in the distance brought a joyful reminiscence of home and family lost to Jo for so long. When she was adrift in the darkness of her fallen life, she had kept the memories boxed up and put them aside on a shelf in her mind, not wanting to allow herself to think how much she missed them or remember how happy her home had been.

Now that healing had come, at last, she was able to open the box again, allowing the comfort and contentment of her memories to wash over her like the warm scent of fresh-baked bread. She rested a hand on the swell of her growing belly, excitement bubbling up inside her for the happiness her child would have.

As they rode up to the ranch house, her father's tall form stepped out on the porch like a sentinel standing guard. Her parents would have been expecting their arrival. Jo had sent a letter when she and Gideon had been married and then had sent word of their plans to visit before leaving Cripple Creek. Yet, her father looked wary and formidable.

"Josephina!" Her mother's alto voice rang out from behind the screen door, and she came barreling toward them, skirts flying. The horses spooked and shied, and chickens scattered in all directions. Jo gave an exasperated chuckle as she pulled Shadow back into compliance. Her mother had never been much of a horse-woman.

Jo dismounted and embraced her mother in a long, tight squeeze. Tears of healing streamed down her face. "I'm sorry, I'm so sorry," she whispered into Ma's hair over and over again until she couldn't speak the words anymore.

"Hush now, child. Hush." Her mother's soothing voice was as calming as it had ever been.

Jo looked up to the wide porch, into her father's stern expression. A shimmer of wetness glistened on his deeply tanned cheeks.

"Pa." Jo's voice broke on the word, and the grim mask split into a grin showing his heartfelt joy for her return more than words could ever say.

He came down the steps to meet her and gathered her to him. The healing embrace made her feel like a child again, safe and loved.

Elaine remained on the porch. With her back pin-straight and hair pulled up into a tight chignon, she was perfect and proper as she had always been. She offered no warm smile of greeting but stood with her arms crossed and face pinched with disapproval. The distance between them stung, but Jo hadn't expected much different. They had never seen eye to eye, and even if she found her parents' forgiveness, it didn't entirely take away the fact she had been a fool and had hurt her family.

By the time Pa released her, Gideon had set the horses to grazing and came over to join the family. He offered a warm handshake for her father and a respectful nod to her mother. Gideon stood beside Jo and slid an arm around her waist.

He whispered into the waves of her hair that now brushed the tops of her shoulders, "Elaine the Pain doesn't seem to have changed much at all." The resulting snicker got caught in her nose and came out as a snort, causing Ma to raise a disapproving eyebrow at whatever joke the two of them shared. It was as though nothing had changed at all, even though her childhood on this ranch felt like it had been three lifetimes ago.

Life was a balance of blending what they once had known and the events and mistakes that had changed them. The result was a new picture of grace they now found themselves in.

Gideon held her back a moment as the rest of the family went inside the house. Then, he wrapped his arms around her from behind, pulling her close and running a hand over her stomach.

"Are you ready to see them?" Jo asked, resting the back of her head against his chest.

"Ma and Jimmy?" Gideon rubbed her slightly protruding belly in a soothing, circular motion.

"Mhmm."

His hand stopped, and he sighed heavily. "Well, I suppose I'd better be. No help for it now, is there?"

"Your ma deserves to know the truth about your pa." Jo patted his hand. "It will be alright. She loves you, and she'll be so happy to have her son back."

Gideon turned her around to face him and tucked a wayward strand of hair behind her ear. "And what about you, Mrs. Cross? You alright?"

Jo smiled and allowed him to pull her into a tight embrace. "More than alright. I am whole."

Continue the adventure of the Cross Family Saga in Redeeming the Outlaw,[1]
available now for pre-order!

Dear Reader,

JO'S STORY OF REDEMPTION has been something on my heart for many years. I am so happy to have had the opportunity to share it with you. It was important to me to share the message that we can still find grace and forgiveness in Jesus Christ no matter how far we have fallen. I believe many Christians struggle with the concept of redemption even after salvation. We tend to view redemption and forgiveness of sins as something reserved only for those at the moment of salvation, but, *thank you, Lord*, that isn't the case.

No matter what you have done or when, if you turn to Christ, you will see, like Jo, that He was there all along and offers grace with open arms. Although there was darkness and pain throughout Jo's journey, I hope that you can take with you the beauty and the light that she found in the end.

In my research, I was heartbroken for the fallen women of this era. A particular point of poignancy came when I learned street walking was often referred to as "the hog pens"

---

1. *https://www.jodibasye.com/redeeming-the-outlaw*

or "hog ranches." I found this piece of history to be a subtle acknowledgment of the story of the prodigal son when he found himself at rock bottom. The connection of Jo's darkest moment in her own prodigal story being brought to that lowest form of prostitution was too heartrending not to include.

On a note of authenticity, I wanted to include as much history as possible in this book. In doing so, I kept the history of Cripple Creek, Colorado and The Old Homestead Parlour House, as well as Pearl DeVere, as historically accurate as possible. However, I did take a small liberty with the character of the madam, Hazel. While a woman named Hazel Vernon did become Madam after Pearl's death, my depiction of her was purely fictional.

Did you enjoy Jo and Gideon's story of Love and Redemption? I hope so!

Would you take a quick minute to leave a review? You can do so on Amazon, Good Reads, or wherever you purchased your copy.

It can be as long or as short as you'd like—just a little something about why you liked the story.

(I only ask that you try not to give away any spoilers! I like to keep my readers in complete suspense.)

Thanks in advance!

FREE BONUS BOOK!

Read Gideon's parents' love story in, Redeeming the Swindler[2] for free by subscribing to Jodi's Newsletter.

Acknowledgments

THE JOURNEY OF BRINGING a story to life is a labor of love and not for the faint of heart. It is a humbling process that involves an incredible amount of hard work, tears, and joy. It is also, most assuredly, not something that can be done alone. I have had so many people come alongside me in this adventure with help, support, encouragement, and prayers that I could not have done without.

To my husband Matt, my mountain man, you are my inspiration. You, above all, have taught me that anyone can learn new things and grow if they are willing to research, roll up their sleeves, and work hard. Your quiet support through this process has been the single most important thing that kept me going. God blessed me beyond measure when he gave me you.

To my girls: Kamryn and Kara. Thank you for being my cheerleaders, asking me how the book was going, brainstorming character names, and browsing cover images with me. For making your own breakfasts and lunches too many days when Mama was swamped with edits. I can't wait to cheer you along with your dreams the way you have done for me.

To my parents and sister, you have been my biggest fans since I wrote my first pathetically tragic poem and have never stopped encouraging me and giving me what I needed to

2. https://dl.bookfunnel.com/bh3ewyytok

move forward in this adventure. Thank you for reading this book long before anyone should have and helping me hone my craft. Your constant prayer has been invaluable to me, and I will forever be grateful.

To my writing peeps: Sara Blackard, Shelly Sulfridge & Maryann Landers: What a crazy, unique gift it has been to be surrounded by writing buddies and critique partners in this tiny Alaskan town. You have pushed me to be better, prayed and cried with me, and patiently sat through my stubborn outbursts. You have made me better than I ever could have been on my own.

Also, a huge thank you to Ranee at Sweetly Yours Press for helping me fine-tune a messy manuscript into what it is now. You took the heart of my story and helped me polish it so the message could shine, even through my own imperfections as a writer. I know it was a big job!

I look forward to continuing to work with you for years to come.

Above all, my ultimate thanks go to the Creator. Thank you for planting the seed of this story in my heart and breathing life into it so that it could bloom. It is only because of your love and the sacrifice of your son, Jesus, that we have hope in redemption. In the famine of our faith, you offer us the Bread of Life and make us whole.

Find Jodi on Social Media:
Instagram:
Jodi Basye (@jodibasyeauthor) • Instagram photos and videos[3]

Facebook:
Jodi Basye - Author | Facebook[4]
Goodreads:
Jodi Basye (Author of Redeeming the Prodigal) | Goodreads[5]
Website:
www.jodibasye.com[6]
Newsletter:
Get your FREE copy of Redeeming the Swindler (bookfunnel.com)[7]
Jodi's Cowboys & Coffee Book Club[8] on Facebook.
We play games, have Book Club discussions with prizes, answer polls, and just have fun!
Come join us!

READ MORE BY JODI BASYE[9]

3. https://www.instagram.com/jodibasyeauthor/

4. https://www.facebook.com/profile.php?id=100068389219890

5. https://www.goodreads.com/author/show/21711469.Jodi_Basye

6. http://www.jodibasye.com

7. https://dl.bookfunnel.com/bh3ewyytok

8. https://www.facebook.com/groups/466780171052260

9. https://www.jodibasye.com/books

About the Author

Jodi Basye is a born and bred country girl with a western heritage and a love for stories that stay true to her cowgirl boots and ranching roots. She is the blessed wife to a rugged mountain man, a homeschooling mama, and writes inspirational western romances and family sagas that span the centuries by her wood cook stove in the wilds of Alaska.

Read more at https://www.jodibasye.com/.